Bernice Rubens won the Booker Prize for Fiction in 1970 for *The Elected Member*, her fourth novel. She was also short-listed for the same prize for *A Five Year Sentence* in 1978. Her most recent novel is *Our Father*, which will shortly be published in Abacus.

In addition to numerous novels, Bernice Rubens has written for the stage, television and films. She lives in North London.

D0519615

Bernice Rubens

MADAME SOUSATZKA

ABACUS

Published by the Penguin Group
27 Wrights Lane, London W8 5TZ, England
Viking Penguin Inc., 40 West 23rd Street, New York, New York 10010, USA
Penguin Books Australia Ltd, Ringwood, Victoria, Australia
Penguin Books Canada Ltd 2801 John Street, Markham, Ontario, Canada L3R 1B4
Penguin Books (NZ) Ltd, 182–190 Wairau Road, Auckland, 10, New Zealand

Penguin Books Ltd, Registered Offices: Harmondsworth, Middlesex, England

First published in Great Britain by Eyre & Spottiswoode 1962
Published in Abacus by Sphere Books Ltd 1982
This edition printed 1987
5 7 9 10 8 6 4

Printed and bound in Great Britain by
Richard Clay Ltd, Bungay, Suffolk
Set in Baskerville

1

All her life, Mrs Crominski had taken anxiety like a
pep-pill. And naturally, over the years, she had become an
addict. She couldn't have lived without it, and even if there
was nothing to worry about she daily took her dose, in
order to ensure a restless, sleepless night, which had for her
become a norm. She carried anxiety about her person like a
built-in shadow, which dogged her even when the sun never
shone.

She rounded the corner into her street. After a half dozen
steps, she could see her own house. Well, thank God, it
wasn't on fire. It was still there, whole, and please God,
Marcus was in it, and please God again, in bed. She hated
these nights when she had to work late, with Marcus by
himself and getting his own supper. Please God he listened
to me and didn't boil a kettle. She could see Marcus's
bedroom window now, and the light shining through the
curtains. Thank God, he's in.

'Marcus,' she shrieked, her key still in the door.

'Momma?' she heard him call.

He's in, and what's more, he's alive. She went upstairs
still carrying her heavy shopping basket, not wanting to
lose any time. She pushed his door, but it was locked.
'Marcus,' she whispered in a panic. 'What's the matter?'

'I'm undressing, Momma.'

'Undressing,' she screamed with relief. 'In front of your
own mother you should be ashamed. A baby he is,' she
addressed the empty landing, 'eleven years old, he should
be ashamed from his mother.' She put down her heavy bag.
'How long you should be?'

'Five minutes.'

She sat down on the leather hold-all, spreading her
hands on her knees.

'Marcus,' she said, 'you ate?'

1

'Yes, Momma.'

'You practised?'

'Yes, Momma.'

'The scales?'

'Yes, Momma.'

'The arpeggios?'

'Yes, Momma.'

'The pieces?'

'Yes, Momma.'

'All twice over?'

'Yes, Momma.'

Mrs Crominski sighed with satisfaction as if she had checked a laundry list and found it complete. 'Homework?' she added.

'Yes, Momma.'

She always felt a slight irritation that things could go smoothly even if she were not in the house. 'You cleaned your teeth?'

'No, Momma.' Mrs Crominski smiled. She heard him unlock his door and jump into his bed. She went unhurriedly into his room.

He lay with the blankets touching his chin. His black hair half obscured the blue embroidered *'Marcus'* on his pillow. Mrs Crominski sat on the bed and Marcus made no move to accommodate her. She balanced on the edge and leaned towards him.

'All right,' he said. He knew the questionnaire that was to follow by heart. 'What did they give you for dinner today?' he asked for her.

'So? What *did* they give you for dinner?'

'Momma, every day they give us meat, potatoes and gravy, cake and custard.'

'Vegetables they don't give you in these fine modern schools?'

'Spinach.'

'Always you forget the vegetables, Marcus.'

'Well, I don't like spinach.'

'Is good for you. Spinach, peas, beans. Every vegetable is good. You had a test today?' she added quickly.

'We had a test yesterday, Momma, I told you.'

2

'Results today, perhaps?'

'Yes.'

Mrs Crominski tried to allow a decent interval to elapse. 'So?' she said, as casually as she could.

'I came second.'

'Second you came,' she said, throwing her arms round him.

'Who is first?'

Marcus struggled to free himself. 'Peter Goldstein.'

'H'm,' said Mrs Crominski, 'the boy with the stutter. Nebisch, let him come first with the stutter. How much he get?'

'He got ninety-six, and Peter Goldstein isn't the one with the stutter, Momma. That's his brother.'

'He got ninety-six without a stutter,' Mrs Crominski mused. 'And you?'

'Ninety-four.'

'Ninety-four,' she said, standing up to add sincerity to her statement. 'You should only do your best and I'm not complaining. You did your best, Marcus?'

'Second is pretty good, Momma.'

'I'm not complaining,' she screamed at him. 'Did I say it's not good? I should complain with such a mark. You did your best. In any case,' she added quietly, bending over him, 'this Peter Goldstein, I'd like to see *him* play the piano. Tomorrow in the concert you will show them. You will be best, best,' she repeated, 'not second best. You go to sleep now. Tomorrow in the morning, you'll brush your teeth twice.'

Marcus's eyes were closed and she thought he'd dropped off to sleep. She looked at him tenderly, regretting all the little hurts she had given him, all the reprimands. The times when she wouldn't let him go swimming because he was late from school. She'd make it up to him tomorrow. Every night when she watched him sleeping, she would make it up tomorrow. She turned out his light and shut the door quietly. She went downstairs with her heavy bag and heavier thoughts about Peter Goldstein.

Marcus sat up in bed and turned his pillow over, blotting out his silk-embossed identity. He brought his right hand

3

out of the blankets and studied it carefully. The black birthmark at the base of his palm, the sundry criss-cross lines that escaped from it like the tracks on a railroad terminal. He turned his hand over and studied his finger-nails. What he saw was not very promising. The only finger left with a fraction of bitable nail was the little one and he wanted to save that till after the concert tomorrow, for a little celebration. He brought out his left hand, knowing only too well what he would find. Each nail had been exhausted. He would have to let the whole hand lie fallow for at least a week before he could reap any profit from it. He studied his right little finger again, and his mouth watered with temptation. He hurriedly put it back under the blanket and solemnly knelt up in his bed, tucking his feet well under him, so that he could sit on them, a position he always assumed when nail-stock was low. After a while he got cramp in his feet, and he stretched himself out under the covers and shut his eyes tightly. He rubbed his knuckles deeply into his eye-sockets. That way he could see a kaleidoscope of colours, and out of the colours would emerge eyes, and out of the eyes, people, and out of the people, pictures. From time to time he would rub his knuckles into his eyes, again, to bring the pictures more sharply into focus or to dissolve them altogether. He thought of the school concert. George Welsh was first on the programme. He would probably sing 'Ave Maria'. He always sang 'Ave Maria', as if it were expected of him. George was a bit of a sissy anyway. Then there'd be all those kids from the lower school with their recitations, and their mothers mouthing the words all having little nut trees but nothing would they bear. Then that prefect Hodges from the Upper Sixth. He'd play the clarinet and all his own form would cheer him, together with the little boys in the First Form who thought he was god. And Marcus would be last. He didn't want to think about his own performance. He only hoped his mother wouldn't arrive late as she did last time. And he hoped his mother wouldn't bring her brown hat or her black hat or her brown coat or her black coat. What else could she wear? Nothing. Perhaps she wouldn't be able to get the afternoon off. Perhaps ... he

4

opened his eyes quickly as if to shut off the thought. He suddenly saw her sitting downstairs having her lonely supper. She had taken off her shoes and she was resting her brown lisle swollen feet on a cushion. He wanted suddenly to run downstairs and kiss her, to make up to her all the little hurts he'd done her. Tomorrow I'll be kind to her, he thought. I'll kiss her in the morning. I'll even kiss her in school if no one's looking. He sat up and turned over his pillow. He put his hand on his silken name and his head on his hand. He felt a scratch on his forehead as a reminder of the bumper harvest on his little finger. He slipped it into his mouth and nibbled at it happily until he fell asleep.

As Marcus predicted, his mother arrived late. And as he feared she wore her brown hat and her black coat. He was sitting on the platform along with the other performers. They nudged him along the line. 'There's yours,' they whispered, as if he couldn't see her. He would have denied the relationship if he could. But his mother was too well known in the school because of her frequent visits to the headmaster. 'Can Marcus be excused the school today, Mister? Tomorrow, he has concert.' Or, 'It's better Marcus shouldn't play football, I think. Swimming yes. Is good for the boy some exercise.' Every week it was something else. He stared defiantly at the ceiling. He daren't look in her direction. Above all, he dreaded that if she caught his eye, she would wave to him. He stared at the brown wooden panels on the ceiling and the noose of ropes and rope-ladders that were always hooked up when the gym was used as an assembly hall. He hated her for being late, for her brown hat and her black coat and the shopping bag that had become part of her wardrobe. And he saw it full, the cauliflower sticking out, and the leeks, and the potatoes underneath. Vegetables, vegetables, vegetables. He felt the weight of it and once again he saw her brown lisle swollen feet. He looked deliberately in her direction and smiled. And sure enough, she waved to him.

The concert was almost over. Marcus was the last item. George Welsh had Ave Maria'd his heart out, and his

5

mother had swooned audibly in the front to establish her relationship. Six juveniles had had a penny, a bright new penny, and had each in the same monotonous way, taken their pennies to the market square, followed one after the other by a proud and mouthing mother. Hodges, the prefect, had brought out his only clarinet solo, and had given the audience, as the headmaster had surely promised he would, a rendering. Marcus was next. When he was announced, murmurs of recognition spread among the audience, and murmurs too of ungrudging praise. Because with all the concerts Marcus gave, he was regarded as a professional and therefore not eligible for comparison.

Marcus sat down at the piano, and waited for the applause to wane. He was about to start, when the back doors of the hall swung open. The whole audience turned around to see the newcomer. She took her place, standing at the back of the hall, and acknowledged the headmaster with a distant nod. Marcus stared at her. In the space of a second he absorbed every detail of her appearance.

The most exciting feature of her face was her forehead, simply because it was invisible. It was covered by a thick mat of black fringe which seemed to grow upward out of the eyebrows. She was covered from neck to toe in black material, of which her handbag seemed to be an extended side-bustle. An assortment of coloured beads and pendants hung over her chest and about her wrists. She was as still and as silent as the two pillars that framed her at the back of the hall. Marcus knew somehow that she was there because of him and he suddenly felt very nervous.

The audience were waiting, but Marcus felt he couldn't begin without her sanction. He looked towards her for some sign. Again she gave an almost imperceptible nod and Marcus started to play. He had chosen a Chopin waltz, mainly because it was popular and one of his mother's favourites. He found no technical difficulties with the piece, and after a while he felt he was playing automatically as if he were manipulating a pianola. He felt the woman's stare on him. He wondered whether the eyebrows were raised under the mat of hair, whether she was smiling, or nodding perhaps. He was sorely tempted to look at her. He stole a glance at the platform, at the row of teachers. None of them were looking at him. All were staring fixedly at the back of the hall. He felt he was being done out of something and he wanted to get the piece over with. He began to hate the woman because she was stealing his limelight. He was surprised to hear that he was approaching the final phrase. The audience had begun to clap after the first of the final three chords. He wondered whether she was clapping too. He decided when he stood up to bow, that he wouldn't look at her, but he found her staring at him all the same. She wasn't clapping. She stood there immobile at the back of the hall. Marcus turned round to acknowledge the applause bursting from the platform. He turned about quickly and just caught her in the act of clapping while his back was turned. She dropped her hands to her sides guiltily and stared back at him.

Most of the audience were getting up and filtering across to the long table at the side of the hall where tea was being served. Marcus watched the woman walk down the centre aisle and towards the headmaster, who had come forward to meet her. They exchanged greetings about half-way. The headmaster looked in Marcus's direction and beckoned to him. Mrs Crominski had seen the signal. Anything that concerned Marcus concerned her, and she was at the headmaster's side before Marcus reached him.

'This is his mother,' the headmaster said, 'Mrs Crominski, and this,' he stretched out his arm to Marcus, 'this is the boy you came to hear. Marcus,' he went on, 'this lady is a great teacher. Madame Sousatzka.'

Mrs Crominski gasped. The name had a definite celebrity flavour. 'Is wonderful, Marcus,' she said, 'such a great lady is come to listen to you.'

Marcus resented his mother for reminding him and he silently begged Madame Sousatzka to forgive her. She smiled at her.

'Mrs Crominski,' she said, 'your son has much talent.' Her English was broken, Marcus noticed, but not like his mother's. His mother's English was broken all over in body and spirit. With Madame Sousatzka each separate word was a minor fracture. 'Who is his teacher?'

7

'Mr Lawrence,' Mrs Crominski said in a tone of declaration. Madame Sousatzka showed no signs of reaction. 'L.R.A.M.,' Mrs Crominski added, as if this entitled the man to at least some sign of recognition. Madame Sousatzka was silent. 'A.R.C.M. Diploma,' Mrs Crominski went on with some desperation. Still Madame Sousatzka waited. Mrs Crominski decided to play her last card. 'M.A. Oxon,' she said. Mr Lawrence was obviously a man who had changed his horses mid-stream. Had Mrs Crominski known Madame Sousatzka she would have realized that the whole of the alphabet after a man's name would have made no impression on her. 'I would like the boy for a pupil,' she said simply.

Mrs Crominski's immediate thought was money, or rather, the lack of it. Marcus hoped fervently that she wouldn't mention it. He was ashamed of their poverty when publicly exposed to a rich party, as he presumed Madame Sousatzka to be. But Mrs Crominski felt no such shame. 'Such money, Madame Sousatzka,' she laughed, 'we don't have.' The headmaster shrugged his shoulders at the irrelevance. 'Madame Sousatzka,' he explained to Mrs Crominski, 'is an old friend of mine. I have known her since she arrived in this country many years ago. Madame Sousatzka does not take anybody as a pupil. Money is quite secondary with her.'

Such a nice Jewish woman, Mrs Crominski thought, and aloud to her, 'My son will pay you back, Madame Sousatzka, a thousand times he will pay you back. Such a profit you will have from him. You will not regret, I tell you.' Mrs Crominski had a talent for looking a gift-horse in the mouth.

Madame Sousatzka opened her bag. It hung like an extra bracelet from her wrist. She didn't remove it from her hand. She unclasped the hook and it fell open. She fumbled blindly through and drew out a white card. When she withdrew her hand, Marcus stared at the open bag. The chaos inside astonished him. It in no way corresponded to her immaculate appearance. He could distinguish by colours at least four crumpled handkerchiefs. A broken comb was caught in a metal compact, spillings of pink powder lay on everything. An open pen had left ink smudges around the lining and some stray hair pins were caught on the inside pocket. Marcus thought of the chaos inside his mother's bag, chaos compounded of the same ingredients, dirty handkerchiefs, papers, pins and bus tickets. Had his mother's bag been open and displayed in public, he would have bolted with shame. But somehow with Madame Sousatzka, it was right and proper. He began to feel very proud of her.

'On Friday at three o'clock,' he heard her say. 'Here on the card is the address.'

'Yes,' said the headmaster to Mrs Crominski in anticipation of her request. 'Marcus can leave school at one o'clock.' He rubbed his hands together and ushered them over to the table for tea. Mrs Crominski beamed at the people around her, all staring at their little group with wonder and admiration. She put her arm round Marcus's shoulder and guided him towards the table. 'Not here, Momma, please,' he begged. She dropped her arm slowly and Marcus felt the hurt in her. She walked on in front of him and Marcus looked at her hat and thought it was the brownest brown he had ever seen.

That night after supper, Mrs Crominski wanted to talk about Madame Sousatzka. But Marcus only wanted to think about her.

'Such a fine woman,' Mrs Crominski said, 'and only the best she takes, I'm told. You should be grateful. And for nothing she takes him too.'

'Why did you have to talk about money, Momma?'

'A lie I should tell? Don't you worry. With the piano you will make plenty of money. You will pay back. A hundred times you will pay back.'

'Isn't she pretty, Momma?' Marcus was talking almost to himself.

'Pretty I wouldn't say. Striking, perhaps. Very funny English she speaks. Not like us. A refugee she is of course. And they can be all their lives in England, they never speak like real English people. Yes,' she mused, 'she's very, very foreign.'

'Let's see her card Momma,' said Marcus, reaching for her bag. Mrs Crominski took the bag from him. 'What's so special about a card?' she muttered, undoing the clasp. She spread the fold of the bag on the table. A brown picture of Marcus's dead father was clipped under the inside mirror. 'He should know,' Mrs Crominski said sadly. 'But he knows. Always, he said, you shouldn't worry, Sadie. When Marcus is big boy he'll take care of you.' Marcus was always being reminded of his father's promise on his behalf. He hardly remembered his father, who had died when Marcus was only three, but Mrs Crominski always kept him by her. 'Your father would be proud of you,' she often said, or, 'Thank God your father can't see you, God bless him, so ashamed he would be.'

'What's so special about a card?' she mumbled, fumbling among the handkerchiefs and papers. She drew it out, already crumpled and stained.

'*Madame Sousatzka*,' she read, '*132 Vauxhall Mansions, W.2*. A long way from Stamford Hill it is,' she said, 'near Hyde Park. Very smart.'

'Let me have it, Momma,' Marcus said, stretching out his hand.

'You'll lose it. Only last week, didn't you lose the housekey?'

'I'll keep it in my room, I promise.'

'Have it,' she said, slightly disturbed by his enthusiasm, 'Too much you shouldn't expect. Madame Sousatzka is a fine lady, a fine refugee lady, but only a human being she is.'

Marcus was staring at the card, transfixed.

'Like me, Marcus, she is, a human being. D'you hear?' she said, though she knew he wasn't listening to her. 'Nothing special she is. Give me the card. I'll keep it.' She snatched it from him. 'Go to bed now. Is late.'

Marcus left the table and went out of the room. She waited for him to reach the stairs before she shouted, 'You forgot something, Marcus?'

'No, Momma,' he shouted back. He'd remembered to kiss her good-night, but he'd deliberately not done so.

'Too busy thinking about Madame Sousatzka, I suppose,' she shouted back.

He went to his room and blew a kiss down the stairs. This was as far as he was prepared to go. He took off his counterpane and turned his pillow over. He lay in bed thinking of the card. 132 Vauxhall Mansions. He imagined a vast castle on the outskirts of the park. And inside was the mistress of the castle, Madame Sousatzka. The walls were hung with tapestries and chandeliers shivered from the ceilings. Marcus sat in a bird-cage on the piano and Madame Sousatzka was stroking his hair through the bars. At first gently, the skin of her palm caressing his forehead. And gradually her hands grew hard and she pressed them deeper and deeper into his scalp. She was hurting him, but he didn't want her to stop. He was consumed with a curiosity as to how it would all end. And suddenly the bird-cage melted around him like a ring of birthday candles, and he woke, sweating, with the strange and terrifying feeling that he had discovered what no one else in the world at any time had ever known.

He heard his mother coming up the stairs. Quickly, he turned his pillow over and pretended to be asleep. He felt his mother bending over him, stroking his hair, her rough lips on his forehead. 'Tomorrow,' he thought, 'tomorrow, I'll make it up to her.'

2

THE week passed as slowly for Madame Sousatzka as it did for Marcus. When Friday came, she sat restlessly in her studio thinking of Boris. Normally at this time on a Friday, Boris would be coming for his lesson. But this was the sixth Friday that he wouldn't come. She decided she would give his hour to Marcus. Boris's music still lay in a neat pile on the piano, a few studies, scales and an album of melodies from the 'classics'. He had had inexorably bad taste, had Boris, but among other faults, she had allowed for that one, too. And even if she thought exclusively of his shortcomings, the pain of his rejection would not leave her. Twelve weeks ago today, he had come to her for the first time. He begged her to take him as a pupil. Madame Sousatzka only took children, but in Boris's case she decided to make an exception. He was a good deal older than she was, and he'd told her he'd played the piano practically all his life.

But practice does not always make perfect, and during his first formal audition, Madame Sousatzka recognized his musical shortcomings, but she was attracted to him, and she kept him on as a pupil, for what he lacked in piano technique he compensated for in other ways. His lessons were on a Tuesday until he decided he needed more of them, so he came twice a week, on a Friday as well. Madame Sousatzka lived for these two lessons.

It was the first and last time in her life that music became of secondary importance. He was her first love, and striking her as it did when she had already reached the age of forty-five, she had a nest-egg of passion to invest in him. He would woo her over the piano, crossly shutting the lid if the keys hampered his gestures of affection. He would tell her stories of the old country and of his mother he had tearfully left behind. At this point, Madame Sousatzka would warm to him in sympathy. It never failed, the old mother bit.

Boris had used it a hundred times before. He told her vivid stories of his childhood that he'd read somewhere or other in a book. He proposed marriage, a castle in the old country, servants, droshky rides. And as an acccompaniment to his proposals, he would play the 'Volga Boatman', a piano piece that at the time was popular in pubs and an infallible encore at amateur recitals. He could really shoot a line, could Boris. Then he suggested a week-end in the country, and when Madame Sousatzka promised many such week-ends after their marriage, he raised one bushy eyebrow and decided he was barking up the wrong tree. Then suddenly, on a Tuesday, he didn't turn up for his lesson. Nor on the Friday. Madame Sousatzka waited patiently each week, until she could no longer remember what he looked like, and all that remained was his voice that echoed from the strings of the grand piano whenever she thought of him. Which was continually.

She took away his pile of music, leaving a dust-framed square on the piano, and buried it on the bottom shelf of the music cupboard. She was excited at the thought of Marcus's coming, but the fact that his mother would come with him disturbed her a little. She had known over-ambitious mothers like Mrs Crominski. Her own mother had been the same, shamelessly pushing her daughter into the public eye. For Madame Sousatzka had not always been a teacher. As a young girl in Germany she'd enjoyed a career as a concert pianist, well known in her own country and considered to be of great promise. But the war put an end to all that, and when she came to England as a refugee just before the outbreak, she had to shelve her career in order to make a practical living. She was twenty and alone. Her parents, along with millions of others, had sat with their backs to the engine in the one-way trains that tip-toed across Europe.

With the help of numerous committees, she managed to find a room in a boarding house run by one of her compatriots who had seen the red light a few years previously. She had begun by giving lessons to children, going to their houses, traipsing along unknown streets from recommendation to recommendation. On the side, she helped out in shops and cafes, and after a few years was able to buy a piano. Meanwhile, she picked up her English, not from any recognized authority, but from other refugees of longer standing. Her voice was laced with a mixture of several European accents, culled from certain and varied relationships of her English apprenticeship, and mixed unsubtly and disproportionately together like a bad salad dressing. The ingredient of German was a foundation to which was added an element of French. This she had acquired from her own piano-teacher in Germany, a Monsieur Laramie, himself not genuine, so by the time it had reached Madame Sousatzka, the Gallic influence was distinctly mongrel. A soupçon of Yiddish she had borrowed from a Mr Bronstein, who ran a delicatessen shop round the corner from the boarding house, and for whom she worked between teaching.

Over the years she had saved a little money and was able eventually to put down a deposit on the three-storeyed letting-house off the Bayswater Road. She changed her name from Süsskatz — it was an obvious mutation — and nailed a brass plate to the door, with the simple inscription, MADAME SOUSATZKA. The change of name doubled the number of her pupils amongst those who sought a foreign caché and gradually her reputation as a teacher grew. She now specialized in prodigies. Marcus would be her tenth current pupil, and the eldest.

It was past three o'clock. Madame Sousatzka had a horror of unpunctuality. It was another fault she had forgiven in Boris. She went over to the window and looked across the square. Mrs Crominski and Marcus were standing against the railings in the centre of the square, looking up at the house. It wasn't the isolated castle Marcus had envisaged. It wasn't in any way different from any of the other houses in the square. It had its equal share of dry rot, damp, bitumen-patched walls; like the others, it shivered on a diminishing leasehold. It was like any other Victorian house that had three years to run and hopelessly faced a full-repair clause. But Marcus was not put out by its appearance. The excitement of seeing Madame Sousatzka again completely overshadowed his concern for how she lived. He tugged at his mother's sleeve and held on to it, because he didn't want her holding his hand, and they crossed over to the house.

Madame Sousatzka welcomed them both equally and she sat them down in the studio. Mrs Crominski made a quick evaluation of the room's furnishings and decided that her imagined estimate of Madame Sousatzka's way of life was grossly exaggerated. She felt a lot better.

'First of all,' Madame Sousatzka was saying, 'it is necessary to forget everything. Everything you learn by your teacher, it is necessary to forget. We start from beginning.'

'Everything?' Mrs Crominski gasped. 'Is impossible. After six years with very fine teacher he should start from the beginning?' This certainly wasn't Crominski economics.

Madame Sousatzka decided she might as well nip Mrs Crominski's participation in the bud. 'Also,' she went on, 'in the lessons, no mothers. This is by me a rule, a strict rule. Not only for you, Mrs Crominski,' she smiled at her. 'All the mothers must suffer a little.'

'You are talking to a woman who knows,' Mrs Crominski warmed to her. 'About suffering I know plenty.'

Madame Sousatzka didn't want to make an issue of it. 'I would like the boy twice in a week,' she said. 'I am very busy,' Mrs Crominski gave a heave of understanding, 'so only time I am able to give lesson is now, three o'clock punctual Friday, and Saturday ten o'clock. Also punctual.' Mrs Crominski heaved again. 'Very close, I know,' Madame Sousatzka went on, 'but each lesson very different. Each lesson we make progress.'

'Is very long way from Stamford Hill,' Mrs Crominski said. 'Also I am not allowed to stay in the lesson. Adds up every week to four journeys, to bring and to take.'

Marcus stared at his mother's brown hat. Not that he needed a bait for his anger. Not only was Madame Sousatzka going to give him one free lesson a week, but two, and here was his mother finding fault. He looked apologetically at Madame Sousatzka. He realized suddenly that recently he had spent a lot of time apologizing to people on his mother's behalf.

'I have solution to problem,' Madame Sousatzka said. She'd worked it all out beforehand. 'Friday night, Marcus stay here in 132 Vauxhall Mansions.' She announced the address as if it were a stately home. 'I have a room. Very nice little room. You will see, Mrs Crominski. Later, I show you. I give him supper and breakfast. After the lesson, Saturday, you come to bring him.'

Now Mrs Crominski was herself a generous woman. And she naturally suspected generosity in other people. Apart from that, the prospect of Marcus staying away from home for even a single night disturbed her. He had never been away from her, but her friends had often mentioned that Marcus was in danger of becoming a mother's boy. Perhaps not a bad thing it would be. 'Is all right that I telephone, every Friday night?' she asked humbly. 'Simply to talk to him,' she said.

Marcus had expected that his mother would refuse to entertain Madame Sousatzka's suggestion. He was so happy with her timid acquiescence that he tried not to look at her brown hat again. He knew well how it would hurt him.

'This week, of course,' Madame Sousatzka said, 'he goes home. We begin next week the two lessons.' She wanted to make some concession in return for Mrs Crominski's agreement. Mrs Crominski was glad for the respite.

'I wait outside now, for the lesson,' she said standing up. She was being painfully obedient and Marcus felt his love for her killing him. Tonight, on their way home, he'd tell her all about his lesson; he'd hold her hand, he'd kiss her good-night. 'But you must, you must,' he said to himself, knowing how fickle were his self-made promises.

'Come,' said Madame Sousatzka, 'I show you the room for Marcus.'

Marcus was not curious about his room. The thought of two lessons a week, a bed, a breakfast and supper with Madame Sousatzka was already too exciting for him. He felt suddenly that the house and Madame Sousatzka belonged to him; that he had never at any time of his life not known her. He sat down at the piano with a sense of ownership. He was surprised to find a metal elevation on

16

the loud pedal that facilitated its use for a short-legged player. He'd never seen one like it before. The stool was very low — Madame Sousatzka's last pupil must have been a dwarf — but he found he could twiddle it to a more suitable height. He wound the knobs on full, rising above the keyboard until his feet dangled helplessly above the pedals. And he thought that if ever he could accommodate that stool-height, he would be fully grown. He didn't hear Madame Sousatzka come in, but he suddenly felt her standing behind him. She turned the knobs and he felt himself descending.

'This height I think is for you,' she said. 'Is comfortable?'

At last he was alone with her, and frightened. 'Yes,' he said, knowing that he would have said 'yes' anyhow.

'Now we will make a beginning,' she said, sitting beside him. 'We will start with the scale. C Major.'

'Which hand?' Marcus asked her. He was staring at the keyboard, afraid to look at her.

'Only one hand you have,' she said. 'The right and the left, they are one hand. They cannot work on their own. You understand, my darrlink?'

Marcus trembled. He didn't understand it at all. He could make a circular movement on his stomach with one hand, and pat his head with the other, both at the same time. It was a favourite pastime during geography lessons. He was tempted to prove to her that she was wrong. But he suspected that there was some truth in her theory as far as being a pianist was concerned. He lifted his hands to the keys. She put her hands over his.

'You must forget everything you have learnt. You want to play for me only with the hands? The hands are nothing, my darrlink. I want in the hands the whole body. When you begin to play, you start in the belly. You must feel it swell, and then the chest, and at last the head, rising, rising.' She paused, her eyes shut, smiling a little. 'You are now at the top of the mountain, Marcus, you relax, you stretch out the hands, and it begins to play.' Madame Sousatzka opened her eyes and relaxed her body, exhausted, her shoulders drooping, her hands limp in her lap. 'You understand?' she said after a while. 'We will try

17

again.' She put her hand on the top of his head, and pressed down. 'Now we will climb the mountain together,' she said, 'rise and push away my hand.'

Marcus lifted his inner body, stretching high, until he could no longer feel her hand on his head. His hands rose involuntarily and without any trembling, he started to play. After one round of the scale, he stopped.

'Go on, go on,' she begged, 'to a scale there is no beginning and no end, a scale is a circle that turns around for ever. Pianissimo,' she whispered on the third time round. He took his hands from the keys. 'Pianissimo, my elephant,' she beamed at him. 'But you must remember, you will not bring the pianissimo from the fingers. Nothing you will bring from the fingers. Nothing,' she thundered, closing Marcus's little fist in her ringed hand, obliterating it in her grasp. 'Nothing,' she repeated. 'They don't know how to do, and who will tell them, these ten poor little worms!'

Marcus felt suddenly sick and he swallowed.

'And where,' said Madame Sousatzka, pointing to his throat, 'and where has the swallow gone, my darrlink? Down, down, down,' she gulped like a novitiate mermaid, 'and it is here,' she prodded his abdomen triumphantly, 'it is from here that the message will come to the fingers. Open the belly,' she cried, 'let it get through. The poor message. It struggles!' Madame Sousatzka let fall a home-made tear. 'Open, breathe, expand, drop shoulder, it comes, it comes,' she screamed, surprised as a successful spiritualist. 'Let it out, let it out!' At this point she released her grasp on Marcus's hand so that his fingers were free.

This system, in which the abdomen was the seat of piano technique, and the anatomical route by which it reached the fingers, was known as the Sousatzka Method, and cost £1 12s. 11d. an hour. And what's more, she didn't take anybody. Not Madame Sousatzka. Her love and respect for music was unquestionable and she was consequently discriminate in her services. Her pupils were talented, some terrifyingly so; all were children, and most of poor parents. Few of them paid. The price was a mere formality. You had to be worthy of Madame Sousatzka's dedication.

After the lesson, Madame Sousatzka put her hands on Marcus's shoulders. 'One day,' she said, 'my Marcus will be the great pianist. Sousatzka will make him. Sousatzka knows. But first, you must be free. Free inside you. Free from all the L.R.A.M.s and all the A.R.C.M.s and the diplomas and the honourable mentions. You will see, my darrlink. But you must work. Only the piano is important for you. The piano and Sousatzka.' She went to the door and called Mrs Crominski into the room.

'You enjoyed it, Marcus?' she said as soon as she came in. 'A long lesson you had, but only scales. No pieces.' Marcus was scowling at her hat again.

'For pieces there is time,' Madame Sousatzka said. 'Plenty time. Sousatzka will make your son the great pianist, Mrs Crominski. She does not teach the piano, she teaches to breathe, to love, to suffer, to live, to die, even.'

'All this she teaches for nothing,' Mrs Crominski marvelled at her generosity.

On their way home, Mrs Crominski pumped Marcus about the lesson. But he was silent. He kept his hands in his pockets, and when they had to cross a road, he hung on to her sleeve. He decided that he would never again make any promises to himself unless he could fulfil them on the spot.

When he went to bed that night, he didn't turn his pillow over, but he hid his embroidered name with his hand. He hadn't told her about the lesson; he hadn't held her hand; he hadn't even kissed her good-night. He tossed from side to side, his mind restless and torn. 'Tomorrow,' he said to himself, 'tomorrow, I will. Yes, I will. I must, I must.'

3

The following Friday, Mrs Crominski packed two little parcels for Marcus to take with him.

'Here, Marcus,' she said, pointing to one of them, 'is pyjamas. Clean pyjamas. Also slippers, dressing-gown, and tooth brush. Don't forget the teeth. I won't be there to remind you.'

Marcus smiled at her. Without any forethought, he was able to throw his arms round her and hug her. He had rare moments like this one and he regretted that they were so infrequent. 'Tomorrow night, Momma,' he said, 'I'll be back here. And then you can remind me. What's in that other parcel?'

Mrs Crominski hesitated. 'Now, is not much, Marcus, but you take it. Is just a little something to eat,' she pressed on quickly, 'perhaps you will be hungry. With strangers you never know.'

'But I'll have supper and breakfast there, Madame Sousatzka said so.'

'And tea? What about tea? These refugees, Marcus, they are different. Tea they don't have. Believe me, you will be grateful at five o'clock for something. Tomorrow you will say how you enjoy it.'

Marcus took it from her and at the same time wondered how he could conceal it. She was putting on her hat and coat. 'Tonight I will talk to you on the telephone.'

'There's no need to ring me up, Momma. Nothing can happen to me. You're going to take me there and you're going to call for me.'

'Only good-night I should say to you,' she said peevishly. She put the two parcels into her leather bag. She didn't trust Marcus to carry them. She would hand them over at Madame Sousatzka's.

When they arrived at Vauxhall Mansions, Marcus

stretched out his hand for the parcels. But Mrs Crominski wanted to deliver him right inside the house.

'But Momma,' Marcus said, 'you can watch me go up the steps. You know I've arrived safely.' For some reason, he wanted to keep Madame Sousatzka and her house to himself.

Mrs Crominski handed over the two parcels. She watched him go up the steps and was disturbed to see the door opened even before he had time to press the bell. She looked at the closed front door for a long time and she felt that it was Marcus who had shut it on her. It was then that she realized that tonight, for the first time, she would be alone in the house. She wanted to stay in Marcus's vicinity until the following morning, but the district frightened her. With its large pillared houses and wide-open streets, it was foreign to her and she feared for Marcus's safety. She began to regret the meeting with Madame Sousatzka and felt that no good would come of the partnership. She felt a sudden longing for Marcus's old teacher, Mr Lawrence, with all the safe letters after his name. But Mr Lawrence himself had said that there was little more he could teach Marcus. She wondered if Marcus would ever feel the burden of his talent as much as she did.

She shut her eyes on the bus as it crossed the alien streets of the West End. She knew by the changing accents around her when it had crossed the borders into North London. When she walked towards her street, it did not occur to her to worry whether her house was still there, or even if it were on fire. Her thoughts were in Vauxhall Mansions, in the little square bedroom; the shoes, with their still-tied shoelaces under the bed and the brown paper from the two parcels on the floor.

But Mrs Crominski was on a false scent. What was to have been Marcus's bedroom, had suddenly during the course of the week been switched to a store-room for one of Madame Sousatzka's tenants. Marcus was to sleep in the basement in the Countess's apartment, where a spare ante-room adjoined her own.

The Countess had been the first of Madame Sousatzka's tenants. She was known to all acquaintances as the dirty

21

Countess and was never in the slightest bit offended. She felt the name was an individual one and she would answer to no other. But among her intimates she was known as Uncle. She had been Uncle from the beginning when she had moved into Madame Sousatzka's house. She had voluntarily opted for the basement. She felt far more at home on a lower level, hemmed in by gratings on the window that she never wanted removed. She had told Madame Sousatzka that she was a Countess, and what's more, a Countess in her own right. And in case Madame Sousatzka didn't fully appreciate her status, she hastened to explain that she had inherited the title directly from her father, since she was an only child, and in order to make clear her direct descendency, she desired to be known by the name of Uncle Countess, which title, she felt, would embrace both the quality and the rank of her status. Over the years, she had become simply 'Uncle'.

She had not cleaned or tidied her room since she had moved into the house years ago. To do anything physical was a great effort for the Countess. She must have been the laziest person on earth. She would sit all day in her rocking-chair by an old and noisy gas-fire. Within leg's reach was a bed, a gas-ring, a few cooking·utensils, and a shelf of foodstuffs. The bare necessities of life all huddled within arm's length, so that the Countess had only to steer her rocking-chair to get on with the business of living. The nearest lavatory to her room was in the garden outside, a mere fifty yards' distance. The Countess looked upon these unavoidable journeys as marathons, and she would sink back into her rocking-chair after these sorties, breathless and exhausted, and furious at the amount of energy she had expended. In all, the dirty Countess was a 'sitter'. She would sit for days looking at a wall. Then her gaze would concentrate on a patch of the wallpaper pattern. She would stare at the small black and white squares so intently, that sometimes she could see only black, or at other times, by way of a change, only white. Wisdom can come from looking at a wall, she would tell Madame Sousatzka.

She was an endless smoker. She had a consignment of cigarettes and newspapers – she was a glutton for newspapers – delivered every morning outside her door. And she would make her journeys to the garden coincide with their collection. There were cigarette ends and ash all over the floor. In fact, the Countess's only exercise was flicking her ash into an ash-tray by the side of her rocking-chair, and very often she missed because she wouldn't stretch that far.

By her side, and reaching almost to the arm of her chair, was a pile of out-of-date newspapers, neatly folded, fresh and crisp as on a stall. For in fact, although they were months old, they had never been opened. Only the back page was of any interest to the Countess because of the crossword. She did as many crosswords as she smoked cigarettes, and one was an accompaniment to the other. On her lap lay the current evening paper, and of this, she only read one page. Politics and gossip could not assuage the Countess's conscience. For she had a conscience. She was acutely aware of the sterility of her existence. The line about conserving her energy kidded no one, least of all the Countess. To read the column headed *'Situations Vacant'* was her daily confessional. It was the last of her good intentions, and even this she dispensed with as quickly as possible. She had a special routine for dealing with the column. She would run her finger down the initial heavy type of each classification. *Assistant* anything didn't interest her. Somehow she couldn't see herself in a subordinate position. Neither could she imagine herself as *Capstan Setter,* and though she assumed she would make a very good *Car Greaser,* she didn't quite see why she had to. A dozen or so *Experienced* followed. This was decidedly not one of the Countess's qualifications, and in anticipation of what she knew by long habit was to follow, she slowed her finger till it rested hopefully on *Intelligent*. This she knew she was. Of that there was no question. Gingerly she lifted her hand to see the rest of the advertisement, only to find that the other qualifications needed were secretarial. The Countess had always considered the two terms antithetical. It was a principle with her. There were only a few 'Intelligent' advertisements, and all too soon her finger caressed the inevitable list of *Jig and Tool.* Jig and Tool bearers were always in demand, and although she had not the slightest

23

notion of what they were, she felt she wasn't one of them. *Messengers* and *Male Cleaners* left her cold. With *Models* she declared herself not guilty, likewise to *Sheet Metal* workers. What a demand there always was for *Time and Motion* experts. She never ceased to wonder what they were, and whether perhaps she was one of them. But the effort to find out was too much for her, so that even though through her negligence they had lost the greatest Time and Motion expert of all time, she didn't consider it worth the effort. *Shorthand Typists* and *Secretaries* occupied almost one and a half columns of close type. She skipped these by contemptuously. Her next stop was *Woman*. This qualification was basic, and there was no doubt in the Countess's mind that she had it, but she never seemed to fit into the packers or cleaners that followed. *Woman* she knew from long practice was her last chance for they were always followed by *Young*, which the Countess took as a personal affront, and she would stuff the paper into an imaginary waste-basket at her side.

The Countess had welcomed Madame Sousatzka's suggestion of having Marcus in her apartment, for her loneliness was sometimes unbearable. She had decided to teach him to play draughts if he didn't already know how. It was an effortless game and obviated the necessity for conversation.

After the lesson, Madame Sousatzka gave Marcus tea and took him down to the basement. 'Is she a real Countess, Madame Sousatzka?' Marcus asked.

'In Sousatzka house, only genuine article,' Madame Sousatzka said.

She knocked on the Countess's door and they went in without waiting for an answer. 'Uncle,' Madame Sousatzka said, 'here is Marcus.'

Marcus was astonished at Madame Sousatzka's mode of address. He himself had been prepared to bow and call the Countess, your ladyship. But when he saw her untidy room, and then the Countess herself, with her hair unkempt, and vast, torn slippers on her feet, he began to be less convinced of her status. He smiled at her and she pointed at the draughts board at her feet. He picked it up, together with the pieces, and assembled a game on a small table near the fire. He moved the table over to her chair.

'Black?' he asked.

The dirty Countess shook her head. Marcus turned the board round so that the white was on her side. He had cottoned on to her lethargy very quickly. They started to play and a whole game had been finished before Marcus realized that Madame Sousatzka had left the room and not a single word had passed between them. They started another game, Marcus asking whatever questions were necessary and taking a nod or a shake in answer. He fully accepted the fact that his relationship with Uncle was to be a wordless one, and he had the feeling that they would get on very well together. He was excited at the thought of telling his mother all about the real Countess in Madame Sousatzka's house. But he felt his mother would disapprove of her. Perhaps after all it would be better if he kept the Countess to himself.

When Madame Sousatzka came to fetch him to supper, the Countess had fallen asleep, her hand still clutching the last black king she had taken from Marcus.

Supper was in Madame Sousatzka's kitchen and her other two tenants were already seated. 'This is Marcus,' she said, 'Marcus Crominski. Remember the name, Cordle,' she said to a white-coated gentleman on one side of the table. 'Is a very good name for very good pianist.'

Mr Cordle stood up and stretched out a bony hand. Marcus took it and felt its gentle pressure. 'I shall be seeing you,' Mr Cordle said. In any other setting, Marcus would have been astonished at such a greeting, but the eccentricity of Madame Sousatzka and Uncle had already conditioned him to such oddities. 'Why?' he asked.

'I am an osteopath,' Mr Cordle said. Marcus didn't know what the word meant, but he was too shy to ask. He hoped he would remember it so that he could ask his mother. Or better, look it up in his dictionary in case it was something his mother disapproved of.

'And Jenny,' Madame Sousatzka was saying. Jenny didn't get up. She stretched out her left hand and took Marcus's in her own. She looked carefully at his palm.

'You're right, Sousatzka,' she said. 'In his hand it's a famous name.' She gave Marcus a broad smile and Marcus saw how young and pretty she was. 'I'll tell Momma about Jenny and Mr Cordle,' he thought, but immediately decided against it. The number of facts he was piling up to conceal from his mother excited him but at the same time made him feel guilty. He knew that he could cry at will, simply by thinking of her lisle-stockinged feet. He hoped he could keep the thought out of his mind at least until the meal was over and he was in bed. Then he would cry and feel better. And tomorrow when they went home from Madame Sousatzka's, even if he told her nothing about Mr Cordle or Uncle or Jenny, he would hold her hand.

Madame Sousatzka placed him at the head of the table and she herself sat at the other end. There was a dish of cold chicken on the table and a bowl of tinned pears, which Marcus took to be for dessert. He was astonished to see Madame Sousatzka, Cordle and Jenny help themselves to both at the same time. When the dishes were passed to him he did likewise, though he was sure he would hate the combination. But he had the feeling that all these people, especially if they lived with Madame Sousatzka, were the right people, doing the right things and thinking the right thoughts. As he looked at the white meat on his plate and the pear juice seeping from its weave, he felt he was one of them. But only partly. He felt, too, an unhappy sense of betrayal of Stamford Hill. He wondered what his mother . . . and with the sudden thought of his mother, even without the lisle stockings, he knew he was going to cry. He ate a mouthful of food quickly, hoping to swallow the lump in his throat along with it. Jenny noticed his discomfort.

'Marcus,' she said, smiling at him, 'next Friday after your lesson, you must come and have tea in my room. D'you like crumpets?'

For Marcus the word was nearer home, miles and miles away from the concept of chicken and pears. His mother bought him crumpets every Monday. He suddenly loved Jenny. Yes, he decided, without any doubt, he could tell his mother about her.

He helped Jenny with the washing-up after supper, and when he went to bed, both Jenny and Madame Sousatzka kissed him. Cordle parted from him with the same words with which he had greeted him. 'I'll be seeing you,' and to his dismay Marcus realized that he had forgotten the word Cordle said he was.

He got into his bed, his mind whirling with thoughts about the Sousatzka establishment. Automatically he turned over his pillow, and then he realized that he was a long way from home. He suddenly remembered the second parcel his mother had given him. He reached under his bed and brought out three clean raw carrots. They make you see in the dark, or they make your hair grow curly. Or was that cabbage? Vegetables, vegetables, vegetables. He munched at one slowly, keeping his hand pressed hard on his hair to stop it from curling. He wondered vaguely how to dispose of the other two carrots. He would tell his mother that she'd been right. He'd enjoyed them. He'd been grateful for them. More lies. One day, when he was older, and loved her with less pain, he would begin to tell her the truth.

4

And so every Friday night and Saturday morning, Marcus
lived with the Sousatzka Method. He grew less and less
interested in his school. Among his school friends and in
class, he felt himself slightly superior. After all, he had
eaten pears and chicken, both at the same time; he felt
himself almost betrothed to Jenny, with whom he had tea
every Friday; he knew a man in a white coat who was
something special, and above all, he spent his week-ends
with a real Countess. The word Cordle had used still
escaped him, and it was not until about six months after
first meeting him that its meaning became clear.

Of late, his mother had been nagging him to hold himself
erect. 'A cripple you will grow up to be,' she warned him.
'Is the way you practise. When Mr Lawrence was your
teacher, with a straight back you played. Also you gave
concerts, it's true. But concerts. And now already six
months with Madame Sousatzka, and a hump he has. And
does she mention a concert? Never.'

'Madame Sousatzka's a much better teacher than Mr
Lawrence,' Marcus defended her. 'Madame Sousatzka
teaches more than just the piano. I've learnt more with
Madame Sousatzka in six months than I ever learnt with
Mr Lawrence. If anyone can make me a pianist, it's
Madame Sousatzka.'

'Madame Sousatzka this, Madame Sousatzka that. Like
she's God you talk about her. And tell me, since she's so
clever, the almighty Madame Sousatzka, tell me please,
what great names have learnt with her? Who is the famous
pupil of the great Madame Sousatzka? Who? I ask you. For
twelve years she is teaching the piano. What happened to
all the pupils? They go afterwards to someone else perhaps?
Someone better, perhaps? All right, so you learnt already
many pieces with her, concertos and so on. But for concer-

tos you need orchestra. You need concerts. You need audience. I'm not satisfied. I'm not satisfied at all,' she concluded. 'Next Friday, I'll have a talk with Madame Sousatzka. About two things I want to know. One is the hump, the other is the concerts.'

His mother's decisive tone frightened Marcus. Above all, he wanted to keep Madame Sousatzka and her household to himself. He didn't want his mother trespassing on what he guiltily considered his private life. 'You don't have to tell her, Momma, I'll talk to her,' he said weakly.

'I can see you talking to the great Madame Sousatzka. She will tell you a hump is in the fashion, and you'll believe her. She'll tell you a concert is out of the fashion, and also that you'll believe. No, I'll see her myself. Next Friday, I'll talk to her.'

And despite all Marcus's pleadings and promises to handle the matter himself, Mrs Crominski forced her way into Vauxhall Mansions the following Friday. While on the bus, she had rehearsed her speech. She wasn't going to ask. She was going to tell, and Madame Sousatzka was going to listen to her. She slowly began to hate her, not only for the hump and the lack of concerts, but because Marcus practically worshipped her.

But when she faced Madame Sousatzka in her studio, all her belligerence melted. There was something disarming about Madame Sousatzka. She was a woman who could be hated only *in absentia*.

'Is it possible we should have a talk?' Mrs Crominski said timidly.

'Naturally.' Madame Sousatzka was very forthcoming. 'We will talk about Marcus?'

'There are one or two things . . .' Mrs Crominski had completely forgotten her speech. She tried to hang on to her determination to voice her opinion anyway. As Marcus left the room, he smiled at Madame Sousatzka and shrugged his shoulders as if to absolve himself from responsibility for anything his mother might say. He decided to go downstairs and talk to Uncle.

'Well, Mrs Crominski,' Madame Sousatzka said when they were alone, 'have you heard your son? Have you heard the music he makes since he is with me? So proud you must be of him.'

But Mrs Crominski hadn't come to discuss Marcus's talents. 'It's about the hump,' she said.

'The hump?'

'Yes.' Mrs Crominski tried to hide her impatience. 'The hump.'

'Where, Mrs Crominski, is the hump?'

'Where else should a hump be? On his back of course.'

Madame Sousatzka laughed and Mrs Crominski's belligerence came slowly flooding back. 'Ha ha,' she echoed, 'so funny it is. A cripple he is, my son. A big joke.'

Madame Sousatzka was genuinely taken aback. 'Mrs Crominski,' she said, taking her hand, 'is no hump, is no cripple, Marcus. Is only for the time being, the bump.' Madame Sousatzka's diagnosis was less severe. 'Listen, I explain. For years he learn with Mr L.R.A.M. For years he is tight inside him. He plays for Mr Letter-Man with straight back. And you think, this is fine, my Marcus has a straight back. But you are wrong, Mrs Crominski. That is not a straight back. That is strait-jacket back. All the muscles tense and tight. I teach Marcus to be pianist, not soldier. You see, the back,' she went over to Mrs Crominski and ran her fingers over her spine. 'The back is like the elastic. It moves. It moves with the head and the hands. With Mr L.R.A.M. Marcus plays the piano with his fingers. The back is not wanted. Therefore is the back straight. But with Sousatzka, he plays with the whole body, with the back also. He relax. The bump is what is left from Mr Lawrence constrictions. It comes out from the body. Soon it will all be gone.'

It seemed logical enough to Mrs Crominski and she was more or less satisfied with the explanation. She realized that none of her prepared speech had been made and she was slightly irritated that Madame Sousatzka had so easily made her point.

'But is simple,' Madame Sousatzka went on. 'Upstairs is Mr Cordle. A very great osteopath. Very often I have the pupils who come to me from letter-men. And very often happens the bump. Mr Cordle will massage after each lesson. Not to pay,' she added hastily, 'In all ways, Marcus is for nothing. A few weeks' massage. All gone then, Mrs Crominski.'

Mrs Crominski smiled. 'You are good to my boy, Madame Sousatzka,' she said. 'Is very difficult to bring up a boy without a father. Especial a boy with talent like my Marcus.' She was beginning to love this woman and she began to understand and forgive Marcus's adoration. 'Another thing I want to talk,' she went on chattily. 'About a concert.'

'Of course, of course,' Madame Sousatzka said quickly. 'Many concerts. But when he is ready, Mrs Crominski. Only when Sousatzka knows he is ready.'

There was such a finality in her answer that Mrs Crominski felt she could not pursue the question without casting doubt on Madame Sousatzka's musical judgment. But she knew that later on she would regret her silence. She couldn't let Madame Sousatzka get away with everything so easily. First the hump and now the concerts. She tried desperately to pick up some threads of her speech.

'Already for six months he is having with you the lessons. Already with Mr Lawrence he is giving concerts. Why for Mr Lawrence he is ready, and after six months with you, with more pieces to play, he suddenly isn't ready. That I don't understand.' Even with this timid protest Mrs Crominski felt she had gone too far. 'Of course,' she added, 'is difference between you and Mr Lawrence.'

'Is big difference,' Madame Sousatzka said, 'for Mr Lawrence he is ready. For Sousatzka, no. Believe me, Mrs Crominski, when Marcus is ready, so many concerts he shall give. And six months, you say. Six months, it is nothing. From the beginning we have started.'

Mrs Crominski had never been convinced of that necessity. She recalled with a smile the regular Wednesday lesson, when Mr Lawrence came to the house, before all this nonsense of traipsing every Friday to the other end of the world and getting a hump for your trouble, even if it was all for nothing.

'When will he be ready?' she said, suddenly angry.

'Mrs Crominski,' Madame Sousatzka made an effort to

be calm. 'If only concerts you want for Marcus, there are other teachers. Plenty other teachers. If for being a great pianist, there is only Sousatzka.'

Mrs Crominski didn't quite see why the two were antithetical. But Madame Sousatzka's calm tone of voice had made her feel ungrateful. 'I'm sorry,' she said. 'Grateful you know we are. You know how it is in the life. Like all the mothers I am anxious for the best for my boy. I am happy you teach him, Madame Sousatzka. Very much he loves you, almost he forget sometimes I am his mother. Yes, is true,' she said and she realized it suddenly for the first time. 'Of course,' she added quickly, 'only sometimes he calls me Madame Sousatzka, now I come to think of it. Not very often he calls me that. Is habit, that's all.'

'Of course,' said Madame Sousatzka, jubilant. No matter how hard Mrs Crominski tried to take back what she had said, she had told her what she had wanted to know. And she immediately set to thinking how she could keep Marcus and his love. She couldn't allow him to play in public. That was out of the question. If he did, his genius would be noticed, taken up by some showman or other, he would be launched and celebrated and she would lose him. There would be other teachers, the lettered ones, recognized by the Establishment, and she would get the occasional card from him at Christmas. She had had too many of those cards from other Sousatzka renegades. Her mantelpiece over Christmas was a tinsel testimony to her failure. Marcus she was determined to keep.

On the bus on the way home, her eyes shut, Mrs Crominski was biting her tongue. She deeply regretted having betrayed Marcus's feelings about Madame Sousatzka. She knew, too, how miserably she had failed in her cover-up. Her failure embarrassed her, and she voluntarily twitched her body. It also made her angry. 'Three more months I'll give that woman,' she said to herself, 'if Marcus doesn't give a concert by then, I'll take him away from her. And the hump. All that nonsense she talks. A bump, she calls it. Glasses she needs. It had better go, and quickly.'

She had to move up to make room for a large gentleman burdened with parcels who sat heavily beside her, stepping on her foot in doing so.

'Bitte,' he said, with some concern.

'You foreigners,' said Mrs Crominski, 'you're all the same.'

Madame Sousatzka looked lovingly at Marcus as he sat down at the piano for his lesson. Since Marcus had been coming to her, the memory of Boris had grown less painful. But she realized, especially now, after her talk with Marcus's mother, the possibilities of losing him. She knew that with his talent, he had a right to a better teacher than herself. She knew that to teach was only a substitute for her, her evolved 'method' only an excuse for having failed to make the established grades. In the beginning she had believed in her method, even though its origins were specious. She had had utter faith in it, but it was difficult to ignore the fact that none of her pupils had greatly benefited from it. Perhaps they hadn't stayed long enough to understand it. Yes, that was it, she convinced herself. With Marcus, if she could only keep him, it would work. She put her arm round his shoulders, outlining with her fingers the slight curve on his back. She remembered that it had been one of Boris's affectionate gestures. 'All the rubbish from Mr Lawrence's teachings,' she said.

'Oh, it's nothing,' Marcus wanted her to know that he didn't attach as much importance to it as his mother.

'In any case, after the lesson, you will go to Cordle. He will take away the bump. He is osteopath.'

Marcus smiled at the recollection of the word and Cordle's first strange greeting, 'I'll be seeing you.' He had seen Cordle very rarely since their first meeting, and he was too excited at the prospect of seeing him again to concentrate deeply on his lesson.

Madame Sousatzka noticed it and half resented Cordle as a competitor for Marcus's affections. She could feel Marcus's impatience with her, and once or twice she caught him looking at the clock on the mantelpiece. She was going to have to fight to keep him. But she didn't want his resentment. She decided to cut the lesson short so that he wouldn't feel that she was holding him.

'Today, such a headache Sousatzka has,' she told him.
'Tomorrow, we have long lesson, yes? You go now to
Cordle,' she said.

'I'm sorry,' said Marcus, highly delighted. Without
thinking, he flung his arms round her and kissed her. 'I
hope the headache will be gone tomorrow,' he said.
Madame Sousatzka clung to him.

'For you and for the lesson, Sousatzka will be better,' she
said. She watched him as he left the room, noting the thin
wet lines on the backs of his knees, like furrows on a young
brow, the half-hearted crease in his short trousers, the
knotted corner of a handkerchief that dropped from a
side-pocket, and the black soft mould of his head. She lay
on the couch and shut her eyes, clinging to his arm-prints
on her shoulders, and trying hard not to think of Cordle's
hands on him.

Cordle lived on the first landing, and Marcus knocked
timidly on his door. Cordle himself, in his white jacket,
opened it. He ushered Marcus into the room and pointed
shyly to a couch at the far end.

'Take off your jacket, will you,' he said, 'and lie down.'

Marcus climbed on to the couch and lay on his back.
Cordle was fiddling with some charts in the corner and
Marcus looked at the room around him. It seemed bigger
than Madame Sousatzka's, and very bare. On the wall
opposite him, there hung an anatomical chart, one of the
many that almost papered the four walls of the room. It was
the picture of the body of a man, shaded in a hundred
different colours. Colour was a great thing with Mr Cordle.
The functions of each bone prescribed its own colour. The
spinal column, for instance, was filled in in blue, because
blue was the imagined colour of balance. The rib-cage was
shaded gradually from black to grey, and the breast-bone
sprouted in a menacing red. All the charts on the walls were
similarly coloured, some in greater detail than others. They
looked like political maps of the world, for to Mr Cordle,
the whole of the discovered universe lay in the body of

Man. In each picture, there were certain unshaded parts, which Mr Cordle had not yet accounted for in colour.

'The undiscovered continents, they are,' he would tell his patients. 'One day, I, Horace Cordle, will discover them. Horace Cordle, the Discoverer,' he laughed, and he would pose himself as a statue in a National Square.

'The body, Marcus, is the world,' he said, walking over to the couch. He switched on a lamp on a table beside him. A pair of curved yellowing rib-bones protected the naked bulb like two stubborn stamens. 'Here,' he said, laying his hand on Marcus's navel, 'is the centre of the Universe. On the chest, spreading over the rib-cage, lies Asia. Take care of Asia, Marcus,' he said, 'it can be the cause of great troubles. Now turn over. I think what we came for is a little pressure on Central America.' He pressed his long, beautiful hands into the small of Marcus's back. If Madame Sousatzka could have her method, Mr Cordle was entitled to his, too.

For an half an hour, Marcus lay submitting himself to Cordle's gentle pressures. He thought of the contrast between his life at school and his week-ends with Madame Sousatzka. He couldn't decide which one was real for him. Now, with Cordle's hands on his back, the boy who sat in a geography lesson or at the science bench was not he. Yet when he was at school, it was someone else he saw at Madame Sousatzka's. And his mother. To which world did she belong? He saw her separate and alone, cocooned in a sheath of purity that had been forced on her. He knew that if he really belonged anywhere, it was with her. And at that moment he loved her very dearly.

5

Mrs Crominski never forgot the promise she made to herself on the bus home from her interview with Madame Sousatzka. Three months she had decided to give her and as the weeks passed, she ticked off in her mind what was left of Madame Sousatzka's reprieve. Another week to go, and still no talk of a concert. She decided that she had better prepare Marcus for the break.

He was practising just before going to his lesson. 'Sounds to me like an angel he plays,' Mrs Crominski said. Marcus knew how she enjoyed listening to his playing and he didn't mind her sitting in on his practice. Every week-end he spent at Madame Sousatzka's, he was aware of her non-participation. Although he was glad for it, it was yet another rejection he had to compensate her for. He stopped playing.

'I've learnt so much with her, Momma,' he said. 'D'you know, I never understood the piano before I went to her.'

'How much is it to understand before you give a concert? Nine months it is already. So many pieces. So much practising. What for, I'm asking.'

'You're impatient, Momma. She says I can give a concert when I am ready.'

'When he's ready, when he's ready.' Mrs Crominski was exasperated. 'For me, you're ready. That's enough. Marcus,' she said solemnly, 'I'm thinking you should leave her.'

'No!' Marcus shouted. It wasn't only Madame Sousatzka he would have to leave. It was Uncle, Jenny and Cordle. It was a whole way of life he would have to surrender. 'No, I'm not leaving her,' he said defiantly. 'She's the best teacher in London, Momma,' he begged, 'I don't want to leave her.'

'So all your life you'll stay with Madame Sousatzka. A beard you'll grow there and still you're not ready. Is no good, Marcus. Money I'm not wasting. That I know. But time. Time. Next week I'll go and tell her. Is time you're wasting and a hump you're growing. Yes, a hump. I don't care what she calls it. Is still there. Have you ever heard such a thing! A boy should go for piano lessons and a hump he gets. Next Friday, I'll tell her, and this time, believe me, I'm not listening to any nonsense.'

'I'll tell her,' said Marcus. 'I'll tell her today. There you are. I'll tell her at today's lesson. Then you don't have to come and see her.'

'Today in any case you can tell her. Next Friday, I go. Tell her I come. Next Friday, tell her, you should be ready for a concert.'

Mrs Crominski put on her hat and coat and prepared to leave. At the door, Marcus looked helplessly at her brown hat. 'Momma,' he said, 'you look better without that hat.'

'All of a sudden,' she smiled, 'he takes notice of his mother.' She took off her hat and patted her hair. 'Is better?'

'It's all right,' Marcus said.

'All right, he says. Is better or not better?'

'It doesn't make any difference,' Marcus said. Mrs Crominski put her hat firmly on her head again.

'Everything you do is wrong,' she said to the mirror. 'You wear a hat. Is wrong. You don't wear a hat. Is also wrong.' She scrutinized her face in the glass. 'Is not a nice hat,' she decided. 'All right, so when you give a concert, I buy a new hat. If by then I'm still alive,' she muttered. She picked up her empty shopping bag.

'Why d'you always have to take that bag with you?' Marcus said.

'Some vegetables I buy on the way home,' she sulked. 'Suddenly he's ashamed of his mother with her hat and her bag. If the great Madame Sousatzka goes out with brown hat and shopping bag, is all right, I suppose. Will I thank God when he leaves her,' she threatened.

'It's got nothing to do with Madame Sousatzka,' Marcus shouted at her.

'Deaf yet I'm not,' Mrs Crominski said. 'I should live to hear my son shout at me. Thank God your father, bless him, can't hear you. And all because of this woman. Suddenly his mother's not good enough for him. Well,' she suddenly shouted at him, 'you want to go to your lesson or not?'

Marcus followed her out of the door. What was it if it wasn't the hat, he thought. He wanted to put his arm round her and protect her until they got to Vauxhall Mansions. But he couldn't. And he hated himself because he couldn't touch her. Tomorrow, he said to himself, tomorrow, I'll . . . He saw a small stone on the pavement and he kicked it violently. Mrs Crominski watched it race past her, barely missing her foot. Marcus shuddered at the interpretation his mother would put on his act. He rushed to her side and took her hand, praying that she would make no comment on his gesture.

'All of a sudden he loves his mother,' she said.

Marcus wondered whether with other boys of his age, it all came naturally.

'Please, how many times, my darrlink, pianissimo. Not like the . . .'

'An elephant?' From long experience, Marcus knew the analogy for his unsuccessful pianissimos.

'You are right, my darrlink,' she said, stroking his hair, 'an elephant.'

Madame Sousatzka bent over the music, her bosom resting on the keys in a distinctly minor chord. She underlined the offended passage with a red pencil. Marcus took this opportunity of looking at her watch which she wore round her neck and which swung like an inquisitive plumbline in the area of her cleavage. Ten past four. Another twenty minutes. Then up to Mr Cordle on the first floor. That would last until five. Then he'd go up to the attic and see Jenny. He decided he would do nothing else but think of Jenny until five. He would execute all his pianissimos gently in her name.

Madame Sousatzka raised herself from the keys in an ascending arpeggio.

'Lower the shoulder,' she said, putting her hands around

him. 'You are not free, my darrlink. How can the message come to the fingers if you do not open the body to let it through? Look at the bump,' she said. 'Is that Mr Lawrence again and all his letters.'

But Madame Sousatzka knew that the slight curve in Marcus's spine was not due to Mr Lawrence at all, but the continual lowering of the shoulder to give the 'Message' a freer passage. Week after week, Cordle tried to put it right. What Madame Sousatzka bent, Mr Cordle would straighten, and the battle for poor Marcus's back was waged every Friday night with the same amount of give and take on each side.

'It's all in a good cause,' Madame Sousatzka would tell Cordle whenever he questioned her method. 'You go for walk,' she would tell him, 'you stick on the straight main road, and what do you see? Cars, factories, smells – no more. But if you go through the lanes,' she whispered, 'the twisted narrow streets, what do you see? Life, Meaning, Beauty. The true message cannot travel on the main road.'

Mr Cordle did not try to disprove her vague logic; partly because he was very fond of her, but mainly because it would have cost him most of his clientele which consisted of all those in the Sousatzka Conservatoire who had taken the 'method' to heart.

'Try it again, my darrlink,' Madame went on. 'This time, I know you will make it.'

Marcus thought of Jenny, of the crumpets she would have ready for him when he got upstairs; how he would tip-toe into her room and she would be sitting with her back to the door, painting her nails. And he'd creep up behind her and put his hands over her eyes, and she'd pretend she was frightened and she would scream, 'Who is it?' and Marcus would know that she knew very well who it was because it had happened every Friday for the last nine months.

'That's much better,' said Madame Sousatzka. 'No more elephants. Now we will make an end with the study.'

The study always rounded off the lesson. Most brass-plate piano teachers would have started the lesson with the study; studies, scales and arpeggios, the drudge work that

39

was written to be got over with, as quickly as possible, as a conscience-saver for both teacher and pupil. With Madame Sousatzka, it was the other way round, rather like a footballer who practises his passes after the game is over and won.

Once more, she bent over the piano to make a re-adjustment of fingering on the music. Twenty past four. Forty minutes to Jenny.

'Now,' she said, leaning back in her chair and shutting her eyes. 'We will both of us listen to it from the beginning to the end. I will listen, you will listen, and it will play. When you're ready, darrlink, tell it to begin.'

She took a deep audible breath. Marcus watched her large nostrils dilating, revealing two small clusters of black hair. When she breathed out, it would be the signal to start. Marcus laid his hands on the piano and waited for Madame Sousatzka's exhalation. She took in an inordinate amount of air, much more, Marcus thought, than was necessary for any practical purpose, and when it was all up there, up in her head, her eyelids closed and her nostrils fluttering, she kept it there, simmering, on an even keel. Marcus waited. He bent backwards and looked at her watch. Thirty-three minutes to Jenny. Madame was certainly record-breaking this lesson. Then it came, suddenly, in a great gush. Marcus pressed the first chord of the study into the piano keys, drowning its release. Now they were off. About half way through, she murmured to him, 'Listen, my darrlink, how well it plays.' There was a time, when Marcus first started taking lessons from Madame Sousatzka, that he resented the 'it' routine. 'It's me playing,' he used to argue with her. He didn't see why anything else should be given credit. One day when she had whispered through a scale passage how lucidly it was playing, he left the leading note high and dry, and went off to the corner of the room. 'Listen how beautifully it's playing now,' he had said to her, while the leading note hung irritatingly unre-solved on the air. 'But you've taken it with you,' she said pleadingly. 'Send it back,' she insisted, 'and let us listen to the last pages.' Marcus had given up. Even though he didn't understand the 'it' fully, he sensed that it was the

40

basis of Madame Sousatzka's teaching, and probably her whole way of life.

Marcus was absorbed in the study. He was no longer thinking about Jenny. He was conscious only of his own participation in the sounds that filled the room. He was happy while playing, though unaware of how well he played. But Madame Sousatzka grew more and more aware, and once again, as so often during the last few weeks, she realized that there was nothing more about the piano that she could teach Marcus, and the fear that one day he would discover it made her shudder. The study came to an end. There was no doubt in Madame Sousatzka's mind about the brilliance of playing. 'It has done well,' was all she could bring herself to tell him, but this time the 'it' did not refer to her method. A slight pang of jealousy prevented her from ascribing the virtuosity of the performance to Marcus. He was still too innocent to detect anything but the most genuine motives in Madame Sousatzka's comments. And even if he had been aware of her envy, he would have forgiven her. He loved Madame Sousatzka for so many things that had nothing to do with the piano. For her house that she let Jenny live in, for the room upstairs that she rented to old Mr Cordle, and for the dirty Countess in the basement; for a whole world of oddities and eccentrics that Marcus was too young to recognize as a world of failures.

When the study came to an end he suddenly remembered his promise to his mother. 'Sousatzka,' he ventured, 'when will I give a concert, d'you think?'

'When you're ready, my darrlink,' Madame Sousatzka tried to be cheerful. 'The concert is the last thing you should think. So much time you have yet. So much Sousatzka has to teach you.' Marcus bent down to tie his shoelace. 'That's what you always say,' he mumbled.

Madame Sousatzka pretended not to hear him. 'Hurry now,' she said, ruffling his hair and pushing him gently from her, 'Cordle will be waiting for you.' There was another half hour before Sally would come for her lesson. Normally Madame Sousatzka spent the intervals between lessons playing herself, or in preparation. But now, she couldn't settle to either. Marcus's questioning had upset her. She didn't want to let him go. He had become part of her. Even during the week, when he stayed with his mother, she felt she was with him. She knew when he was biting his nails, and as he did so, she followed the contours of the birthmark on his right hand, and the flattened domes of his thumbs, smooth as mushrooms. She wondered whether he was talking to Cordle about the concert and the thought of Cordle's gentle hands on Marcus's back sickened her. She went over to the piano and started to play the study that Marcus had just finished. And as she played she heard how clearly he had outgrown her. She stopped playing suddenly, and gathered up Marcus's music; his study book, his scales and his book of sonatas. She wound her arms round the pile and pressed it to her body, clinging to it frantically as if she had already lost him.

6

'Oh, it's you,' said Mr Cordle in surprise, as Marcus entered the room. Marcus had been coming to Mr Cordle's consulting room every Friday for the last three months, but Mr Cordle always greeted him as if he was entirely unexpected. 'Now, what can we do for you?' he said.

Both Marcus and Mr Cordle knew very well what they could do for him, but the question was a formal opening to each session. The 'we' added a professional touch to Mr Cordle's lay activities. The other part of 'we' was related in Marcus's mind to Madame Sousatzka's 'it'. It was as if the house was haunted by two disembodied operators.

Cordle moved over to the couch and laid his hands on Marcus's bony frame, massaging deeply into his shoulders, working his way gently into the slight curve of the spine. 'She's been at it again,' he grumbled to himself. 'We can't go on like this. In half an hour she destroys what I take weeks to repair. I shall have to talk to her again.' He pressed his hands up and down the curve, muttering, 'Sousatzka, Sousatzka' to give his movements a certain waltzing rhythm. Sometimes he would change his beat, and thunder, 'Forte, forte' instead, and with the new time-signature Marcus would feel the massage take on a marching measure up and down his spine. 'Now let's take a plunge into the Arctic Ocean,' Mr Cordle said. He took a cold wet flannel and pressed it around Marcus's neck to give a semblance of reality to his fantasies. Marcus shivered. 'We'll be warm in no time,' Mr Cordle said, protecting himself in the plural, and he rubbed Marcus's neck until a tingling warmth filtered through the boy's body.

'Let's have a look at Russia, shall we,' he said, in his best rack-side manner. Marcus turned over. He was a boy who responded conscientiously to his cues. He knew the routine by heart. Mr Cordle laid his hands across Marcus's chest. 'Oh dear, we are skinny, aren't we,' he chided, thumping his fingers between the jutting ribs. 'Here, have some chocolate.'

Marcus sat up on the couch. The offer of chocolate always marked an interval in the session. 'And when are you going to give this concert of yours?' Mr Cordle always asked this question every week at chocolate time. It was another way of stating that Madame Sousatzka was afraid of losing her prize pupil to the public.

'Next year, I suppose. Madame Sousatzka says I'm not ready yet.'

'D'you think you're ready?'

'Sometimes I do. I'd like to play for lots of people. I get fed up with practising on my own, with no-one listening except Madame Sousatzka. But maybe she's right. I haven't learnt everything yet.'

'You'll always have a lot to learn. You'll never stop learning. If Madame Sousatzka has her way, you'll never be ready. Have you started on a programme?'

'I know lots of pieces. They could be made into a programme. I know concertos, too, but however will I get a chance to play them?'

'Never,' said Mr Cordle. He pulled what was left of his hair over his head as a fringe, and played with an imaginary watch round his neck, 'Never,' he mimicked in the Sousatzka guttural, 'You'll never be ready.'

Marcus laughed, but he quickly checked himself with the thought that he was being disloyal. He remembered his mother's threatened visit and fleetingly thought that it was justified. When away from her, he found it so easy to be on her side. 'She's in my way,' he said suddenly, 'I could be earning money. I could be famous. I'm ready. She knows I'm ready but she won't let me go. I'll leave her. I'll go to someone else.'

Mr Cordle put his hand on Marcus's shoulder. He felt responsible for the boy's sudden rebellion. 'She's taught you everything you know,' he said quietly, 'it would be ungrateful to leave her. Maybe she's right. Perhaps you aren't ready. She knows what she's doing. You're still young. You've got a lot to learn. Lots of things, other than the piano.'

'But she called me a genius. Only this week, she said I was a genius.'

Mr Cordle sighed. 'You see that picture over there,' he pointed to a sheet on the opposite wall. It was the plan of a man's body and embedded in each bone, muscle and joint was a line which extended to the outside of the body and which ended in a name of the part to which it belonged. The titles were neatly and symmetrically placed together, assuming the contours of the human frame around a hollow man. 'When I was a boy,' Mr Cordle said, 'about your age, I suppose, that chart used to hang by my bed. And every night I looked at it and I cried. I cried for that man hemmed in by a battery of labels. Those lines you see travelling out of the body,' he went on, pointing to the chart with a long pole, 'I was convinced that they were arrows. The blood was pouring through the body because of them. And there he was, hanging by my bed, crucified with labels, dying a little more every day, and there was nothing I could do about it. My mother came in one day to kiss me goodnight, and she saw that I was crying. She asked me why and I told her it was because of the man dying on my wall. She laughed and stroked my cheek and told me I was too imaginative. I saw a picture of myself in my mind, like the man on the chart, and at the end of the line it said, Imagination. You can kill a man with labels, Marcus. That was the first time in my life that I started to die. That was my first arrow. I've had lots since and each time it hurts a little more. Dying gets harder and harder,' he murmured, and Marcus was horrified to hear a break in his voice. Marcus only vaguely understood what Mr Cordle was getting at. He wished he'd never mentioned the genius business. It was bound to lead to some theory or another.

'Lie on the couch,' Mr Cordle said softly. His tone of command frightened Marcus. For some odd reason, he felt he was about to sacrificed. He walked towards the couch and felt Mr Cordle's hand. But Mr Cordle turned his face as if to hide something and lightly lifted Marcus on to the bed. Marcus lay there, terrified. Mr Cordle looked down on him and a tear from his cheek dropped on to Marcus's shirt. At the sight of Mr Cordle's weeping Marcus felt safer. He stretched out his hand and clasped Mr Cordle's knuckles, as Madame Sousatzka so often did to him.

'I'm burdened with labels, Marcus,' Mr Cordle confided. 'I have to shake them off before I die. That's the process of dying, Marcus. Shaking them off, shedding the labels one by one, until Man is free, pure and in space, until he is free of all his packaging. Until there is room for the only label that really matters.'

'Which one is that?' said Marcus, who felt he ought to keep the conversation going if for no other reason than to divert Mr Cordle's attention from anything more violent.

'When I die,' Mr Cordle went on, 'I want to be lying unburdened, except for that one label.' He put a finger gently on Marcus's navel. 'Here the label will be,' he whispered, 'and the label will be called Man, the centre of the Universe.'

Marcus stared at Mr Cordle's bent head. The crown was completely bald, shining like a peeled hard-boiled egg. There was a tiny speck of dirt in the middle, and Marcus's eyes were riveted on the black dot in the centre of all that shining cleanliness. He stared at it for what seemed an eternity, and a surge of compassion overcame him. And out of pity for that poor little speck of dirt in the middle of all that whiteness he began to cry.

'Turn over,' Mr Cordle suddenly said. 'Back to business. Let's go back to the North Pole.'

Marcus gratefully turned over. He wanted to shut out the last five minutes from his mind. He tried to think of Jenny, but when he imagined her, he saw her cluttered up with labels. He closed his eyes and the portly figure of Madame Sousatzka blotted his vision. But he fared no better with her. The labels dangled from her as from a giant Christmas tree. Then he thought of himself. Where was the label that Madame Sousatzka had pierced him with? His heart, his head, his finger maybe? He felt suddenly tired and overburdened with scraps of knowledge and experience that lead a child to think he understands everything. Mr Cordle's hands were gentle on his back. He knew he was going to fall

46

off to sleep, but he wanted to do nothing about it. He heard Mr Cordle call his name, once and then twice, very softly. He thought he heard a door close, and even a fleeting thought of Jenny couldn't keep him from sleep.

Marcus's first thought on waking up was that he had been sleeping for many days. Firstly because he was hungry, and secondly, the feeling of utter remoteness. Mr Cordle was shutting the door quietly behind him. He turned round, surprised to find Marcus awake. 'I thought you'd sleep till tomorrow, at least,' he laughed.

'How long have I been sleeping?'

'Not ten minutes,' Mr Cordle said. 'I just saw Jenny on the stairs. She's waiting for you.'

Suddenly Marcus remembered in detail their strange session together. He looked quickly for the chart on the wall. But the space that it had occupied was bare now, a pure white space in an off-white frame. Marcus thought of the dirty mark on Mr Cordle's head, and wondered whether he had washed it off. Mr Cordle had obviously regretted his outburst and had removed all evidence of it whilst Marcus was asleep.

'You'd better wash your face before you go up to Jenny's,' Mr Cordle said. 'You look as if you've been asleep for a week.' Mr Cordle giggled with embarrassment. 'Don't forget your exercises,' he said automatically. He seemed to realise that there was no point in trying to believe that nothing had happened. 'Marcus,' he said pleadingly, 'forget all that nonsense about the labels. It's just a theory I have,' he laughed. 'I'm working it out. Sometimes I don't understand it myself, but it's something I feel.'

'Does Madame Sousatzka know about it? The labels, I mean.' Marcus tried to laugh too. If Mr Cordle himself was prepared to ridicule his own theory, Marcus was ready to give him support.

'She knows,' Mr Cordle answered. 'She says I'm right. I think she understands it better than I do.'

Marcus didn't want to be drawn into any further discussion. He was heartily sick of labels anyway. 'I'll be late,' he said. He went over to Mr Cordle and touched his arm. 'I'll see you tomorrow,' he said, reassuringly, as if he felt that Mr Cordle feared that he would not come again.

'Yes,' Mr Cordle muttered, 'tomorrow. Tomorrow,' he brightened up suddenly, 'we'll take another look at America.'

Marcus didn't bother to wash. He ran up the stairs to the top landing. He paused at Jenny's door to get his breath back, then tip-toed quietly into the room. Jenny was sitting as always by the gas-fire, painting her nails. Marcus crept up behind her and put his hands over her eyes.

'Oh!' Jenny screamed in mock horror. 'Who is it?'

Marcus released his hold and she turned round to look at him. 'Oh,' she said in surprise, 'Marcus, it's you. You know, you act like a real man.'

Marcus felt a fluttering inside his navel. She took his hands in hers. 'What's the matter, Marcus?' she said. 'You're trembling.'

'Jenny,' he said, 'I think I'm growing old.'

7

Marcus didn't know anything about Jenny except that
she was always in her room on Friday nights, painting
her nails in front of her gas-fire with the kettle boiling
and the crumpets on the table in the bay window. There
was a telephone in the room, too. Marcus only noticed it
because of its strange position. Jenny's gas-ring had a
double burner, and the 'phone stood on the jet next to
the kettle, and Marcus often wanted to light the gas
underneath to see if it would start ringing. Jenny was the
only one in the house who had a private 'phone. The
dirty Countess who lived in the basement, Mr Cordle,
even Madame Sousatzka, who was after all the landlady,
had to resort to the telephone box on the first landing,
armed with pennies and adaptable accents. Somehow it
never occurred to Marcus to ask Jenny why she had a
'phone of her own. He probably felt that Jenny was
entitled to something that the others didn't have. In any
case, Marcus had never heard it ring, never on a Friday
anyway, so perhaps she looked upon it as an ornament.
Which was why he was startled this Friday when
suddenly, only a few minutes after he had come into her
room, the telephone started ringing. Jenny was surprised
too, and she got up quickly from her seat, and turned off
the kettle as she picked up the receiver, as if the
operation of the one depended on the non-operation of
the other.

'Hullo,' her voice was tentative and questioning. She
listened for a while, glancing nervously at Marcus as he
picked up a magazine from the floor. 'You know I never
work on Fridays,' he heard her say. Then another long
silence.

'I don't mind, Jenny,' Marcus whispered. She waved
away his offer with her hand. 'I really don't, if it's

important.' She would let him take the crumpets down to his room in the basement, and he'd play draughts with the Countess till it was bedtime. But the thought of missing a Friday night with Jenny and of upsetting his week-end routine made him miserable and, in spite of his offer, he looked at her pleadingly.

'No, it's impossible,' he heard her say. 'It'll have to wait until you come back. I'm sorry, Felix, but you know Fridays are out.' She said good-bye sadly and as she put down the receiver, she re-lit the gas under the kettle.

'I'll go, really I will,' Marcus said with enthusiasm, knowing that his departure was no longer necessary.

'Friday night is for you, Marcus. It has been for almost a year. In any case, I hate changing a routine. It brings bad luck, especially on a Friday.' Jenny was very superstitious. She was always on to Marcus if one of his socks was inside out, and she was forever touching whatever wood was in sight to ward off the evil spirits. 'Take a crumpet,' she said. 'The kettle's almost boiled. Bring the plate over here. We'll have it by the fire.'

'What work d'you do, Jenny?' It was the first time Marcus had thought of asking her.

Jenny laughed. 'All kinds of things.'

'What things?'

'I help people out. Give them a hand.'

'Doing what?'

'Oh, all sorts of things. How's Sousatzka today?' she added quickly. 'Not ready for your concert yet, I suppose?'

Marcus grunted. Somehow he felt this Friday wasn't going to be like the others. Jenny seemed to be terribly nervous, and she was being awfully cagey about her job. She couldn't settle down with her nail-painting, either. Then there'd been that 'phone call, and now she was on about the concert, just like Mr Cordle, and his mother. 'No, I'm not ready,' Marcus said angrily, 'and I don't want to talk about the concert any more.'

Jenny smiled. 'We're both on edge today, aren't we? Come on,' she laughed, 'let's make the tea, and when you've drunk yours, I'll read your tea-leaves.'

Jenny had never read his cup before, though he had heard from Mr Cordle that she was a professional cup-reader. Madame Sousatzka, too, used to swear by her, which probably accounted for the odd unwashed cups which lay about the studio, guarding their secrets until Jenny was ready to reveal them.

The prospect of having his future read excited Marcus. He wanted most of all to know about the concert. He prepared himself to have faith in everything Jenny would tell him, and with each mouthful of tea, he swallowed a measure of disbelief. At last he strained the tea from the cup, leaving a pattern of leaves that lined the bottom and one of the sides, its intricacy promising a wealth of forecast. 'Here, Jenny,' he said challengingly, 'what does all that say?'

Jenny casually looked inside the cup whilst taking a pair of spectacles out of her bag. Marcus had never seen Jenny in glasses before. She looked quite a different person in them, and what with the 'phone call, the tea-reading, and now the glasses, Marcus felt Jenny more and more a stranger.

He looked quickly around the room for something that was familiar to him. The crumpet plate was empty, the nail varnish had somehow vanished. He looked back at Jenny and the frown folded underneath her glasses removed her once more from him. He soon had the unaccountable feeling that if she was a stranger to him, then perhaps he wasn't Marcus any more. He quickly looked at the palm of his right hand where it joined the wrist and recognized in the middle the small brown birthmark. Reassured, he stretched out his hand and snatched the glasses from Jenny's face. She seemed not to notice their removal and continued to stare fixedly into the cup.

'It's her,' she screamed suddenly, 'it's Sousatzka. It's her. I could tell her anywhere.'

'How can you see her without your glasses?' Marcus asked, waving them in the air.

'You don't need glasses for a vision,' Jenny said, half

to herself. 'She's there. I can see her. Though there are thousands of people around her. Hundreds and hundreds of people. And they're trying to make her move away, because she's hiding something. They're angry,' Jenny had begun to pant with excitement. 'Move Sousatzka,' she shouted, 'Move. Oh no. Don't. Please,' she stuttered.

'Don't what?' Marcus whispered, caught up in her excitement. 'What's she doing now?'

'Yes,' Jenny went on breathlessly, 'good heavens, it can't be. It is, I can see him,' she went on, rather like an engrossed radio commentator forgetful of his audience.

'Who can you see?' Marcus pleaded with her. 'What's going on?'

'Nothing,' Jenny said, suddenly relaxing in her chair and breathing calmly as if at last exorcised. 'Nothing. Just a crowd of people like I said, and Madame Sousatzka in the middle.'

'Was it at my concert?' Marcus asked eagerly.

'Maybe it was,' Jenny was startled, suddenly understanding the meaning of the vision. 'Marcus,' she said, leaning forward, 'how long are you going to go on learning with Madame Sousatzka?'

The 'phone rang and Jenny jumped up from her chair. 'I'm going,' Marcus said. This wasn't a regular Friday night at all. 'I'll go and play draughts downstairs.'

Jenny quickly put her hand on his shoulder. Though she was anxious to answer the 'phone, she was more anxious that Marcus should stay with her. Holding him with one hand, she unhooked the receiver with the other.

'Hullo?' she questioned. There was no answer. 'Hullo,' she said, again and again, angrily at first, and finally with relief. 'You see,' she said, putting the receiver down, 'There's no-one there. They must have got the wrong number.'

Marcus sat down again, though he wasn't happy with Jenny any more. And why were they all on about Madame Sousatzka all of a sudden? Mr Cordle with his labels, and now Jenny with her vision. He didn't want them to talk about her any more.

'I won the two hundred yards breast stroke on Monday,' he said.

'Did you, love?' Jenny was genuinely pleased. 'Did you get a medal or something?'

'I got a cup. Maybe I can whip it out of school and bring it to you next Friday. Would you like to see it?'

'Yes, I'd love to see it. You can have your tea out of it, and I'll read your tea-leaves,' she laughed.

'Jenny,' Marcus leaned towards her, 'about those things you saw in my cup. Are they true, I mean, has anything ever come true, what you've read, I mean?'

'Course it does. You haven't got any faith. Cordle's mother died, didn't she? I read it in his cups three weeks before it happened and he didn't even know she was ill. Then a friend of mine went on holiday and her husband was drowned. I could have told her that before she went. I saw it in his cup.'

'Didn't you tell him?'

'No, of course not,' said Jenny. 'You can't go against fate. If it's in the cups, it'll happen, and there's nothing anyone can do about it.'

'Don't you ever read anything happy in cups?'

'I read your concert, didn't I? That's happy, isn't it?'

'But it wasn't happy for Sousatzka. You know it wasn't.'

Jenny didn't answer. Absentmindedly, she blew on her finger-nails to dry them.

'Shall I wash up for you, Jenny?' Marcus said, getting up. He always washed up for her on a Friday.

'No,' Jenny shouted, almost falling out of her seat as she stopped him taking the cups away. 'I'll do it myself later,' she said quietly. Marcus sat down again and they said nothing to each other.

'I think I'll go down and have a game of draughts,' he said after a while, not able to bear the silence any longer. He was hurt but not surprised that Jenny made no move to keep him.

Marcus walked down the stairs dejectedly. On the top flight leading from Jenny's room the banister was of wrought iron with unadorned metal supports. He took a pencil out of his pocket and strummed it along the rails. He felt lonely and the noise comforted him. As he neared Mr Cordle's room on the second landing, he put the pencil away and tip-toed past his door on to the stairs. From here onwards, the stairway became more respectable. It was encased with hardwood and Marcus had to walk silently and alone.

Madame Sousatzka was fumbling with the telephone on the first landing. In all her years as a box hirer, she had never understood the vital difference between Button A and Button B. She was shouting frantically to an unhearing recipient while the pennies dribbled back into the hole. Suddenly she caught sight of them. 'Oh, I'm sorry,' she said to no one in particular, and she reinserted them. As each penny dropped, Madame Sousatzka counted hastily, repeating the number she was going to dial between each penny. Marcus watched her turn the dial with a red pencil.

'Hullo,' she shrieked after a while. 'Now I've got you,' her tone of voice seemed to say triumphantly. She pressed Button B. The pennies wearily stuttered down the slot and Madame Sousatzka wearily picked them out again. 'I'm sorry,' she mumbled, and Marcus turned to go downstairs.

As he reached the hall floor, he saw the shadow of a man climbing the front steps, and scrutinizing the names of the bells on the side of the door. Not that it would have helped him. None of the bells worked, neither was there a knocker on the door. Only those in the know could gain access to 132 Vauxhall Mansions, by heaving one shoulder on to the front door. Even Madame Sousatzka used to do it when she'd forgotten her keys, and on entering she would shove the door with her other shoulder to even out the pain.

Marcus watched the man press on the bells, and he sat on the bottom stair, listening to the silence in the house. The man pressed again after a few minutes and stepped back a little to look up at the front windows. He pressed for a third time, leaning his ear against the glass panel.

Marcus smiled. He felt the man had been patient enough to deserve an entry. He turned the metal knob of the door and pulled, but the door had for so long been used to rough treatment that it refused to respond to any conventional handling. 'Push,' Marcus shouted through the hole that had once been a letter-box. Marcus stood back while the visitor pushed. And in a second they were facing each other in the hall.

'Hullo, hullo,' screamed Madame Sousatzka again from upstairs. There was a silence and Marcus heard the familiar sound of falling pennies. Marcus stepped behind the visitor and shut the door. With Madame Sousatzka upstairs, and he alone on the hall floor, he felt a sense of authority.

'What do you want?' he asked the man.

'Jenny?' the man asked. He had obviously never been to the house before and he was a bit nervous about coming at all.

'Jenny who?' said Marcus jealously. Although his evening had been a failure, he still felt that being a Friday, Jenny belonged to him.

'I don't know,' the man said simply. 'Just Jenny.'

Marcus realised for the first time that, after almost a year, he didn't know Jenny's second name either.

'You must be Marcus,' the man said, trying to establish a better right of entry. 'Jenny's told me about you.'

'What did she say?' Marcus said eagerly. He loved Jenny suddenly for having told strangers about him.

'She told me that I must hear you play, and that if I think well of you, I must get you a concert.'

'Hullo, Marion darrlink,' Madame Sousatzka was triumphant on the first landing.

Marcus looked around. Once Madame Sousatzka had managed to get through, she'd be on the 'phone for ages. 'Who are you?' Marcus whispered like a conspirator.

The man bent down and whispered in Marcus's ear. 'Felix Manders.'

It was a name that to Marcus was a legend. All the great artists depended on his name for their concerts. In Marcus's mind, he owned all the concert halls of the world. Somehow, he'd never imagined him as a man at all, dressed as he was in a dark grey suit with a red carnation in his lapel; nor smiling, as he smiled at Marcus then, modestly and self-effacingly. He had never worn a suit or a smile. He was always a shadow behind a performer, sometimes on a pianist's shoulder or on a 'cellist's lap. Marcus wanted to run to the stairs and shout, 'Madame Sousatzka, come down at once. Felix Manders is here. Felix Manders has come to Vauxhall Mansions.' But for some reason or other, he wanted to keep the secret between them. 'Mr Manders,' he whispered, 'come inside. I'll play for you now.'

But auditioning was obviously not the object of Manders's visit and he was impatient to go upstairs and see Jenny. 'Another time,' he said kindly, 'I'll make an arrangement.'

'No,' Marcus pulled him by the sleeve. 'I'll play to you now. I'll play you the study I'm learning. Please listen.' He was dragging Mr Manders into Madame Sousatzka's room. 'Sit down,' he said, almost pushing him into the great armchair behind the piano. 'It won't take long. Then I'll take you up to Jenny.'

Mr Manders was clearly embarrassed. He found himself in a very awkward position. He'd been caught and was the subject of very gentle if unconscious blackmail. 'All right,' he said, 'just the study.'

'I will listen, you will listen, and it will play,' Marcus said. Saying this was another way of crossing his fingers for luck. He pressed into the opening chord. It was probably the first time in his career as an impresario that Mr Manders had been offered a study as a selling point. Not that it mattered except conventionally so. Mr Manders couldn't have told Czerny from Chopin. He had built up his business, like many commercial patrons of the arts, on the maxim, 'I don't know anything about music but I know what I like'. And strangely enough, what pleased Mr Manders very often turned out to be what an undiscriminating public liked, and he was always careful to dress up his product with a gimmick or two.

He had one famous pianist on his books who played from a deck-chair. One of his singers sang with her hands on her head 'to keep the sounds from soaring', she had said, 'beyond my control'. She went down awfully well, especially in the provinces. But his greatest catch of all was his lady 'cellist, who, for her audition, had played side-saddle. He'd got her a lot of work, mainly recitals, because she was not too popular with orchestras. The rank and file of the 'cello section, most of whom could play her off her saddle, looked upon her as a traitor. But she made a good living, and Manders his commission.

He looked at Marcus and wondered what he could make of him. His playing sounded brilliant enough. He was especially impressed by the scale and arpeggio passages, above all when they were fortissimo. Quiet playing didn't interest him. He wanted fireworks and display. The boy had talent; anyone could see that, but it took a man like Manders to visualise him in short velvet pants passing, as he quite easily could, for nine years old. He began to concoct phrases for his press hand-out. 'An ordinary, simple boy. Plays cricket for his school. A good swimmer. Loves his mother. Mischievous like any other ordinary little boy.' (Find examples from *Schoolboy Adventure* here.) 'Heard the great Paderewski by accident from his cradle, and determined from that moment to play the piano. Was playing before he was crawling. His technique is terrifying.' (Good word.) 'The problem of parents faced with a genius as a son.' (A natural for the Sundays.) Letters to the Editor. 'My Joe could read when he was three months old. Can any reader beat that?' There was no end to it. Besides, Mr Manders could do with a prodigy. His present one was nearing twenty and was getting more and more difficult to push. Although he looked younger, his voice had broken years ago, and he was obliged to keep his mouth shut at interviews while Manders talked for him. His legs were hairy, too, and they looked a bit silly beneath those short velvet trousers. No. As long as you could push a prodigy, it was good business. Mr Manders made his decision immediately. 'Come and see me,' he said aloud, although the study that Marcus was playing was not yet finished. 'I think I can help you.'

Marcus didn't hear. He didn't even notice Mr Manders stand up. He didn't hear the door open, or even feel Madame Sousatzka standing behind him. She waited for the end of the study.

'Manders,' she said, addressing him as if he were a recently articled clerk, 'What are you doing here?'

Madame Sousatzka had never met Manders, but she knew his face well. It was a face known to thousands of concert-goers. It appeared in the auditorium a few minutes before a concert was about to begin and it sat on a gangway seat, fitted with hearing aids and reserved for the deaf. It took a last look around with satisfaction, and usually closed its eyes until the interval. 'What are you doing in my room?' she asked again.

'He came to see Jenny,' Marcus said, 'and when he told me who he was, I said I'd play to him.'

Mr Manders heartily wished he'd never set foot in the house. His relationship with Jenny was strictly a clandestine one. He'd only come because he was going away and he wanted to see her before he left. He wanted to take Madame Sousatzka into his confidence, but the boy was in the way.

'Jenny?' Madame Sousatzka enquired. This was a new one on her. She thought she knew all Jenny's clients. 'Jenny?' she repeated, suddenly realising the opportunities of the situation.

'That's right,' Mr Manders confessed weakly.

'You come to give Jenny an audition?'

'In what?' Marcus asked.

'You run off, my darrlink,' Madame Sousatzka told him. 'I want a little talk with Mr Manders.' Manders was trapped and he knew it. He smiled at Marcus as the boy left the room.

'Shall I tell Jenny you're here, Mr Manders?' he asked.

'No, that's all right. I'll see her later.'

Marcus shut the door. Manders took out his pen and tapped it on his fingers. He tried to assume the authority he felt in his agent's office, but it was difficult standing up. He could hardly take a seat with Madame Sousatzka standing over him. But she sat down, on the piano stool, which Marcus had twiddled to its highest level. Perched high on the seat, she motioned Manders to sit down. He sat on the low armchair opposite her. He felt he was almost sitting on the floor. Madame Sousatzka stared at him without saying a word. Her right hand felt the piano keys, and as she stared at him she casually played a scale. She paused as she reached the top, and then as casually came down again. Then, staring hard at him, she struck the tonic chord. 'He's not ready,' she said.

'But of course the boy's ready, Madame Sousatzka.' Manders leaned forward as far as was anatomically possible on his low seat. He was smiling and relieved that Madame Sousatzka didn't want to talk to him about Jenny. 'He's more than ready. If he doesn't come out now, he'll grow stale. Why don't we launch him while he's still young?'

'We?' asked Madame Sousatzka. 'He's still my pupil. He still has much to learn.'

'Rubinstein has a lot to learn,' Manders said, though he couldn't frankly say what. 'So has Horowitz. So has . . . Well, all great artists have a lot to learn. But they learn by experience. And what experience can this boy get, if he doesn't concertise?'

'Mr Manders,' Madame Sousatzka said, with great condescension, 'to play the piano is not only to play the notes. You are a businessman. About music,' she waved her arm contemptuously, 'you know nothing. Some people, they sell clothes; some other people, they sell furniture. You, you sell the artists. That is your business. You dress up the artist, so he sells very good. Only last week you had a black man playing the piano in the big hall. I heard him. He played the piano, Mr Manders, like I drive the train, and believe me, Mr Manders, I don't drive a train. But he's black. Very good. That's different. Now you want to take my boy, put him in little velvet trousers, take with him his special elevated pedal, put him in the Festival Hall, and make a lot of money. It doesn't matter if the boy cannot play well. Then, when he is older and he must wear the long trousers, you drop him. Perhaps he is playing even better by then the piano. But you say to him, "I'm sorry, they won't buy any more." Then what? Answer me that, perhaps, Manders. Then what?' she repeated angrily.

'If you've no wish to see the boy launched just yet, I agree with you, and I'm prepared to wait until you think he's ready.' Mr Manders did not want at that moment to fall into Madame Sousatzka's bad books. What with the

Jenny business, there was too much at stake. He had to keep in with her. 'Of course, you know more about music than I do,' he flattered her.

'That I am hoping,' she said, 'That at least I am hoping.'

Mr Manders laughed feebly.

'You can go to Jenny now,' she said, 'and leave the boy alone.'

'Of course, of course, Madame Sousatzka,' he answered. He got up and leaned over the piano. 'It would be a little awkward,' he whispered, 'in my profession, you know, if it were to get around about, well, you know, Jenny?'

'Leave the boy alone,' was all Madame Sousatzka would give him. In return for her silence Manders was prepared to leave Marcus alone for ever. He felt he'd struck an easy bargain. 'Not even when he's ready,' he laughed.

'When he's ready,' she said, showing him the door, 'he won't need an agent.'

When Manders had gone, Madame Sousatzka sat crumpled in the low armchair. She felt alone and frightened, like a self-appointed monarch who sees his realm crumble. And what's more, the enemy had struck at the capital. None of her other pupils had Marcus's gift. And apart from that, there was Marcus the boy. He was the son that Boris might have given her. He was the grandson, born to survive her parents. He was the continuation of a broken line, like the trail of a diced worm which renews itself with a simple inviolable faith. But she knew too that she would lose him; that he had never really belonged to her; that not all her love for him had given her the rights of possession. She had a sudden terrible longing for Boris. She opened the piano and began a quiet Russian love-song, singing it gently with his half-remembered words. Outside it was getting dark. A large van pulled up outside one of the houses in the square.

Madame Sousatzka went over to the window. Two men were carrying a mattress into the van, and another two followed with a kitchen table. Then a woman came out of the house carrying a flower vase and suitcase. She was followed by two small children who stopped to pick all the flowers out of the front garden. They all got into the van and the driver shut the doors. Then they drove off quietly.

The whole operation had taken about five minutes. Madame Sousatzka stared at the abandoned house. Each front room window was covered with net curtains, empty shrouds, a semblance of habitation. She was suddenly filled with hatred for the family that had stolen out of the square. She felt herself betrayed, and she closed the curtains quickly. She stared at the piano and at the study that Marcus had just played to Manders. 'It's not fair,' she sobbed, and she sat on the elevated stool, perched high and moaning, like a stranded sea-gull.

8

When Marcus left Madame Sousatzka's room it occurred to him to stand outside the door and listen to their conversation. But he was too restless to stand still for very long. Mr Manders was going to help, him. He'd said he would. He had to tell somebody. His mother, he thought, and he was happy that he'd thought of her first. She would be ringing him up anyway, as she did every Friday night, but he couldn't wait for her to call. He would ring her himself. He ran upstairs to the 'phone box.

'Momma,' he said, as she answered.

'Oh my God,' she screamed. 'What happened? You had accident? I said no good would come of that woman.'

'No, Momma,' Marcus said, instantly regretting that he had phoned her. After her remark about Madame Sousatzka, he even dallied with the idea of not telling her at all. 'Everything's all right,' he said without enthusiasm. 'It's just that I've got some news.'

'So? What is it? Tell me.'

'Guess,' Marcus teased her.

'I should guess, he tells me. Listen Marcus, you tell me at once, or I shall scream,' she threatened him.

'Momma,' he whispered, his excitement flooding back, 'I'm going to give a concert.'

'A concert? Where? What? How?'

And so Marcus told her all about Manders and how he'd played for him.

'A concert,' Mrs Crominski said. 'At last you're ready. What does she say, Madame Sousatzka?'

'I think she's a bit angry. She's talking to Mr Manders now.'

'Angry she should be?' Mrs Crominski was incredulous. 'Ah,' it suddenly became clear to her. 'Now I understand. Now everything I understand. I'm coming,' she said decisively. 'Yes, I'm coming,' she said, anticipating his objections. 'I'll get my hat.' She put the 'phone down before Marcus could protest. He regretted having told her. He could see her pulling down her brown hat in front of the mirror. He knew she was thinking what a horrible hat it was. He knew she was pained that Marcus hated it. He wouldn't tell anyone she was coming. He would pretend he was surprised to see her. He tried not to think about it.

He wanted to talk about Manders to someone else. Jenny? There wouldn't be much time with her. Manders was going up. And what did Mr Manders want with Jenny anyway? Mr Cordle? The memory of the labels was too fresh in Marcus's mind. Old Cordle would go on about it again. There was Uncle. He'd go downstairs to her.

By the time you reached Uncle's apartment, the stairway had given way to concrete. It was impossible ever to surprise the Countess. She had fourteen stone steps to count before you arrived, and even if you managed to muffle them all, you still had to negotiate the area of cracked lino in front of her door. Uncle would have heard a fly land on that lino and she would call 'Who's there?' long before you reached her door.

Marcus ran down the stone steps. 'It's Marcus,' he called, anticipating her question, and saving her the trouble of opening her mouth.

She did not look up when Marcus came in. He stood in front of her breathless with excitement. He waited for her to ask him what had happened. But Uncle was especially tired today. A stomach upset had necessitated several journeys out of doors, and a raised eyebrow to Marcus was all that she could muster.

'Mr Manders is upstairs,' he panted.

Another raised eyebrow.

'You know, Mr Manders,' said Marcus, who was as familiar with her means of communication as he was with Mr Cordle's crazy terminology. 'The impresario,' he went on. 'I played to him.' Having exhausted her eyebrows Uncle opened her mouth, wide enough, she hoped, to express amazement.

'Yes, honestly,' Marcus said, laughing. 'He said he's

going to help me. I'm going to give a concert.' He put his arms on her shoulders and spun her chair round, disturbing the rhythm of her rocking. He knelt down in front of her. 'I'm going to give a concert,' he said, slowly and deliberately, so that it would sink right inside the dirty Countess.

Poor Uncle didn't have a feature left with which she could ask all the questions she was dying to put to Marcus. And she spoke very quickly, as if she were short of time, rather like a car-driver who, seeing his petrol gauge veer to empty, accelerates. 'Does Madame Sousatzka know?'

'She was there. She heard me.'

'She let you play?' Uncle was incredulous. So Marcus told her the whole story. 'They're up there now, talking about me.'

'More likely they're talking about Jenny.' And suddenly the Countess burst out laughing. Laughter was obviously what she conserved her energy for, because it was a violent laugh, young and full of strength.

'What's the matter, Uncle, d'you think Madame Sousatzka won't let me? Will she stop me, Uncle, will she say I'm not ready?'

Uncle put her hand round his shoulders. Coming from her it was a generous gesture, and Marcus appreciated this unsolicited donation of her energy. Moreover, she bent forward and kissed him on his forehead. It was a field day for Uncle. No doubt she would spend a week recuperating.

'It's all right, dear,' she said to him. 'She'll come round. You'll see. I'll talk to her. You'll give your concert. And we'll all come. Cordle, Jenny, Sousatzka and me.' She paused for a well-deserved half-time. 'I'll wear my tiara,' she laughed. 'I'll tell everybody that I'm your week-end landlady. And after the concert, we'll have a grand party, and I'll dance with Cordle, and you'll dance with Jenny, and Madame Sousatzka will dance with . . . she'll dance with,' Uncle went on in mock seriousness, 'She'll dance a quadrille with Mr Felix Manders.' And then Uncle did an unbelievable thing. She actually got up, lifted Marcus to his feet, and held out her hand gracefully for the dance. Marcus took the tips of her fingers and the Countess hummed a stately minuet. They managed to find an uncluttered patch of floor to execute the dance, dictated by the Countess's humming and her obviously expert guidance. When the dance came to an end the Countess took an imaginary chiffon handkerchief from her wrist and, waving it sadly across her face like a flag at half-mast, she curtsied low to Marcus, who very seriously bowed in response.

And it was thus that Madame Sousatzka found them, when she came unnoticed into Uncle's room. She clapped her hands and the dancers turned round, astonished. Uncle managed to remember that first and foremost she must sit down, and she returned to her rocking-chair, leaving Marcus gaping at Madame Sousatzka in the doorway.

Her eyes were red and her fringe dishevelled. She stopped clapping and Marcus saw a crumpled white handkerchief in her fist.

'What's the matter, Madame Sousatzka?' he said, going up to her. Madame Sousatzka stretched out her arms to him as he approached and held him closely to her. Then she began sobbing all over again, silently, without saying a word.

'Come and sit down, dear,' the Countess said without turning her head. 'Marcus, go to your room for a while. I'd like to talk to Madame Sousatzka. You can get out the draughts whilst you're waiting, and set the board. I'm white, don't forget,' she laughed, 'Jenny says black's unlucky.'

Marcus went to his room, which adjoined Uncle's, and led directly from it. He shut the door behind him and sat trembling on his bed. The thought of eavesdropping this time did not enter his mind.

'It's Manders, isn't it?' said Uncle, when Madame Sousatzka had sat down.

Madame Sousatzka nodded her head sadly. 'Yes, it's him. I want to do what is right for the boy. You know that, Uncle. What is right for him.'

'What is right for him, or what is right for you?' Uncle said, coming to the point right away. Madame Sousatzka's answer was a loud wail. She knew that Uncle knew the dilemma, and Uncle knew that she knew. 'We'll see Jenny,' she said. 'We'll have a session. It'll solve everything.'

Madame Sousatzka shrugged.

'Didn't it solve Cordle's problem? Follow the glass, that's what I say. It's never been wrong. You go and see Jenny.'

'It's urgent,' Madame Sousatzka said. 'You think she will do it tonight for me? Tonight you can come?'

Uncle thought for a minute. She was always free but she was never ready to admit it. 'I could be free tonight,' she said generously. 'And ask Cordle. He's always willing. Ask her to arrange it tonight. At ten o'clock, when Marcus is in bed.'

'He's a nasty one, that Manders,' said Madame Sousatzka suddenly. 'A business man. He is like the others. I told him that. Human beings for him are like the things in the shop.'

'There have to be people like Manders,' said Uncle, 'otherwise what would happen to all the Marcuses?'

'So many Marcuses there are not,' Madame Sousatzka interrupted her.

'In any case, Sousatzka,' she went on affectionately, 'he will have to advertise Marcus as your pupil. Think of all the good that will do you. You will be the most famous teacher in London. All the little Marcuses will come to you.'

'No, no,' Madame Sousatzka began to cry again. 'There is only one Marcus. He is different. When he come to me, he play only with the fingers.' Uncle secretly wondered what on earth else one would play the piano with. 'Now,' Madame Sousatzka went on, 'he play with everything; his mind, his body, his . . .' she was at loss for words, 'with everything he play. Without me, he is nothing.'

'But he doesn't belong to you,' Uncle said. She was already very tired from her unaccustomed exertions and would gladly have left the decision in the hands of the glass. 'Arrange it for tonight, my dear. I'll come up to Jenny's at ten o'clock.' At the thought of the four flights of stairs she would have to climb to get to the session, she turned sideways in her chair and dropped off to sleep.

Madame Sousatzka got up quietly and went over to Marcus's door. 'Marcus,' she called softly. She opened his door and found him lying on the bed, playing draughts with himself. 'No, no,' she whispered, seeing him make a

66

misguided move. 'Look, the black will take the two white.'

'But I'm black,' Marcus said.

'Who plays the white?'

'Me too, of course,' he laughed, 'but somebody has to lose.'

Madame Sousatzka sat down heavily on the bed, disturbing the board and disarranging the pieces. Marcus collected them into a little red bag.

'Uncle's asleep,' Madame Sousatzka said. 'Shall I play with you?'

'I don't feel like playing any more,' Marcus said. 'I'd like to practise. Can I use the piano now?'

'Yes,' she said sadly. 'But only the studies you must practise. And not just because of the concert. In any case, you hear? In any case.' She kissed him on the top of his head and tip-toed uncomfortably out of Uncle's apartment.

Outside the door, she fumbled in her purse for pennies and clutching them in her hand she climbed the stairs to the telephone box on the first landing. She realized she couldn't go up to Jenny's. Manders was probably still there and she didn't want to meet him again. In any case, she had never interfered with Jenny's business, because she wasn't curious about it.

She put in her pennies before dialling the number, and she held her thumb on Button A on the ready. The fact that she was right this time was purely accidental. From the landing she could hear the telephone ringing in Jenny's room. She listened for a long time. She visualised the room, and was sure that had Jenny been in, the 'phone could have been reached by now from the most distant part of the room. Yet she let it ring. Jenny never went out on Fridays. She heard Mr Cordle breathing heavily behind his door. He was probably painting one of his charts. Suddenly the ringing from upstairs stopped. Madame Sousatzka heard a very drowsy 'hullo' through the receiver. She pressed Button A. 'Jenny?' she whispered. Jenny whispered back. 'It's me, Sousatzka. I wondered, tonight, if the glass is at home?'

'Tonight?'

'Yes. Is very important. Did he tell you? I must know

67

what to do. Uncle will come, and I go now to Cordle. Please Jenny. I know I have to make an appointment. But I make appointment now. Emergency case,' she spluttered, suddenly inspired by the instructions for dialling Police, Fire and Ambulance on the board above the telephone.

'Don't worry,' Jenny laughed. 'At ten o'clock. I'll have it ready.'

Jenny put the 'phone down, and Madame Sousatzka heard her walking about her room upstairs. Then she too placed the receiver, and out of habit pressed Button B. 'Cordle,' she called from the landing, 'I come to see you.'

'Wait, wait,' he shouted in panic. 'I'm painting on the door.'

Madame Sousatzka waited outside until Cordle let her in. He had on a gold smock with paintbrushes sticking out of the large front pockets. The chart on the door had been newly painted. For some reason or other, Mr Cordle had embarked on oils. Normally, he covered his charts with poster paints. He was obviously more serious about this new one.

'You discover a new colour?' Madame Sousatzka asked conversationally.

Cordle rubbed his hands together. 'Sousatzka,' he whispered, 'I think I've got it.' But Sousatzka was too worried with her own problem to show any enthusiasm over Cordle's new discovery. 'I've got it,' Cordle said again, thinking she hadn't heard him. 'It will change my whole method. And it was Marcus who first gave me the idea.'

At the sound of his name, Sousatzka showed a sudden interest. 'It is because of him I come to you,' she said.

'Are you changing your method, too?' Mr Cordle asked, frightened. He felt that since his profession was more or less dependent on hers there ought to be some kind of liaison between their two methods.

'No.' Sousatzka was adamant. 'The method is the same.' And she told Mr Cordle all about Mr Manders. 'Uncle says we must ask the glass. Jenny is making it for tonight. You can come, Mr Cordle?' she pleaded.

'Of course I'll come. I'm a great believer in the glass, especially as in my case when it was impossible to make a decision. But Sousatzka,' he warned, 'what the glass says, you must obey.'

'I know, I know,' said Madame Sousatzka, almost breaking down. 'That is the trouble.'

'What is it you want?'

'I want what's right for my boy.' There was a silence. Cordle didn't know how to advise her, and like the Countess, he preferred to pass on the responsibility.

'The glass will help you,' he told her. 'I'll be upstairs at ten o'clock.'

He drew the chart gently away from the door to let Madame Sousatzka through, and she walked slowly down the stairs to her room. Marcus was practising a study and the brilliance of his playing sickened her. She waited outside the door until he'd finished, correcting him in whispers as he proceeded. When he had finished, she heard the rustle of music sheets. He was singing to himself. She recognised it as a Beethoven Piano Concerto and she felt defeat and a terrible despair. He had at last found the music and she heard him playing the opening bars. She didn't want to listen but her tired defeat glued her to the door. She heard footsteps on the landing and she realised that it must be Manders coming down. She didn't want to see him again, neither did she want at that moment to join Marcus in the studio. She ran into an alcove at the bottom of the hall and watched him come down the stairs. When he reached the studio door he stopped and listened. He was smiling. Sousatzka could have killed him. He had no right to trespass on her bond with Marcus like a cheap adulterer. He had no right to listen to him outside her door. He had even less right to smile.

It seemed hours before he turned away and left the house. Marcus was still playing, singing the orchestral score as he went along. Then he stopped in the middle of a difficult passage. He tried it again but still without success. Madame Sousatzka began to smile. She listened as Marcus repeated the phrase, slowing the speed, testing new fingering, and each time entangling himself more. She started to laugh as she heard him set the metronome and try it again. But the machine had ticked away the whole passage before

Marcus was half-way through. Then she heard him bang his fists again and again on the piano in his annoyance, and she drowned the pedalled din with loud laughter. She went on laughing long after the noise from the piano had ceased. Uncle, Cordle and Jenny heard it echo through the house, like the muffled shriek of a ghost-train.

Through the windows of the studio Marcus saw his mother coming up the front steps. None of the bells worked and she didn't know how to get in by just pushing the door. No-one was expecting her, so if he didn't open the door she would have to go away. He let some time elapse. He knew she was pressing the dead bells and waiting. He saw her out there, with her brown hat and her shopping bag and her impatience. He was determined not to let her in, and he knew at the same time that he would regret it. If he were to shut her out from his private world, not a lifetime of hand-holding and kissing would make up for it.

He gripped the sides of the piano stool, chaining himself to his seat. She would go away and tomorrow he would explain to her that the bells didn't work, so nobody had heard her.

But Madame Sousatzka was still outside in the hall. She had seen a shadow behind the glass door, and Marcus heard her opening it. He felt himself blushing. He got up quickly, looking around for evidence to remove. He felt there should be something to hide, a letter, a photograph or a diary. But there was nothing. All the evidence was inside him, and he knew that that way it was far harder to conceal. He started to play again, very loudly, to give himself an excuse for not hearing her come into the room. When he heard his mother's voice he stopped playing abruptly, and pretended astonishment. But he felt that neither his mother nor Madame Sousatzka believed him, and he overdid his surprise to convince them.

'You said nothing to me that your mother comes, Marcus,' Madame Sousatzka said, slightly angry.

'I forgot to tell you. I was too excited about Mr Manders and I forgot.'

'Marcus,' Madame Sousatzka said. 'This Manders. He is not right for you. First thing. Second thing, I hear you play Beethoven fourth. Is too difficult. You are not ready.'

'Of course it's not ready yet. I couldn't play it tomorrow. But with lessons and practice I could play it easily.' He was suddenly glad that his mother was there.

Mrs Crominski realised with some relief that at least she would have Marcus on her side. She could afford to give way a little. 'Now Marcus,' she said, 'Is important Madame Sousatzka says what she thinks. After all, Madame Sousatzka is the teacher.'

Marcus was horrified at what he took to be a change of side. 'But Momma, I know I can play it. I know I'm ready.'

'Oh, is a problem,' Mrs Crominski said happily, looking forward to the discussion. Having opposed Marcus to Madame Sousatzka she had put herself in the happy position of arbitrator. 'All right,' she said, 'so that piece isn't ready. Suppose we agree, Madame Sousatzka. Is plenty other pieces. And even for this piece' – she didn't want to risk naming it in case she got it wrong – 'is time to be ready. Not tomorrow is the concert.'

Both of them looked at Madame Sousatzka. It was undeniably her turn.

'For me, is even bigger problem than is for Marcus,' she said. 'If Marcus plays bad, is bad for Marcus. But for Sousatzka, is much worse. For Sousatzka's reputation, is bad. For Sousatzka's living.'

The discussion had taken quite an unexpected turn. To pursue the question of the concert, now, seemed like depriving Madame Sousatzka of her livelihood.

'But why should Marcus play bad?' Mrs Crominski asked.

'For me, he is not ready.'

'So no concert?' Mrs Crominski said, and her tone was threatening.

'That I do not say. Perhaps when he is ready. We see.' The glass was going to decide for her, but she didn't want to tell them about it.

'When shall we see?' Mrs Crominski pressed on.

'Tomorrow, perhaps.'

Mrs Crominski had the good sense not to press her further. She knew that the tone of threat in her voice had not been lost on Madame Sousatzka. She knew that Madame Sousatzka had made her decision, and she was prepared to give her more time to announce it so that it wouldn't look as if forced on her. 'Next week is plenty time, Madame Sousatzka,' she said. 'I understand for you is a big decision. Take time. Overnight you do not decide these big matters. Take a week. A fortnight, perhaps.' Mrs Crominski was handing out allowances with easy charity, the sort of generosity a victorious wife can afford to mete out to a discarded mistress, and Madame Sousatzka hated her for it.

She tried to smile. She didn't want Mrs Crominski to know that the decision had been forced on her. She would ask the glass anyway, and if the glass decided there was to be no concert, she would listen to the glass, whatever the consequences. She wanted Mrs Crominski to go. She wanted to be alone with Marcus for a while.

'Well,' said Mrs Crominski, standing up, 'we have talked what is necessary. Now I go. Perhaps you want to talk to Marcus.' She went over to Marcus to kiss him, and Marcus tried to turn his face away. His mother had won, and though she'd fought on his behalf, all his feelings went out to Madame Sousatzka. He too wanted to be alone with her. Mrs Crominski left the room practically unnoticed, while Marcus and Madame Sousatzka stared at each other helplessly.

She walked over to him, putting her hands on his shoulders. 'Sousatzka is losing her Marcus,' she said.

If only she hadn't said it, Marcus thought, we could have gone on with the lie together. He turned away from her. 'I don't understand,' he said. 'Why can't I give concerts and still have lessons with you?'

He suddenly thought of Peter Goldstein and his stuttering brother. What would they be doing now? Probably practising in the garden for the school match tomorrow. He wished he could be with them, with all the others, getting filthy on the football pitch, getting detentions, or staying in after school to help with the Christmas decorations. He looked sadly at his bitten fingers. There was never any nail-stock when he really wanted it. Why didn't Peter Goldstein bite his nails? Why didn't *his* mother wear a brown hat? How could he eat his spinach? Did he have a Madame Sousatzka who came to him almost every night and left him exhausted? He'd ask him, he'd ask him on Monday during prep. Then perhaps he'd be accepted as one of them. They wouldn't keep thinking he was someone special. 'But you are special, Marcus,' he said to himself. 'You're chosen.'

9

At a quarter to ten that evening the dirty Countess set out on her journey. She wanted to be the first to arrive, to have a word about the session with Jenny beforehand. She reckoned if she took two minutes for every stairway, she would reach Jenny's room with five minutes to spare, and not unduly exhausted. But Mr Cordle had similar ideas. He too wanted a word with Jenny before the session started, and as the Countess climbed the stairs that led to Cordle's apartment, he came out of his door. 'You're early,' they said to each other simultaneously, and, both thwarted, there was nothing to do but to go up together. But Madame Sousatzka had beaten them to it. She was already in Jenny's room.

She had dressed for the occasion. She wore a long red velvet dress that reached down to her ankles. A black nondescript fur curled around the hem, and drooped into a tired train at the back. She was obviously very nervous and paced the floor clutching her hands, stopping very often and looking at the door like a prima donna whose partner has overlooked his cue.

Jenny, too, wore her seance uniform; a long black sheath dress that wound itself tightly around her ankles so that it looked like a rolled umbrella. Cordle was still in his white coat, and Uncle's exhausting afternoon had left her with little strength to change her clothes, but they shuffled in trying hard to look as if their carriage was waiting at the door. Madame Sousatzka looked at them long enough to show that there were no hard feelings, though they reasonably deserved some.

Jenny had rearranged the room to suit the severity of the occasion. The black curtains were drawn and two green lamps at each end of the room threw the shadows of the four participants on to the walls. In the middle of the room was a green baize table and four identical chairs were symmetrically placed on each side. Around the rim of the table, evenly spaced, lay the letters of the alphabet. And in the middle, turned upsidedown, stood an ordinary tumbler. Beside it was a small bowl of French chalk. There were four extra chairs around the gasfire. They grouped around it, taking their seats for the initial stage of the session.

'Are we ready?' Jenny asked.

Cordle fidgeted in his chair to find a comfortable position, and Madame Sousatzka draped the folds of her fur-lined hem around her feet. A strong smell of mint pervaded the room. The ceremony of mint-tea drinking preceded every session and was intended to relax the participants and to induce concentration. No-one was allowed to speak after being handed their glass of tea. Each glass was marked with the owner's name on a piece of adhesive tape. While drinking, they were supposed to concentrate on the problem they would put to the glass that evening. Although Uncle didn't publicly admit it, the mint tea didn't work with her. It made her relax all right, but into a reverie that had absolutely nothing to do with the problem in hand.

She invariably had the same day-dream, which she would consciously induce with the first sip. She was sitting in a street cafe in Paris and Paul was by her side. He was fingering the red feathers of the boa around her neck. 'Are you glad we're married, Louise?' She remembered trying to say 'yes' but her happiness choked her. She put her hand over his and he kissed it, and when he looked up at her, two single red feathers sprouted from his moustache. She laughed at him and he smiled and she was sitting in a street cafe in Paris with Paul by her side. He was fingering the red feathers of her boa . . . As she looked at him she grew aware of Mr Cordle, staring at her accusingly, as if conscious of her illegal thoughts.

But in fact Cordle was no more concentrating on the problem than she was. All Mr Cordle was doing was making a speech, between sips of tea, to the community who had erected his statue in the park to honour his discoveries. Cordle's past life was best left buried, and his day-dreams concentrated on what might yet be. 'I am grateful, very grateful,' he said, 'for the way in which you have shown your appreciation. And I am honoured, deeply honoured. I have spent a lifetime working on my theories, and when at last I made the great discovery that the essence of Mankind is . . . is . . . I am grateful, very grateful, for the way in which you have shown your appreciation, and I am honoured, deeply honoured,' he caught sight of a tear in Madame Sousatzka's eye and marvelled that his oration had so moved her.

But of them all, only Madame Sousatzka was thinking of the glass. Supposing, as she inwardly feared, that the glass advised her to allow Marcus the concert? She would have to obey. It was bad luck to go against the glass. And then what? The concert and a great success, and offers from all over the world. New teachers, new methods and new investigations. Marcus would be lost to her and every so often she would get a letter of gratitude and a card at Christmas. She didn't even feel the hot tear that slid down her cheek, only a vast hole in her stomach, the sad and stubborn pain of rejection.

Jenny was looking at her and hoped, for her sake, that tonight the glass would make a misjudgment. She knew what Marcus meant to Madame Sousatzka, and so much of it had nothing to do with the piano. But Felix was right. It was wrong for the boy to hibernate, and Marcus would never thank her for it. Somebody would have to be hurt and Jenny tried hard to decide which one. She loved them both. She began to wish that she had never met Manders. She remembered the old days, when she used to wait outside nearby, on the whore-road that skirted the park, and how Manders had pulled up his car and asked her the way to Oxford. Did she look as if she needed to know the way to Oxford, with her tight skirt, her peep-toe shoes, and the fox-fur cape that Beatie had bequeathed her when her own cat-days were over? Anyhow, she'd offered to keep him company. He wasn't going to Oxford anyway, but they drove around for a bit and they talked. She was grateful to him that he hadn't immediately got down to business, that he had treated her as if she were a respectable girl who was just a bit lonely. That's why she liked him, and why perhaps it had lasted for so many years. She looked at her watch, a gift from another client, also a regular, a businessman from the North whose wife didn't understand him.

She usually allotted ten minutes for thought-acclimatization, as she called it. To give more was dangerous. Thought becomes idle and wanders. She tapped her finger on her glass, which was her signal for them to come to. Both Cordle and Uncle jumped at the noise and their first realization of the matter at hand.

'I think we can begin now, but before we begin, I think we must decide who will ask the questions.'

There was some discussion. Uncle declared Sousatzka to be an interested party, and therefore partial, at which Sousatzka explained to Uncle that as Marcus's week-end landlady, she also was not completely disinterested. Cordle, too, would be personally affected by the tumbler's decision, and so it was left to Jenny, who was considered the least partial of them all. Jenny took her seat at the table. Madame Sousatzka sat opposite her, with Mr Cordle and Uncle on the other sides.

They sat in silence for a moment, then at a sign from Jenny, they lifted the index finger of their right hands, and dipped them together into the bowl of chalk. Then they placed them lightly on the tumbler.

'Is there a spirit in this house?' Jenny asked. There was no answer.

'Do you know why we are here?' Jenny tried again in a low voice.

Uncle sneezed and the glass trembled. 'It knows,' said Cordle.

'Whose problem are we concerned with?'

They waited and concentrated. Even Uncle had come back from Paris for the occasion. Then slowly the glass began to move. It knew where it was going but it took its time. It moved slowly to Madame Sousatzka's corner and stopped with assurance at the letter M. But not for long. Barely touching the letter, it moved away to the other end of the table where Jenny was sitting, and paused at the letter A.

'It's Manders,' said Uncle.

'Could be Marcus,' said Jenny solemnly.

They all looked at the glass, which seemed to have retired. Jenny repeated the question, and the glass obediently set off again. It passed the letter N and came to rest at R, but only for a moment, after which it skidded to the C, U and S in quick succession.

'Marcus,' Madame Sousatzka breathed, as if it hadn't been quite clear, and whether from its own volition or from external pressure, the glass returned to the middle of the table.

'What is Marcus?' asked Jenny. It was a question posed only as a formality. Jenny didn't for one moment doubt the authenticity of her tumbler. It had served her well for many years. It had always been right, and she guarded it and respected it as a child does a long-service conker.

The glass began to move again, this time unmistakably and assuredly to the letter P. 'That's enough,' said Jenny. She brought the glass back into the centre. It had proved itself to be genuine.

'Excuse me,' said Uncle, who had to sneeze again.

'You're not concentrating,' Jenny accused her.

'That's not true,' Uncle said. 'It's this French chalk.' She had been thinking of nothing else but Marcus and out of pique she took herself once more off to Paris.

Jenny braced herself. The next questions were decisive, and she wanted to give the tumbler time to compose itself. 'We're not all ready,' she said. 'One of us is not here. Let us come together. Let us join in concentration for the best results.' She waited again. 'Pour your minds into your finger-tips. Uncle, come back,' Jenny whispered. Uncle was in the process of changing trains, but she shook herself out of her reverie and concentrated on the tip of her finger.

'What should Marcus do?' Jenny asked, quietly and deliberately. At that moment the 'phone rang. Madame Sousatzka, who was nearest, picked it up with her free hand, shouted 'Out', into the receiver and promptly put it down again. But the peace had been disturbed. They all rose and returned to their chairs by the gas-fire, while Jenny put on the kettle. No-one said a word.

78

It was a bad omen, and Madame Sousatzka began to feel that whatever the glass advised would be unreliable. But there was the risk of offending it. They had to go through with the session.

Jenny collected their used glasses and looked at the tea-leaves, each in turn. Three of them were of little interest to her, and she rinsed them under the tap. But Madame Sousatzka's she put aside for further scrutiny, and she reached for a clean glass from the shelf. She poured out fresh glasses of mint tea and the ceremony started again. This time it was difficult to relax at all, and Jenny sensed their restlessness. 'Drink up quickly,' she said, 'we mustn't keep the tumbler waiting.'

They drank in silence. Jenny was first to finish, and while waiting for the others she went over to the sink to pick up Sousatzka's old glass. What she read in the tea-leaves was exactly the same as she had read in Marcus's cup in the afternoon, except that in this vision Marcus was visible. He was crouching underneath some furniture, surrounded by hundreds of people.

She quickly washed the glass and all trace of the misfortune she felt was bound to follow. 'Are we ready now?' she asked, collecting the glasses.

Uncle was sitting staring into the gas-fire. Somehow with this glass of tea she hadn't been able to see Paris. Instead she was on the verge of thinking of Madrid two years later. The day they'd sent a message from the Embassy where he worked to say that Paul had collapsed. She tried not to let her thoughts carry her to the vision of his utterly dead body on the Chippendale couch of the Embassy drawing-room. She was grateful when Jenny called them back to the table.

Madame Sousatzka took her seat first and the others followed. Jenny went once more through the preliminaries and the answers were the same. The decisive question could not be delayed any longer.

'What?' said Jenny deliberately. 'What should Marcus do?' All eyes were on the glass. Slowly it started to move, at first in a small circle, and gradually widening in diameter until it was skidding almost uncontrollably within a few inches of the rim of the table. Their fingers went with it, and the top of the glass looked like a Catherine Wheel, with Jenny's red-painted nail briefly smudging Cordle's, which lay next to hers.

Sousatzka didn't want it to stop; she hoped that its speed would gather and that it would fall from the table and smash to pieces. She hated it and willed its destruction. Cordle was concentrating as never before, and even Uncle grew aware of the vital decision the glass was about to make. Then gradually it slowed down, moving further towards the centre. Then suddenly it stopped revolving and, as if magnetized, it moved towards the letter C, where it stopped sadly as if it couldn't help it. It wanted to get it over with, and the next letters of the word 'concert' were visited reluctantly and quickly by Jenny's tumbler. When it had spat it out, like a dirty word, Jenny brought the glass back to the centre and they all took their fingers away.

All except Madame Sousatzka. 'Cordle,' she said, piercing him in the eye, 'Cordle, you pushed.'

It was an unforgivable accusation. It cast suspicion not only on this session, but on all the others in which Cordle had participated.

'That's a lie,' he spluttered, 'a downright lie.' No one would ever have believed that Cordle could lose his temper. None of them had seen him like this before. He looked down at his hands and rubbed them gently as if they'd been hurt, then quietly he added, 'Don't I need him back, too?' He got up and went over to the gas-fire.

Uncle and Jenny looked at Madame Sousatzka. She had begun to cry. 'I'm sorry, Cordle,' she wept. 'It wasn't true. I don't want to believe the glass. That is all. We need him. Both of us. Tomorrow will I telephone Manders.'

Each of them wanted to console her, even Mr Cordle who had understood her outburst and had already forgiven her. But what could they say? Mr Manders was her executioner and she was going to make an appointment with him in the morning.

'I'll make some tea before you go,' Jenny said quickly to break the tension. She ran the tap quietly and got the cups ready with the minimum of noise. Then she put on the kettle and the steady sound of the gas relieved the silence in the room. Suddenly Jenny started to hum. She was humming a well-known folk-song, putting in a word or two here and there. Uncle began to tap her fingers to the rhythm and Cordle shifted forward in his seat. Then at the third verse he joined in shyly, craning his neck towards Jenny, singing slightly off-pitch as in a mating-call. Only Madame Sousatzka sat silent, her hands trembling on her knees.

Jenny poured the tea using a strainer, which was not her custom, but she didn't want to give them a reason to ask her to read their cups tonight. She was tired anyway, and tomorrow she'd have to work.

Madame Sousatzka blew on her tea noisily, then lifting her cup forward and away from her, she said in a broken voice, 'Let's drink to our Marcus and his future.'

'Just listen to that,' Jenny said, laughing with relief. 'That's a real toast. But we can't drink such an important toast with tea. Wait a minute,' and she ran to her cupboard and brought out a bottle of champagne. She shut the cupboard door, then after some hesitation she reopened it, and brought out a second bottle.

'This is really worth a celebration,' she said, forgetting her fatigue, concerned only with making the most of the tumbler's decision. 'Cordle, this is your job, I think.'

She gave him the bottle and Cordle tore off the silver foil. He pressed his thumbs under the wire and aimed the neck of the bottle at the door. He shut his eyes tightly as if, had he had his fingers free, he would have stuffed them in his ears.

For a moment, Uncle was back in Paris, but Madame Sousatzka sat sadly, her cup of tea still raised. 'To Marcus,' she whispered, and she took a sip and put her cup on the floor.

Cordle was treating the cork as if it was a dislocated bone. He coaxed it this way and that, reluctant to dismiss it. 'Fire!' Jenny shouted. Cordle giggled. 'You're the boss,' he said, and the cork went flying across the room with a loud pop.

The champagne bubbled out of the bottle. Jenny had forgotten clean glasses, and it was poured hastily into the dregs of mint tea.

'To Marcus and his future,' Cordle squeaked, already drunk with the fumes.

'To Marcus,' they all said, raising their glasses. 'And to our dear Sousatzka,' Uncle added, clinking her glass to hers. 'To Sousatzka, who is responsible.'

'No,' said Jenny. 'We must have a fresh glass for Sousatzka. The next one. This one is for Marcus.'

Cordle emptied his glass quickly, eager to give some justification to his intoxicated mood. Uncle sipped hers gently, flitting from one Embassy couch to another. Jenny tackled hers professionally, savouring the mint bouquet. 'Come on, Sousatzka,' she said, 'drink up. We've got another bottle to get through.'

Sousatzka was sipping gingerly, but at Jenny's encouragement she finished it in one gulp. She tottered a little, slipping on the fur hem of her dress. There was a loud ripping sound, and then silence. Suddenly Madame Sousatzka laughed, and picking up her skirt she tore off the whole hem of fur and placed it delicately round Uncle's neck. It was Uncle's ticket to Paris again. She would be busy for the rest of the evening.

'I never like this dress, anyway,' said Sousatzka, 'I buy a new one for the concert. Another drink for the concert,' she added, raising her glass. There was a desperation in her sudden gaiety. She was determined not to spoil the fun. But so was everybody else in the room, each trying to feed the atmosphere of jollity that had been forced on them.

Jenny refilled the glasses. Uncle had put her feet on Jenny's chair. 'Come and sit here,' Cordle said, daringly touching his knee. Jenny obliged as part of the job.

Sousatzka giggled. 'And me?' she pouted.

'Have the other one,' said Cordle generously, tapping his free knee. He couldn't have known what he was letting himself in for. Madame Sousatzka, tipsy as she was, put her whole weight on to Cordle's knee-cap. He let out an hysterical, painful laugh, tipped them both over and joined them rolling on the floor.

Uncle watched them disdainfully. They had temporarily disturbed her dream. She flicked her ash on to Cordle's trousers and lurched across to the table to refill her glass.

The others on the floor indicated that she should fill theirs too, and Uncle came down on the floor to join them.

Cordle was much in demand because of his minority status. Uncle put her arms around his neck, touching Sousatzka's fingers which were already there. Jenny was lying flat on her back, her feet resting on Cordle's knees. She was singing a song, a song she always used to sing on outside work, to while away the hours of back and fore pacing during the slack times. She would allocate herself a certain number of verses, plus the repeated chorus, before she would give up and go home. But invariably she went on singing until the end, because it was a song that told a story, and it was bad luck to leave it untold. The others were listening to her, humming the chorus, trying to learn the words. But it was the song of Jenny's Union, unknown to those outside the trade.

'Let's dance,' said Cordle weakly, when the song was finished. He wanted himself fully exploited. Gently he removed Jenny's feet and disentangled himself from Sousatzka's and Uncle's embrace. He opened the other bottle of champagne and refilled the glasses. 'To the future,' he said, not being able to think of a vaguer toast. Half of him wanted to stagger out of the room and go downstairs and shade Paradise into his chart in bright purple. The other half willed him to stay. He felt that some indefinable opportunity waited for him in this room. Without much difficulty he opted for the latter half. 'May I,' he stumbled over to Sousatzka, 'have this waltz?'

He started to sing in questionable three-four time. Madame Sousatzka joined him, putting him more securely into the waltz beat. He held her at arm's length, as if a crinoline separated them. 'Do you come here often?' he asked.

'Yes,' she giggled, 'every week I come.'

With her reply, Jenny's room, which had for Cordle become a State ballroom, was reduced to the local Palais de Danse. He adapted himself quickly. 'What d'you do for a living, love?'

'I am a teacher,' she said proudly. 'I am *the* teacher. The teacher of that great pianist who now is playing all over

83

Europe. I am his teacher.'

'Oh,' said Cordle, trying to place the new location suggested by her answer. But seeing the two drunk wallflowers wilting against the cupboard he said, 'Let's have a Paul Jones.' He grabbed them and joined their hands with Sousatzka's and started them off in a circle. He himself pirouetted in the centre, humming like a top. Although he was drunk, he was acutely aware of his dilemma, that if he ever stopped whirling, two of the ladies would be offended. And so he spiralled to the floor and lay there prostrate and exhausted. He saw three disappointed faces staring down at him, like the swollen head of a giant sunflower. He couldn't distinguish one from the other, and Uncle's fur collar seemed to encircle them all. Suddenly a third of the face disappeared and he was conscious of a great weight on his body. He felt cold metal on his neck, and touching it, he knew it was Sousatzka's watch. He rolled her over to his side, and they lay there giggling.

'I'm drunk,' said Madame Sousatzka, anxious to give some justification for her amorous mood. Cordle said nothing. There was only need for one of them to take the responsibility.

He put his arm round her and drummed his fingers on the fat that covered her spine. Jenny had gone over to her bed. She had refilled her glass and lay face downwards, cradling it on her pillow. Uncle just about made the table, and she sat down heavily in front of the tumbler. There was a sudden heavy silence in the room, broken only by an occasional sigh from Madame Sousatzka on the floor.

'It reminds me,' Uncle said dreamily, 'of a party we had in the Austrian Embassy in 1905. I wore my black organdie. Everybody drank so much, all the people who next morning would be our enemies. Only Paul was sober. And then the awful thing happened. I was standing there, underneath some painting or other,' she moved the letter L for Louise to the side of the table. 'Paul was there' – she did likewise with the letter P – 'and that dreadful English General was in the middle.' She took the tumbler and put it between the two letters. 'Drunk as a lord he was, tottering on his little feet.' She swivelled the glass from side to side.

' "He's not good enough for you, my dear," he said. "Won't touch a drop because he can't hold it." He touched Paul's lapel. "A man who can't take liquor," he spat out at him, "he's not a man. You're not worthy of her," he shouted, putting his arm around my shoulder. Paul was very calm, but I could see that he was angry.' Uncle was whispering now, and both Sousatzka and Cordle were sitting on the floor listening to her. Jenny leaned over the bed-rail. 'I knew he was angry because of the vein that stuck out on his forehead. "You're drunk," Paul said to him. "Drunk, am I? I'll show you how drunk I am," and with both his arms he lifted Paul from the ground.' At this point, Uncle turned the tumbler on its side and with it she scooped up the letter P. The couple on the floor stood up for a better view, and Jenny crossed over to the table. Uncle was in a trance. Her whispering was unbearable. 'So I put my arms around Paul and I screamed trying to drag him away. All the others at the party crowded round us.' With one swoop of her hand she scooped the remaining letters into an untidy pile in the centre of the table. 'At last Paul got himself free,' Uncle gently took the letter out of the glass, 'but I could see he was defeated.' She crumpled the card in her hand. 'I couldn't bear that, not that look on his face. I took off my shoe – it had a pointed heel – and I hit that General on his face. I hit him and I hit him and I hit him.' With the card in her hand, she pushed the glass towards the edge of the table. She was shouting now hysterically. 'I hit him, till he fell on his back.' She swept her hand over the table and the glass crashed into a thousand tiny pieces on the floor. With her other hand, she swept the rest of the cards after it, and clutching the crumpled letter P in her hand, she beat her forehead in an agony of remorse and remembrance.

In a way, Uncle's breakdown was a relief to them all. They could now drop the act they were each playing and become themselves again. The crash of the glass had sobered them. Jenny began to cry with a kind of rage at the loss of her glass, and anger at not being able to scold Uncle. She tried vainly to piece the glass together, but Cordle told her to let it be.

'You'll cut your fingers,' he said gently. But Jenny

insisted, picking up the splinters one by one. Then she took
another glass and poured them inside, like ashes in an urn.
She held it up to the dim green light, like a penitential
candle, and then gently consecrated it to the mantelpiece.

'Poor Paul,' Uncle whispered. Sousatzka put her arms
round her, stroking the fur collar. 'Come Uncle,' she said,
'we must all of us go to bed.'

Cordle went to the door and held it open for the two
ladies. Madame Sousatzka's train dragged through the
door, her arm firmly round Uncle's waist. Mr Cordle
nodded to Jenny with a miserable smile, and he closed the
door after himself.

Jenny stared at the door for a long time. Then she
switched off the lights, leaving only the small night-light by
her bed. She lay awake in the luke-dark, watching the glass
that stood on the mantelpiece, upright and bare as a dead
tree.

'Tomorrow, I'll buy a new one,' she decided. 'We're
going to need a tumbler in this house.'

10

Madame Sousatzka had arranged to meet Manders the following Saturday in his office. She had written to Mrs Crominski informing her of her decision, and suggesting at the same time that her presence at the interview was not strictly necessary. Mrs Crominski had replied. To the first, natural, she was delighted; to the second, natural she understood. She hadn't really understood it at all, but she was still prepared to make concessions to the loser. She decided it would be Madame Sousatzka's last fling.

Madame Sousatzka was a little nervous of tackling Manders on her own, and she had asked Jenny to go with them.

Marcus was up early at the piano, and Sousatzka was still in her bedroom dressing. She had tried on her entire wardrobe, trying various combinations of colours and accessories. The women's magazine lay open on the bed with an article entitled 'Start from Scratch'. Madame Sousatzka took everything off until she reached the scratch condition. Tabula Rasa. 'The first thing you must do if you have an important date is to start from scratch,' the article said. Well, she'd done that, hadn't she, and it was an uncomfortable position to remain in for long. What now? 'Now,' the article continued, 'sit down and think.' Madame Sousatzka sat down and thought. She was much too cold to concentrate deeply on anything. She considered after a few moments of meditation that she'd been loyal enough to the article, and she leaned over to read what followed. 'If your date is a formal one, there's nothing quite to beat that indispensable little black dress,' Madame Sousatzka rushed to her wardrobe. Yes, she had one of these indispensables, that by any standard of good taste is most readily dispensed with. She surprised it off its hanger and quickly put it on, more for the sake of warmth than conformity. She went back to the article. 'With a little black dress, you can go to town on accessories,' it dared her. Well, this was more in her line. She draped a heavy horse-brass round her neck, and swathed her arms in a smithy-full of heavy copper bracelets, and topped the ensemble with a large red velvet hat. 'Let yourself go with the bracelets and bangles,' the article had said. She had followed it to the letter.

A new paragraph signified the next stage of the operation. 'Now take a good look at yourself,' it challenged. Madame Sousatzka felt she'd rather not go that far, but a sense of duty compelled her to follow its advice to the bitter end. Looking at the results in the mirror, she felt she would have done better to reverse the advice of the experts, to have worn her red velvet dress and gone easy on the rest. So she took everything off and started over again.

She ended up with exactly the ensemble she had intended to wear in the first place. She had gone to town on absolutely everything. She looked so much like a shop-window display that it was unnerving to see her set herself in motion towards the door and manoeuvre herself down the stairs into the hall.

Jenny was already there. She was wearing her black indispensable – the magazine had been borrowed from Jenny, who had taken it from Cordle's waiting-room.

Cordle had come to see them off. Uncle was shouting from the bottom of the basement stairs. It was the most she could manage so early in the morning. 'Best of luck,' she was calling at irregular intervals. 'Are you gone yet?' she asked hopefully, impatient to get back to her rocking-chair. 'The taxi's just come,' Jenny shouted back. 'Good luck then,' said Uncle, and hearing the front door slam she retired to her room. Cordle saw them all out, down the front steps and into the taxi. He waved to them sadly without saying a word, as if the taxi were a tumbril.

Marcus sat between the two women. He was the least nervous of them all. He rarely rode in a taxi and each time it was an adventure. He would count the length of the intervals between each meter-change, and it would always vary. The meter was not his personal anxiety, so after a while he ignored it.

Madame Sousatzka grew impatient at the crawling pace. For her, the business of hailing a taxi was far more fun than driving in one. She would often, in a crowded street, shout 'Taxi!' into a line of traffic, having made sure that the cab was already hired. She felt people around her in the bus queues marvel at her potential. She leaned back in her seat, playing with her watch chain, one of the sundry pendants hanging round her neck.

Jenny was impatient, too. For her, riding in taxis was part of the game, especially in the old days of street pick-ups. She remembered how she used to give the cab-drivers her address and how they never failed to wink knowingly back at her. She found this acknowledgment outrageous; she tried whispering her address, or shouting it with confidence, or dropping it casually with determination, but always it met with the same response, the one-eyed confirmation of 'I know what you're up to, luv, but it's none of my business so hop in the two of you and I'll see you right.' The winking cabby had become a recurring image in her dreams and even when she exchanged the pavement for the telephone, she could never obliterate from her memory the demoniac cyclops at the wheel.

They had at last overtaken a bus they had been forced to trail, and the cab-driver turned down one of those back streets known euphemistically as the short cut. When, after much meandering, they got back on to the main road, they found they were only a few yards ahead of their original point of departure. Madame Sousatzka glared at the ticking meter. Not only was she going to her own funeral; she was paying her expenses, too.

'Are we nearly there?' Marcus asked. Madame Sousatzka left the meter unguarded for a moment to look out of the window. 'Almost there,' she said, relieved. The taxi suddenly turned into a side street and pulled up outside a block of offices.

'This is it,' said Jenny, patting her hair. 'Come on, Marcus, we'll wait for Sousatzka in the hall.'

'No.' Sousatzka was adamant. Marcus especially now was her charge. 'We will all go together.'

Marcus and Jenny waited while Madame Sousatzka

fumbled in her bag. She looked repeatedly from her bag back to the meter, to ascertain that it hadn't pulled a fast one on her. She was astonished in any case by its reading. She worked out the ten per cent tip aloud, while the driver watched her patiently. After much verbal calculations, she gave him the fare and the tip, separately and exactly.

'You sure you wouldn't like a re-count, lady?' the cabby asked. But his sarcasm was lost on her. 'No, I'm absolute sure, and thank you.' She managed a smile, and taking Marcus's hand she led him up the steps into the hall.

In the centre of the hall was a desk and sitting behind it, operating a switchboard, was a middle-aged lady. Her nose, her chin, and her finger-nails were lethally pointed. Her long, greying hair was parted severely in the middle and wound itself into snails over her ears. Over these were ear-phones that clamped her head like a vice. She was flicking the switches up and down, and stopping up various holes with plugs, all the time resting one hand on her knitting, which lay in front of her. When she saw Madame Sousatzka arrive, she nodded. Or rather, she gave a series of nods in all directions, first at Marcus, then to the switchboard, down to her knitting and up to the ceiling. Her nodding was thoroughly articulate and indicated 'I'm sorry to keep you waiting, but do take a seat, you can see how busy I am, and if I don't attend to this switchboard, there'll be hell to pay.' This last was indicated ungeographically by the nod at the ceiling. So they sat down and waited.

After about five minutes, Madame Sousatzka got nervous. With all the restless plugging and switching the woman was doing, she expected the whole board to explode at any moment. She got up to draw attention to her continued existence. Another nod from the woman, less articulate this time and with less confidence. Madame Sousatzka nodded too, with great vigour; communication had been re-established. She sat down again, fingering her watch. They were already late for the appointment. In a way, this didn't displease her. She didn't want to show Manders that she was too eager.

Jenny was getting restless and Marcus was fidgeting.

The woman didn't seem to let up with her plugging and switching. She was obviously completely controlled by the machine.

Madame Sousatzka could stand it no longer. She got up and motioned to the others to follow her. They would find their own way to Manders's office. She sailed through the hall past the woman's desk, Marcus and Jenny timidly trailing her. The woman stopped her plugging, and gaped after them, realizing that she didn't even know whether they were friend or foe. She dropped all her wires and even unclasped her head. She was conscious of desertion and the possible penalties, but she had to warn whoever it was, and she hoped to God there was someone, who was expecting them. She thumbed through the large appointments book, checking the time and the date. To her relief, she found only one appointment scheduled for eleven-thirty. Mr Manders with Madame Sousatzka. She flung on her vice and stabbed the neglected, twitching switchboard with a plug, like a matador administering the *coup de grace*. She hoped she'd make it before they did. 'Mr Manders,' she cooed, 'Madame Sousatzka is here.' She didn't specify exactly where she was, but there was no doubt about her presence in the building.

'Could you tell her to wait for a few minutes and apologize?' Manders cooed back. 'I've someone with me at the moment. I'll ring when I'm ready. Come in,' she heard him say as he replaced the receiver.

The poor woman suddenly saw the results of her inefficiency. A pointed tear wriggled down her cheek. She got up in a panic and fled from her desk, even leaving her knitting behind, and the switchboard belching and blinking like an over-jacked fruit machine.

Things were no calmer on the third floor, Room 23, to which Madame Sousatzka and her party had instinctively found their way, as if by smell. When Sousatzka came into Manders's room, he did not at once see Jenny behind her.

'Ah, Madame Sousatzka,' he sung, in his best impresario manner. 'This is my wife,' he said, turning to the woman who sat with her back to the door. At this point Jenny presented herself in the doorway with Marcus. This was a meeting he had spent careful years avoiding. He hadn't expected Jenny to come anyway, and his wife had only dropped in casually because she happened to be in town. He decided to ignore Jenny completely and hope that Sousatzka would have the sense to introduce him.

'And how is Marcus?' he said, going up to him, to give Sousatzka a little time. But Madame Sousatzka was dumb, and Jenny stood around, ungreeted and unannounced. 'Ah, Jenny, you've come too,' Manders said, because somebody had to say something. 'Meet my wife,' he challenged her. He might as well go the whole way now. There was no avoiding it.

Mrs Manders flung out a limp hand as if it didn't belong to her, like a fisherman flinging a little one back into the sea. Jenny caught it and stared her straight in the eye. She was a shrewd-looking woman, and small too, Jenny was convinced, because she stubbornly remained seated. She was expensively dressed, and she fingered her clothes as if checking on her compensation. Her face, even in youth, had never been beautiful; not because of her features, which were well-moulded and defined, but because of the meanness of her expression, which age had underlined with wrinkles.

She stared for a while at Jenny's feet. Then she turned her head towards her husband. 'Felix,' she said, as if scolding him, 'put me in the picture. Madame Sousatzka is the teacher, Marcus is the pupil, but who is Jenny?'

He waited for Madame Sousatzka to supply Jenny's references. But Sousatzka was staring at the ceiling. The silence was beginning to betray him. 'Why, Jenny's another pupil,' he laughed weakly. He regretted it the moment it was out. He knew that at some time or another she would be called upon to prove it. Marcus gasped audibly, and Manders made frantic gestures to him over his wife's head, to keep his mouth shut. He winked at him matily, as if to imply that this was only a game. Marcus shrugged. He wasn't particularly interested in what they were saying. He was vaguely looking round to find where they kept the piano.

'A pupil,' Mrs Manders beamed, 'and no doubt as

talented as our little Marcus here.' Mrs Manders was already asserting her rights of property. Madame Sousatzka instinctively called Marcus over to her.

'There is in England no pianist talented like Marcus. Jenny is only a beginning.'

Marcus saw Manders wink at Madame Sousatzka gratefully. He caught Mrs Manders's eye, and she raised her eyebrows at him distastefully. Then suddenly Marcus understood what the game was all about. 'She's not a beginner,' he laughed, wishing to join the game thoroughly. 'She plays the orchestral parts of concertos, while I play solo. Don't you, Jenny?'

'Well, I try,' she said. She thought that if she was going to pass as a pianist at all, she might as well be a competent one.

'Well, now isn't that nice?' said Mrs Manders. 'Felix, d'you think I could hear them some time? I know, why not let Jenny come over on Friday with Marcus? You could hear Marcus first and then we could have a little concert. I have quite a salon at home, you know,' she turned to Madame Sousatzka. 'Every Friday. The greatest musicians have played in my drawing-room. You must come too, my dear,' she added as an afterthought. Madame Sousatzka shuddered at the thought of great musicians surrounded by chatter and pretty things on toast. 'Salon' was a dirty word in her vocabulary.

Mrs Manders stood up, as if she had settled everything. She was as small as Jenny had expected. She flung out her old fist again in all directions as a gesture of farewell. 'Will you be dining at home tonight, Felix?' It was a question meant to impress. With it went the information that Mrs Manders had good silver.

'I'll ring you, my dear,' he said, slightly taken aback by his wife's terminology. 'I've so much to do today.'

'Well, I really must go now,' she insisted, as if they were trying desperately to keep her. 'I left my car unlocked.' Jenny obediently noted yet another possession. 'And Andre will be furious if I'm late. My dressmaker,' she volunteered. Jenny made another note. 'Goodbye, then, till Friday.' Marcus ran to open the door for her. For some reason or other he pitied her. 'What a sweet little boy,' she said, fondling his head. 'Good manners so rarely go with talent.'

When she had gone, Jenny turned on Manders. 'Now what?' she said. 'I could have been anything. I could have been his mother. I could have simply been a friend. How am I going to learn the piano in a week? I'll just have to be ill, that's all. I won't go.'

'You've got to come,' said Manders almost angrily. He suddenly saw the intriguing possibilities of the new situation, and they half delighted him. 'She'll start being suspicious if you don't come. Look,' he went on, 'I didn't expect you to be here, Jenny. I didn't expect my wife, either. I just said the first thing that came into my mind. I'm sorry.'

'Well, I said you were a beginning only,' Madame Sousatzka exonerated herself.

They all turned to Marcus. 'Madame Sousatzka doesn't take beginnings,' he said, defending himself. 'She wouldn't have believed that.' He already felt himself head of the conspiracy.

'Well, my boy,' Manders said, 'you got us into it. You can get us out.'

They all took it for granted that there was no explanation due to Marcus. They knew he understood the situation and had seemingly accepted it. 'It's easy,' Marcus said. 'This week you have an accident. You burn your hand. Not really though,' he smiled at Jenny. 'You were making tea and the steam from the kettle burned your hand while you were taking it off the gas. It burnt your skin off. Might as well make it a wound that will take a long time to heal.'

Manders was impressed by the boy's attention to detail. He had in him the makings of a perfect liar. 'You bandage your hand, you can even have it in a sling; you can't play, it's simple.'

But Jenny had objections. 'I'll be expected to talk about music even if I can't play, and I can't suddenly burn my hand and lose my voice all in one week.'

'I tell everything you must say,' said Madame Sousatzka, who wanted a hand in the game, too. 'I will ask you certain questions, and I will tell you how the answer is.'

'But supposing *she* asks me, Mrs Manders I mean?'

'We'll all answer for you,' Manders said in a fatherly way. 'We'll manage. It can't be helped. It was a mistake, but we'll have to make the best of it. And now let's get down to business.'

'Where's the piano?' Marcus asked.

Manders laughed. 'No piano here, my boy. I've heard you anyway. The audition,' he turned to Madame Sousatzka, 'is a mere formality. I have no doubts that the boy can play,' he said with some authority, 'and if *I* have no doubts, then there's no question of the boy's ability.'

Madame Sousatzka was irritated by his arrogance and she wanted to protect Marcus from his unjustified assumption of authority. 'Is it absolute necessary that Marcus will stay?' she asked. 'He can wait for us downstairs. This is just a business, darrlink. For you it is boring. Go down and talk to that nice lady at the machine in the hall. She will let you play with it, perhaps.'

'That's an idea,' said Manders. 'Wait for us downstairs. I want to take you all out to lunch,' he said expansively. 'Not a business lunch, Madame Sousatzka. We will talk of other things.'

Marcus put his hands in his pockets as they would not be needed, and he left the room.

Madame Sousatzka, who had been standing all the time, looked around for a chair. Manders drew up a couch to his desk and motioned her to sit down. He moved to the chair that his wife had just vacated and placed it behind Jenny. He returned to his swivel chair at the desk and fumbled with irrelevant papers, scrutinizing them and sorting them with a professional air. 'We'll launch him with a splash, I've decided,' he said enthusiastically. 'The Festival Hall. Nothing less.' Jenny gasped. Manders waited for Madame Sousatzka's reaction and her gratitude. But Sousatzka, whatever she felt, was determined not to show it. 'A recital?' she asked casually.

'Oh no,' said Manders, realizing the reason for her lack of immediate enthusiasm. 'An orchestral concert. I will launch him in a big way. A big conductor, a big orchestra, in the Festival Hall.' Madame Sousatzka noted that suddenly he was undertaking the launching alone. She said nothing, and Jenny was surprised at her lack of reaction.

'He will play the Beethoven Fourth,' Madame Sousatzka announced.

'Never mind what he'll play,' said Manders. 'What will he wear? That's more to the point. I suggest,' he went on, determined to ignore Sousatzka's dumbfounded expression, 'a black velvet suit and an Eton collar. His hair should not be too neat, and preferably longer than is usual. I have tentatively scheduled a date in February. It's one of my boy's concerts, but he's had to cancel it. I'll put Marcus in his place. That gives us two months; he can grow his hair by then. Black patent shoes,' he went on, 'with perhaps a silver buckle. But my wife will see to that. She's rather good at that sort of thing.'

Madame Sousatzka stood up. She had had enough. 'My Marcus is not a male model,' she shouted, desperately reclaiming him. 'What he should wear is not important. That is not my business. My business is the piano, Mr Manders. I will see he gives such a concert, you never heard anything like it. That is all that matters to me.'

'Well, of course, we all know he'll play well,' Manders soothed her, 'but in this business, we take that for granted. There are so many pianists, Madame Sousatzka,' he confided to her sadly. 'They all play well. They all have talent. But these days, with such competition,' he raised his voice as if he were addressing a board meeting, 'they have to have something more. Our Marcus is a child' – Madame Sousatzka noted their joint account – 'I intend to sell him as a child, as a child prodigy, but first and foremost as a child. As for the Beethoven Fourth, and I know it well,' he added quickly, forestalling Madame Sousatzka's disbelief, 'almost all pianists on my books play that one – I don't think somehow that Marcus is, well, mature enough. I think a little Mozart would sell better. The double image of child prodigies,' he said. 'And after all, Mozart is a lot easier for a youngster.'

Madame Sousatzka exploded at his abysmal ignorance. 'Mature you want him to be? I also want him mature. And when he is mature, he will play Mozart. Not before that.

You think that to play the piano is only the technique. So he can play Mozart, you think. Simple. There is more to the business, Mr Manders, than black and white notes. For Mozart, you must be the great musician, you must have lived and suffered, tried and failed. You must know the joy, the hatred, the betrayal.' Madame Sousatzka obviously felt herself a more suitable candidate for the Festival Hall. 'My Marcus is a little boy. He is not ready for Mozart. And I don't care how many of your boys play the Beethoven. Marcus will play it better.'

'Oh, what's the difference for Heaven's sake,' said Jenny. 'Let's not argue. Felix,' she said gently, 'let Madame Sousatzka have her way with what Marcus plays. What does it matter as long as he plays well?'

Because it was Jenny's request, Manders was willing to make the concession. 'All right, Madame Sousatzka,' he said, 'have your own way. But as an impresario, I give you my opinion, gained from long experience, that a child playing Mozart is an infallible best-seller.'

Madame Sousatzka sat down again. She was not interested in Manders's opinions and she let it pass.

'Now there is the question of contract,' Manders said, picking up a blue folder from the desk. 'We needn't go into details. They're rather boring.' Madame Sousatzka opened her mouth in the shape of a contradiction, but pressing on Manders said, 'You can take a copy home with you and study it at your leisure.'

'How much you pay Marcus for the concert?' Sousatzka asked innocently.

'How much do *I* pay?' Manders gasped. He hadn't realized Madame Sousatzka was so naïve. 'D'you understand, Madame Sousatzka,' he said gently, 'that the general procedure in our business, especially with a new, unknown artist, is that the artist pays *me* to launch him under my aegis, and that he will receive a percentage of the profits, that is, if there are any. Now in Marcus's case,' he hurried on, dreading her interruptions, 'I am making an exception.'

'He *is* the exception,' Sousatzka said. 'How much you pay him?'

'I don't know,' Manders said, slightly irritated. 'He is an

exception because I ask nothing of him in the beginning. I undertake all expenses; the Hall, the orchestra, the conductor, the advertisements, the publicity; I risk it all. And Marcus will be paid out of the profits after I have got my money back.'

'So you lose nothing,' Madame Sousatzka said.

'Madame Sousatzka,' Manders was angry now, and a soothing look from Jenny calmed him a little. 'I stand to lose everything,' he said. 'Without an audience, there is no profit. And you must have a big audience even to cover expenses. You never know. He is unknown. He plays the Beethoven Fourth. Not so popular as a Mozart.' He was beginning to regret letting Sousatzka have her say regarding the programme. 'But suppose they want to come. Suppose even, they like the Beethoven Fourth. Then that night, it's raining, or foggy, maybe.'

'In February, no fog,' Madame Sousatzka sneered with the confidence of a weather forecaster.

'But we can have rain. Anything can happen.' Then realizing that his argument was weakening, he shouted, 'Madame Sousatzka, if you think that you can get a better deal elsewhere, you are obviously at liberty to take it. But I doubt it. I doubt it very much. It's a cut-throat profession, Madame Sousatzka. You won't find many as generous as I.'

'He's right, Sousatzka,' Jenny said, who had had personal experience of Manders's generosity. 'In any case, Marcus isn't only playing for money.'

'That I know, Jenny. That I know very well,' Sousatzka said. 'I know what Mr Manders wants to do. I appreciate it. I take home the contract and I will look at it.'

'Can I then go ahead with my arrangements?' Manders asked.

'Yes, you can go ahead,' Sousatzka permitted him. 'For a concert in February, in the Festival Hall, to play the Beethoven Fourth.'

The reminder depressed him. Jenny put her arm round his neck and he smiled weakly.

'What about that lunch you promised us?' she said.

They picked up Marcus in the hall. There was a

lunch-hour let-up on the switchboard, and as they passed by the desk the woman hid her face in her knitting. She watched them disappear out of the front doors, and when they'd gone, she furtively took out a cheese sandwich and nibbled at one corner, like a little old mouse who knows the coast is clear.

11

On the following Friday, as they were getting ready to go to
Vauxhall Mansions, Marcus tried to hide his nervousness,
his excitement and also his guilt. No one had told his
mother about the salon. He knew that she had a right to be
there. But if she came there would be so many complica-
tions, not the least being the Jenny affair. In any case, he
couldn't see her fitting in with those kind of people; he
would have been ashamed of her. And it was this that
worried him more than anything.

She was straightening her hat in the mirror. 'Today, such
a nice hat I saw, Marcus,' she said. 'I thought for the
concert I'd buy it.'

'What colour is it?'

'Brown.'

'Oh Momma, I hate brown. Why don't you have a
change?'

'It *is* a change. Only in colour is the same.'

'Let me choose a colour for you,' he said. He felt
suddenly that the whole future of their relationship depended on the colour of her hat.

'I like brown,' she said. 'Is my colour. Anyway, I already
bought it,' she smiled.

'Let me see.' Marcus wanted to know the worst right
away.

'No. Is a surprise for you,' she chuckled like a child. 'At
the concert you will see it. You will be proud.'

Marcus doubted it. His mother had last bought a hat for
his ninth birthday pantomime treat. That was almost three
years ago. He looked forward dismally to yet another three
brown years.

He picked up her shopping bag. Marcus wondered
fleetingly whether she would bring it to the concert. He

would have to hide it somewhere.

'Let's go,' he said helplessly. He felt less guilty about the salon now. It was all her fault. If she insisted on buying a brown hat, what chance was she giving him?

But on the journey to Vauxhall Mansions the guilt came flooding back. As she took out her black purse to pay their fares on the bus, carefully counting out the brown pennies, he moved closer to her; as she took the tickets and stuffed them into her bag, where they no doubt joined the tickets from their first journey to Vauxhall Mansions almost a year ago, he said suddenly under his breath, hoping and fearing that she would hear, 'I love you, Momma.' And when he left her at Vauxhall Mansions, he kissed her. He watched her out of the Square and was disturbed that he didn't feel any easier.

He pushed the door open with his shoulder, and even before stepping into the hall he called out, 'Madame Sousatzka,' like a password.

'We're downstairs,' Cordle's voice came from the basement. Marcus ran down to Uncle's room. Everyone had collected there for the dress rehearsal. A strong smell of antiseptics filled the room. Marcus noticed that Jenny's raised right hand was covered with a sticky yellow ointment. Cordle was bandaging it with meticulous care, gently avoiding pressure on the imagined burns.

'You like Beethoven?' Sousatzka was saying.

'Oh, I think it's lovely,' said Jenny.

'That won't do at all,' said Cordle. 'Beethoven isn't lovely. It's great, it's moving, it's prophetic, but it isn't lovely. Try again.'

'Do you like the Beethoven?' Madame Sousatzka asked gently.

'I think it's great, it's moving, it's prophetic.' Jenny was putting her heart and soul into the part. She even managed a squeal of pain as Cordle tightened the bandage.

'Very good,' said Uncle, who had elected herself examiner. 'Now what about something more specific? about the concerto itself.'

'Yes,' said Madame Sousatzka. 'Already we practised that. What, my dear,' she said, turning to Jenny, 'do you think of the opening bars?'

Jenny bounded in on her cue. 'I think it is the greatest opening ever written, it is pleading, it is lonely.'

'Bravo,' shouted Uncle, 'You should be a music critic, Jenny.'

Marcus sat on the floor near the Countess. 'Who are your favourite composers, my dear?' he asked in a treble voice, flinging out a limp hand.

'We haven't done that one,' said Jenny. 'You'd better give me a few names.'

'Just say Bach,' Cordle advised her. 'She won't know a thing about Bach.'

'I know something by Bach,' Jenny exclaimed. 'It's a song. "Jesu, Joy of Man's Desiring." I used to sing it in the school choir.'

'Everybody sings that in school choirs. Don't mention it,' said Cordle. 'If she asks you what is your favourite piece of Bach, say Brandenburg Five, as casually as you can. That'll impress her. D'you get it? Brandenburg Five. Let's practise.'

'What's your favourite piece of Bach?' Marcus squeaked again.

Jenny twisted round in her chair. 'Brandenburg Five,' she threw off casually, flinging her bandaged arm in his direction.

'Bravo,' said Uncle again, awarding an extra mark.

'I hope everything is all right,' said Madame Sousatzka.

'Everything'll be fine,' said Cordle. 'As long as Jenny doesn't speak unless she's spoken to. Anyhow, she can always change the subject or one of you can interrupt.'

'As long as you don't leave me alone with her,' said Jenny.

'Don't worry. You stick with me,' Marcus told her. 'I'll do all the talking.' He suddenly felt a proprietary right in Jenny. He sensed that she was depending on him. She put her injured arm round him.

'Not that one,' Cordle said, 'you're not supposed to be able to lift it. I think you'd better put it in a sling to remind you.'

Suddenly Jenny remembered that she had a client at four o'clock. 'You'll have to take the bandage off, Cordle, and do it again before we go. Otherwise it's going to get disarranged.'

Cordle undid the bandage with the long-suffering patience of his profession. 'I'll never make as good a job of it the second time.' But secretly he was happy to find an excuse to do it again. He loved bandaging. It was a clean, neat and tidy job, especially when there was no wound to sicken you. He found it very satisfying to unroll a virgin bandage, crossing it this way and that to get a neat little fit. He often regretted that his special skill did not call for more bandaging, and he fleetingly considered how he could justly incorporate it into his profession. He unwound Jenny's bandage lovingly, trying to roll it back into its original shape. But once deflowered, it had lost its pristine symmetry. He threw it away into Uncle's wastepaper basket, gleefully anticipating a fresh roll.

Jenny left them for her meeting: Marcus decided to practise, and Madame Sousatzka announced that she would start dressing. She ran after Jenny to borrow the magazine. Uncle and Cordle settled down to a game of draughts. Uncle was gently rocking in her chair, and from above them in the studio they could hear Marcus practising.

'What do you think of Beethoven, Uncle?' Cordle said.

'I think he's great, he's moving, he's prophetic,' she laughed.

When they arrived at Manders's house they found a number of cars parked outside. Marcus pressed the bell and a series of vulgar nursery chimes answered him. The door was opened by a man they assumed was a butler. He wore a new white coat, and looked unnervingly like Cordle. He practically forced the two women into the cloakroom, while Marcus waited outside.

Sousatzka and Jenny let a decent interval elapse before they came out again. The butler was looking at his watch, as if he was timing them. He was sniffing all the time, and they weren't too sure whether it was a sniff of better breeding, or whether Jenny's ointment was too overpowering. He asked for their card.

103

Jenny smiled at him. 'We haven't got cards,' she whispered confidentially, as if to say that socially they were really on his level. 'Just say Madame Sousatzka and party.'

He raised his eyebrows, convinced that they were gate-crashers.

'We are expected,' said Madame Sousatzka, on her dignity.

'What did you say the name was?' he asked haughtily. He obviously didn't wish to be one of them.

'Sousatzka,' Marcus said in a clear voice, wondering how a man could be so ignorant, never to have heard the name before. 'Madame Sousatzka.'

The butler sniffed again, took a deep breath, opened the lounge door and stood against the post. 'Sousatzka,' he threw off contemptuously, as if he were announcing the arrival of a greyhound, 'and party,' he finished, stressing the anonymity.

He was astonished at the welcome Mr Manders accorded them. He came forward and took their hands. He winked at Jenny. 'My dear,' he said, 'what's happened to you?'

'She burnt it,' Marcus said. He felt, since he was the author of the play, he had a right to launch it.

'How was that?' Manders asked with concern.

'Nothing very exciting,' Jenny said. 'Just steam from the kettle.' Both Marcus and Madame Sousatzka nodded.

'You can certainly smell it,' Manders whispered.

'Oh my dears,' Mrs Manders swept towards them. 'How nice of you to come. We've been waiting hours for you.' She flung her arm in the direction of her sundry guests. She started to sniff and then noticed Jenny's bandage. She put her hand on Jenny's thumb. Jenny shrieked with the pain. Manders thought she was overdoing it.

'It only happened yesterday, and it still hurts.' Marcus smiled at Jenny, silently congratulating her on her script embellishments.

'I'm so sorry, my dear,' Mrs Manders sympathized. 'You won't be able to play for us. But our little Marcus is all right, I notice. I hope you're ready, my dear. We're all just dying to hear you.' She indicated her guests again. They all looked perfectly healthy and quite happy as they were, drinking, talking, not even noticing the new arrivals. Mrs

Manders's greeting to Madame Sousatzka was an after-thought. 'You must be quite nervous, Madame,' she said. 'Do sit down.'

She shepherded Marcus and Jenny to the other side of the room. Manders followed them. Madame Sousatzka turned around and found a chair that had been discreetly placed behind her while her back was turned. Another white-coated flunkey appeared with a single glass of sherry on a large silver tray. She sipped it quietly. She suddenly felt very hot, and realized that her chair had been placed against a radiator. She surreptitiously turned the knob to 'Off', and noted happily that it was the only form of heating in the room. A little black dachshund suddenly appeared on her floor area. In her embarrassing isolation, Madame Sousatzka could have kissed it with gratitude. It was a godsend. There is nothing quite like a dog for a nervous wallflower. It was someone to talk to, so that if others looked her way they would see that she was occupied. She began to talk to the dog, cunningly putting out her foot so that it couldn't get away. 'Hullo darrlink,' she said. 'You come also to hear the music?' Not surprisingly, the dog gave no answer. Madame Sousatzka tried again. 'Oh, such a beautiful face you have,' she said. She hated the sight of dogs, and this one was particularly hideous. 'Are you hungry?' she asked, as the dog made to get away. At that moment she would have given her right arm for the dog to eat, if only he would stay in her area, but he slid off and Sousatzka just managed to kick him for rejecting her. She was left once again in public isolation. She got up with the intention of going. 'Manders,' she shouted.

'Why, my dear Madame Sousatzka, what are you doing over there? Do meet Mr Phillips,' and he grasped the person nearest his grasp. 'Come and join us.' He brought her forward, calling Jenny and Marcus into their circle, effecting as many introductions as he could, talking all the time for fear Madame Sousatzka would interrupt him. She had decided meanwhile to stay. She had plenty on Manders and he knew it. It would keep.

'Madame Sousatzka,' an old gentleman croaked nearby. 'The teacher. My dear, I've heard of you, but I thought you dead,' he said chattily. He began to sniff audibly, as though he were still suspicious that Madame Sousatzka was in a state of *rigor mortis,* but it was only because Jenny was standing nearby.

'It's my ointment,' she explained to him. 'I've burnt my hand.'

'Oh dear, I am sorry,' he said. 'What did your doctor put on it? I'm a doctor you know,' he went on to explain. 'I'm always interested in other doctors' opinions.' Jenny rose to the unexpected occasion. 'What would *you* have put on it, doctor?'

'Why, aureomycin of course.'

'Well, my doctor must be very clever,' said Jenny. 'That's exactly what he gave me.'

The old man laughed. 'Yes, I thought so. Smells like it,' he said. 'The treatment of a simple burn doesn't call for much imagination, alas. Now, you keep it well covered. Well, well, well,' he turned to Madame Sousatzka again, 'so it's your pupil we're going to have the pleasure of hearing tonight. And what do you hope from this lad here?' He put his professional hand on Marcus's head. Marcus had the kind of head that invited people to fondle or shelter it. In fact, when no one's hand was there, he felt unfinished. The old man's hand was comfortable and fitted nicely, and Marcus was sorry when he took it away.

'Marcus will be the great pianist,' said Madame Sousatzka. 'You will hear him. You will see.' She looked away from the old man and was horrified to see that Mrs Manders had got hold of Jenny. She nudged Marcus. 'I think Jenny wants you, my darrlink,' she said, and Marcus, knowing his cue, rushed over to Jenny's side.

'I think it's very becoming,' Jenny was saying, very much at home. 'I was getting rather tired of those very long dresses.'

Marcus felt he wasn't needed and he returned to Madame Sousatzka. Again he felt a hand on his head, an ill-fitting one this time, and he turned to find Mr Manders.

'Well, young man,' he said, 'are we ready? If we go on talking much longer, we'll forget what we came for, won't we? Come and have a look at the piano. Do sit down,' he said to those in his vicinity, pointing at the gilt chairs that lined the walls of the room.

The old doctor took Madame Sousatzka's arm and guided her over to a chair. 'May I sit next to you, Madame Sousatzka?' he asked. 'I should be most honoured.'

'Natural,' she said, though she would have preferred to stay at Marcus's side. She watched Manders lead Marcus away, his hand on the boy's shoulder. The old man held the back of her chair while she sat down. Other guests were drifting towards the chairs, keeping their groups and conversations intact. Soon all were seated. The flunkey was clearing away the glasses, otherwise there was no sound or movement in the room.

'A most obliging audience,' Manders said, 'but we're not quite ready yet. We have to adjust the pedal for our little man here.' He got down on his knees and tried to fit the elevation on to the sustaining pedal of the piano. Marcus was handing him the screws. Everyone watched them in silence. Manders pushed the pedal this way and that, but it wouldn't fit exactly. 'It'll take a little while,' he said underneath his arm to the audience. 'Go on with your conversations.' Another silence. The guests were fascinated by these extra preparations.

Madame Sousatzka looked across the room and shuddered to see Jenny planted right next to Mrs Manders, out of shelter, completely on her own. Jenny threw a nervous glance at Sousatzka, and a still, small prayer. It was this moment of piercing silence, broken only by a whispered oath from Manders under the piano, that Mrs Manders chose to begin her cross-examination. And it was going to be a public one.

'And who is your favourite composer, Jenny?' Mrs Manders asked. Her voice was low and alone, and it rang through the room like a drum roll. Everybody looked at Jenny. Marcus dropped a screw and joined Manders on the floor to look for it. He no longer wanted to be in at the kill. Madame Sousatzka clenched her fists and prayed silently. But Jenny recognized her cue.

'Bach,' she said with confidence. She looked at Mrs Manders, hoping to see the impressed look on her face that

Cordle had promised her. But Mrs Manders's face was blank. 'What especially do you like of Bach?' It was as if Mrs Manders had been eavesdropping at the dress rehearsal.

Jenny hesitated professionally, as if she were weighing up in her mind the comparative virtues of all of Bach's output; with her knowledge of Bach, it didn't take very long. She heard strains of the old school choir. It was a lovely tune. It made everything right in the world. All those little scrubbed pig-tailed girls with steel-rimmed spectacles loving Jesus. It was tempting. But with Cordle's warning in mind, she reluctantly cast it aside. 'Brandenburg Five,' she said, as if it were a momentous decision.

A few guests gasped, and Mrs Manders raised her plucked eyebrows. 'I prefer number four, myself,' she said.

Jenny was flabbergasted. She suddenly realized that if there was a Brandenburg Five, there must, by the law of nature and chronology, be a number four. What's more, numbers one, two and three. She would be there for a week. Jenny raised her eyebrows in her turn. There was nothing else she could do.

'I thought, being a pianist,' Mrs Manders went on, 'your preference would have been for a piano composition. And after all,' she turned to her audience by way of explanation, 'the Brandenburgs are hardly for piano.'

They had all underestimated Mrs Manders. Her knowledge of Bach obviously went further than 'Jesu, Joy of Man's Desiring'. Jenny looked at Madame Sousatzka helplessly.

'They are all arranged for piano,' Madame Sousatzka rallied.

'Of course,' said Mrs Manders, as a victor generously conceding on a small point. 'But I find that number four is far more interesting.'

It was Jenny's turn, and there was no getting out of it. 'Do you?' she said, as if the woman were mad. 'Well, I prefer number five,' she said, sticking to her guns.

'Why?'

Madame Sousatzka prayed vigorously, her heart palpitating. Manders and Marcus were in communal prayer under the piano. But Jenny didn't let them down. She hadn't yet been called upon to express her views on Beethoven. If it arose later on it was a problem that could be dealt with at the time.

'Why?' she repeated, incredulous that Mrs Manders should be so ignorant as not to know the answer, 'it's great, it's prophetic, it's moving.' Jenny fervently hoped to God it was apt.

'Moving?' Mrs Manders repeated, equally incredulous. 'Hardly an adjective I would apply to Bach.'

'Wouldn't you?' said Jenny, full of pity. 'I would.'

'Would you, my dear? Why?'

Dammit, Jenny thought. She could see that the only way to get the upper hand in this conversation was to become the questioner. If there were any more 'why's', she was going to say them. But at the moment she had to cope with Mrs Manders's last question. Why indeed, she thought. She desperately tried to think of something that had moved her. 'It reminds me of my childhood,' she said. Damn the dress rehearsal. She was on her own.

'Why?' Mrs Manders was nothing if not persevering.

Well, this was easy; she didn't need Cordle or Sousatzka for this one. She was just about to launch into a moving account of her childhood; they'd asked for it, and they were going to get it, and anyway, it was a wonderful way of changing the subject – when a little woman on the other side of the room felt the need to voice her opinion. She obviously felt it to be of great importance and well-studied, because she spoke breathlessly, as if her discovery was the fruit of long and painful research.

'I like Mozart best myself,' she panted. 'I do think Mozart is so pretty.' She pronounced Mozart with a soft 'z'. She was obviously not prepared, since she liked him, to admit that he was a foreigner. 'There is something about Mozart,' she added, deep in thought, 'that is so elegant.' Madame Sousatzka could have strangled her.

'What's the matter with Brahms?' another woman said peevishly. She spoke as if she were Brahms's mother. Madame Sousatzka and Jenny sighed with relief at their acquittal. Manders and Marcus started again on the pedal.

'Brahms is all very well,' a dowager said generously, 'but we have some great moderns, you know.'

'Who?' Mrs Manders was at it again.

The dowager had waited for this moment. It was a moment she obviously manoeuvred in all the salons she attended. 'Webern, for instance.' Silence. From her long experience of the drawing-room the dowager found that the reaction never varied. Always a flummoxed silence.

'Come, come,' said an old gentleman whom the dowager had never seen before, 'you're not really serious?'

The poor dowager had never been taken up on her opinion. It had always been, out of ignorance, accepted. She hoped the old man wasn't going to make an issue out of it.

'A lot of noise he makes, that's all,' the old man went on. 'We're talking about the aristocrats of music,' he said, looking at her as if she had betrayed her class, 'not these upstarts with new-fangled ideas. Webern's like an abstract painter with no academic knowledge.'

'But we must keep up with the times, you know,' the dowager laughed. 'Abstract art can be as profound as Leonardo.'

'You'll be saying next,' the old man chuckled, 'that concrete music is greater than Beethoven, or that pop singing is greater than opera.'

'They each have their place,' the dowager insisted, and she shrugged her horsey shoulders like a beatnik granny.

'I think we're all set now.' Manders emerged triumphant and sweating from underneath the piano. Marcus crept out after him, and sat on the piano-stool testing the pedal. He looked around at Madame Sousatzka, communicating an invisible 'thumbs up' sign, then at Jenny, with an equally invisible 'well done'. Cordle and Uncle would have been proud of her.

Madame Sousatzka went over to the piano with the obvious intention of taking over from Manders. She fussed around Marcus, whispering advice in his ear which left the audience in no doubt as to whose property Marcus was. She straightened up and faced the audience. Manders was beside her, and they both opened their mouths to speak at the same time.

'The floor is yours,' Manders conceded gallantly. 'Perhaps you will introduce him, if I may be allowed to introduce you first.'

Madame Sousatzka stepped back, and Manders took the floor. 'Madame Sousatzka,' he said, 'is one of our finest teachers. Her teaching methods, as you know, are regarded by some as being most unconventional. Be that as it may, we, the audience, and especially myself, in my own particular way, are interested in results.' He strove vainly in his mind to find some great example of a Sousatzka product. But failing, he passed on quickly to Marcus. 'Madame Sousatzka herself tells us that Marcus is her prize pupil.' Well, we shall see, he wanted to say, partly because it seemed an obvious remark to conclude with, and partly because he could think of nothing else. With Madame Sousatzka breathing down his neck, he thought that he had already said enough. 'We look forward to hearing him,' he said weakly, and almost collapsed into the nearest armchair.

There was a faint, polite applause as Madame Sousatzka stepped forward. The women in the audience were examining her minutely. Already they felt hostile towards her, with the natural hostility of the buyer towards the seller. They tried to find fault with her appearance. But it was difficult. Although unconventionally attired, she looked extremely attractive, and they found it undeniable that Madame Sousatzka was a beautiful woman. Their hostility grew. They went on with their dribbling clapping even though Madame Sousatzka was obviously ready to start. They were not going to make it easy for her. 'Sh,' Jenny suddenly hissed with authority.

Madame Sousatzka smiled and began to speak. 'I have nothing to say to you,' she said gently. Most of the guests settled comfortably in their chairs prepared for a long speech, having heard that opening before. After all, they thought, most people have nothing to say, but they can take an awfully long time saying it. 'That is true,' she went on, as if reading their thoughts. 'I don't know how to make the speech. All my life I teach the music. Marcus here will make for me the speech.' She touched him gently on the head and sat down next to Manders. The audience were won over and they applauded her.

Marcus waited until they had finished. 'I will play a Chopin study,' he said. This announcement was followed by thunderous applause. Not only could he play, he could talk too. They settled in to listen.

Marcus repeated his talisman to himself. 'You will listen, I will listen, Sousatzka will listen, Jenny will listen, and it will play.' And miraculously, it seemed to Marcus for the first time since he had begun playing the piano, that it *did* play. He seemed more and more to dissociate himself from the sounds that filled the room. He heard them and was pleased. Occasionally, he adjusted a note here and there, he encouraged them, he watched them perform, listening to their strange permutations of sounds and rhythms. He felt light and detached as if he had become his own shadow. And at the same time, he felt afraid. Would it ever desert him, the body, would it not perform any more? Would it cease to play? But it went on, it seemed of its own accord, and he was listening and he was happy. And when it had finished it stopped and Marcus returned to the last chord, pressing his fingers into the notes, claiming them as old possessions.

He heard the clapping, and turned to look at Madame Sousatzka, who was coming towards him. There were big tears in her eyes. 'It played, my darrlink,' she whispered to him, 'and it played like an angel.'

'Encore, encore,' the audience was saying, and shouts of 'Bravo' came from Manders's quarter.

Marcus waited for them to settle themselves again. 'Variations,' he said, 'on a theme of Handel, by Brahms.' The Brahms fan in the audience heaved triumphantly. Jenny crossed her legs, arms, and all her fingers.

Marcus started on the theme. It dropped out of the tips of his fingers in its simplicity, ornamented occasionally by a casual trill. Marcus listened and heard it as if for the first time. He smiled. It was still working. After each variation,

Jenny uncrossed a pair of fingers, until by the end, she had uncrossed everything.

The audience, led by the Brahms fan, crossed over to the piano, eager to shake Marcus's hand.

'You've got quite a property there, Manders, old boy,' a young man, obviously in the trade, gave Manders his verdict.

'Alas, in partnership,' Manders whispered, nodding in Madame Sousatzka's direction. She was sharing the congratulations with Marcus.

Suddenly a 'phone rang. And Marcus remembered his mother. She must have phoned him tonight, as she did every Friday night to say goodnight to him. And he hadn't been there. What could Cordle have told her? Cordle didn't know they were trying to keep it from her. He felt a sudden fear at having been found out. He dared not think how he could explain it to her. He wanted to get away. He wanted to sit for a while by the 'phone-box on Cordle's landing. He wanted most of all to get out of this room, and away from all these people who didn't know the first thing about brown hats and vegetables. He felt a lump in his throat and he opened his mouth wide so that the air could dissolve it.

'You are so tired,' Madame Sousatzka said, mistaking it for a yawn.

'Yes,' Marcus said, jumping in on his cue. 'I want to go back. I want to go home.'

'Home?' Madame Sousatzka whispered.

'Yes. Home.' Marcus practically shouted at her.

'Is too late,' she said coldly, 'to go home. When we get to my home, we 'phone your mother.'

'What d'you think Cordle said to her?' he asked, as if accusing her.

'I don't know. I forgot to tell him,' she said weakly. 'We all forgot. So easy it is to forget.' She knew that her omission to cover up their evening was a further setback to her future with Marcus. She realized how important it was for them to get away. 'Marcus is tired,' she announced sadly. 'We must go now.'

'But Jenny,' Manders risked, 'you can stay a little?'

'No,' Jenny said, 'we'll all go together.'

When they got back to Vauxhall Mansions, they found Mrs Crominski pressing the dead bells.

Madame Sousatzka opened the door with her key, and they all trooped silently into the studio, as if the meeting had been previously arranged. Madame Sousatzka and Jenny stood against the piano and Mrs Crominski faced them. Marcus hovered in between, as if unwilling to join the accusable.

'So a party you've been to,' Mrs Crominski said.

'Some party,' said Jenny disdainfully. She thought it best to belittle the whole affair.

'Please?' said Mrs Crominski. 'I don't think I have the pleasure.'

'This is Jenny,' Marcus said. 'I've told you about Jenny, Momma. She lives upstairs.'

'She lives upstairs. Is that all she does? Lives upstairs? Yet she goes to the party and all she does is live upstairs.'

'I happen to know Mr Manders,' Jenny said gently. 'I went because I was invited.'

'So you were invited. But Mrs Crominski isn't invited. What is my boy, I'm asking. An orphan is he perhaps? Or perhaps Madame Sousatzka, they are thinking you are his mother?'

Marcus looked at Madame Sousatzka, imploring her to say something. She walked over to Mrs Crominski and as she came towards her, Mrs Crominski felt her anger decline. She hoped she wasn't going to touch her. She knew that she would weaken, and on the bus on the way home she would painfully repeat to herself her prepared, unspoken speech. But Madame Sousatzka was already taking her hand.

'Mrs Crominski,' she said gently, 'the whole business of the party is not so important. Not so important at all. Is all a business which is made before a concert. The most important is the concert. You will be there. You will be proud.'

'Tonight at the party,' Mrs Crominski insisted, 'I would be proud. Such a secret it is, the party. Such a secret his mother shouldn't know. Now suddenly it isn't a party. Now suddenly it isn't important.'

'But it wasn't,' Marcus said, going up to her. He noticed

for the first time that she was hatless. 'You would have been bored, Momma,' he said. 'We were all bored. It was full of business people. There was nothing to eat. I just played to them and we went home. Didn't we, Jenny?'

'That's right. Manders does it all the time. Before every concert he gives, the artist has to go to his house and play. It's like an audition.'

'So it wasn't a party?' Mrs Crominski asked weakly.

'Of course not.' Marcus jumped in on her surrender. 'I just played, that's all.'

'Then I'm sorry,' Mrs Crominski said, 'for all the fuss. You understand, Madame Sousatzka,' she said, 'I'm anxious for my boy, that's all.'

Don't apologize. Please, please, Momma, Marcus said to himself. You're right. You should have come. They didn't want you to come. Jenny, Sousatzka and I . . . I didn't want you to come either.

'Momma,' he said, 'Tomorrow I'll tell you all about it. I'll play to you what I played tonight. Then you won't have missed anything.' He suddenly felt free with her. She could have walked into his classroom at school, even with her hat on, and he would have happily greeted her. He looked forward to the concert when he could say to everybody, 'This is my mother.' At last he would be like Peter Goldstein and the others.

'Tomorrow,' he said, 'at home, we'll pretend it's the audition. You can be Madame Sousatzka, and I'll be me and all the others.' He was bubbling with his sudden sense of freedom.

'Why wait until tomorrow?' Madame Sousatzka said. She felt she could afford to make a concession. 'After tonight's playing, is not necessary tomorrow a lesson. Now you go home with your mother.'

'But I want a lesson tomorrow,' Marcus said. He was suddenly confused. He didn't feel free any more and he was hurt that Madame Sousatzka seemed to find it so easy to send him away. 'I can go home tomorrow, after my lesson,' he sulked.

Madame Sousatzka put her arm round Mrs Crominski's shoulder, lining herself up with her. 'Tomorrow,' she laughed, 'Madame Sousatzka is not teaching.' Marcus scowled at her and she felt a sudden thrill at his anger. 'Sousatzka is not at home tomorrow,' she teased.

'All right,' he said, furious. 'If you're not teaching tomorrow, you're not teaching next Friday or any other Friday. I'm not coming any more,' he shouted.

Madame Sousatzka broke into hilarious laughter, and Mrs Crominski joined her.

Only Jenny was silent. 'Put your coat on, Marcus,' she said quietly.

'I'm not coming any more,' he threatened again through their laughter. 'It won't be so funny next Friday.'

'Marcus, Marcus,' Mrs Crominski said. 'So rude you are. Say to Madame Sousatzka you are sorry.' The sudden link-up between his mother and Sousatzka terrified him. Even Jenny, by helping him on with his coat, was on their side. He felt completely isolated from them all. He hated his mother and he hated Madame Sousatzka and he almost hated Jenny. He looked forward to being alone in his bed, and concentrating on his isolation. He was positive that this night Madame Sousatzka would not come to him, that he'd put his head on his pillow, and like Peter Goldstein and all the others, he'd go straight to sleep.

But when, after their silent journey home, he blew his mother an invisible kiss down the stairway, he climbed into bed hoping that she would come. And when she did, he welcomed her for having taken no offence at his outburst. He fell asleep looking forward to his next lesson.

12

Madame Sousatzka had been sitting at her piano almost all night. She hadn't been playing. Occasionally her fingers would rest on the keys and silently depress them. She stared at the keyboard helplessly and hated it. The open piano score of the concerto stared at her from the stand. Ever since Manders had arranged the concert, the score had been there, and after each lesson a new piece of advice or warning had been scrawled across it in red pencil. A few bars preceding a difficult passage had been pointed with warning arrows, and the passage itself was ringed in scarlet. A few of the printer's pleas for pianissimo were scratched out where Madame Sousatzka had disapproved of the editor's interpretation. And the same with certain crescendo arrows which Madame Sousatzka had once or twice inverted. All night she had been going through the score, occasionally playing it on the wood of the piano. She knew immediately Marcus's reaction to every passage. She knew what he would look forward to, and what he would be glad to be finished with. And these latter passages she went over and over again, drumming her fingers on the piano lid, trying to make it easier for him, trying to infuse his sleep far away in North London with new confidence. She would smile for him when a difficult passage had been well dealt with, and leaned back in her chair, while the orchestra took command of the score. And to the imagined sounds of the orchestra she gave all her attention, leaning forward in anticipation of the cadenza. Until the final chord, which announced that the orchestra was retiring for a while to leave the arena to the soloist. And always after the majestic chord came the terrifying split-second silence. Madame Sousatzka had been through the score at least a dozen times during the night, and each time this pause had become longer and more terrifying.

It was getting light and though the curtains were still drawn the sun filtered through the cracks. She heard the clatter of milk bottles on the door-step, and she drew the curtains. The sunlight staggered into the room and she was conscious of the wrinkles on her neck and under her eyes. She wondered whether the milkman was going to the concert, or whether he'd even heard about it. She went quickly to her desk and took out two complimentary tickets from the drawer. She opened the window, and leaned out.

'Milkman,' she called, 'you go to the concert?'

He straightened his back and looked at her, astonished that another human being was sharing this hour of the morning. 'What concert?'

'My Marcus. He plays tonight. The Festival Hall. You want to go?'

'Ah, good morning, Madame Sousatzka,' he said. First things first. 'I saw it advertised. Good luck to the lad. You'll need an extra bottle of milk today.' Business before pleasure.

'You want to go?' she said, less enthusiastically this time. She held out the tickets towards him.

'Can't afford it,' he said hopefully. 'Not on this job.'

'I give to you,' she said, thrusting them out still further. 'You are married?' The milkman shook his head. 'A fiancée?' Madame Sousatzka smiled at him. Again a mournful shake. 'You must have a friend,' Madame Sousatzka said desperately.

'My brother,' the milkman said, tracing his shadow on the steps with one foot.

'You bring the brother, then,' Madame Sousatzka said triumphantly, handing the tickets to him.

The milkman looked at them. 'Twenty-five shillings!' he gasped. 'Fifty bob altogether.' He was clearly calculating what allowance he could make on a sale.

'You come? I see you and the brother?' said Madame Sousatzka eagerly.

The milkman looked at her guiltily. 'Of course,' he decided. He already began to look forward to it. He wondered what he would wear and how he could get in touch with his brother. 'Thank you, Madame Sousatzka,' he said, 'I'll hurry on the round so I'll be ready. Wish the boy luck for me. You too,' he added, with unconscious understanding. 'The Festival Hall,' he muttered, picking up the empties. 'Twenty-five bob a throw.'

Madam Sousatzka closed the window, and suddenly felt very tired. It must be six o'clock, she thought. There would be time for a little sleep before the rehearsal at ten-thirty. She lay, fully clothed, on the divan, silently figuring the cadenza on the silk cushion, and she fell asleep at the end of the final trill. And as she slept, she had a terrifying dream.

Marcus was still trilling and the conductor raised his baton for the orchestra to prepare their entry. But Marcus went on trilling. The conductor looked at him, raising his eyebrows and his baton. 'The lights are green,' he hissed. 'They won't get any greener.' But Marcus went on trilling. The audience were getting restless. And suddenly the milkman got up and took his brother's hand. They were both in evening dress, and they carried a milk crate between them. They hurried down the steps to the platform. 'Stop it, Marcus,' the milkman pleaded. But Marcus went on trilling. 'It won't stop,' he said. 'Ask Madame Sousatzka to stop it.' 'It's playing beautifully,' said Madame Sousatzka, 'Let it play.' The trill got louder and louder until it sounded like a high-pitched road drill. The conductor stood on tip-toe and raised his baton as far as he could and crashed it to his side. The orchestra came in, unwilling to wait any longer for their cue. 'I told you to get an extra bottle of milk today,' the milkman said. Marcus was still trilling, and the orchestra meanwhile finished the concerto. They left the platform, desk by desk, as in the Farewell Symphony, and the conductor followed them. And then the audience, until the Festival Hall was empty but for Madame Sousatzka, and Marcus at the piano, still trilling. 'It plays well,' she said into the empty hall. Marcus stopped playing and turned to smile at her. Madame Sousatzka turned over and opened her eyes. She wiped the sweat from her forehead and she got up and closed the piano. She threw open the window, and sat looking out into the street, waiting for the day to begin.

*　*　*

Mrs Crominski delivered Marcus to Vauxhall Mansions at nine o'clock. Both Marcus and Madame Sousatzka had asked her to come to the rehearsal, and both hoped that she would decline. Which she did, but for her own reasons. She was terribly nervous. For a whole week she had been trembling at the thought of the concert, and trembling, too, that Marcus might notice it. She felt she couldn't face the concert and the rehearsal too. She had nagged at Marcus to find out whether he needed her to come. 'If you'll feel better I'm there, then natural, I'm coming.'

'If you want to come, Momma,' he had said, 'then come.'

'I'm not talking about wanting. Is for you I come, if I come, if you feel better.'

'I don't *need* you to come,' he said, 'just come if you want to.'

'Of course he doesn't need when Madame Sousatzka is there,' she sulked.

'I don't need her, either,' he lied. 'She's coming because she wants to.'

'Then I come too,' she said, terrified.

'It's not necessary, Momma. You rest, and you'll enjoy the concert.'

She had made no further protest.

As she was leaving Madame Sousatzka's, she threw her arms round him. She was practically hysterical with worry and fear for his performance. She kissed him frantically, knowing that she had to say something before leaving, and not having the faintest idea what to say. 'Best of luck' perhaps, or 'Don't worry'? Marcus freed himself from her kisses. 'Don't worry, Momma,' he smiled, 'everything will be all right.'

She started to walk down the front steps. She still hadn't said anything to him. She stopped and turned to look at him. He was smiling, and waving. She was shocked into the vital necessity of saying something, no matter how ridiculous it was. 'Don't forget the soft parts,' she said helplessly.

He watched her go, her shopping-bag flopping against

her lisle stockings. He turned quickly into the house, dragging his hand over his eyes. He could forget everything else, everything he had ever learnt, but above all he mustn't forget the soft parts.

Manders arrived at ten o'clock to pick them up. Normally, he didn't go to his clients' rehearsals, but he didn't trust Madame Sousatzka to hold her tongue if she disagreed with the orchestra's interpretation. Although no war had yet been declared, he already felt himself the peacemaker.

'Well, how d'you feel, my boy?' he said, as they settled into the back of the car. He signalled to his chauffeur to take off. 'It's a fine day,' he announced. 'Should have a good house. How d'you feel?' he asked again.

'A bit nervous,' Marcus said,

'Well, that's natural, isn't it?' he said. 'I've found in my experience,' he turned conversationally to Madame Sousatzka, 'that the greatest artists are always nervous before a concert.' Madame Sousatzka showed no particular interest in his discovery. 'In fact,' he tried again, 'if one of my boys isn't nervous, *I* get nervous,' he laughed feebly. The car slowed down at the lights. Marcus shifted between them, rubbing his knees to ease the pain. 'It always gets them there,' Manders said appreciatively. 'In the knees. Or the stomach. Or both,' he warned, smiling.

Madame Sousatzka shivered. She had it everywhere, and so probably did Marcus. She put her arm round his shoulder and they melted in their nervousness together.

Manders couldn't feel with them. The tickets had gone well. In spite of the choice of programme, people were coming. He'd managed to throw in the Beethoven Fifth as an extra bait. Almost everyone was familiar with at least its opening bars, and recognizing the tune would give them a comfortable sense of culture. The orchestra had carped a bit, but he'd managed to get his own way. Tickets sold, a fine day, and the Beethoven Fifth for the casuals. In his mind, Marcus had already nothing to do with it.

The chauffeur pulled up at the artists' entrance of the Festival Hall. Manders told him to call back at one o'clock for them. They went inside together to the lifts. A lonely double-bass player was waiting at the grille. He looked at Marcus and recognized him as one to be dealt with at the concert. He nodded reassuringly, and smiled. It was the closest Marcus had ever been to an orchestral player, and his heart swelled with sudden love for the whole double-bass section. He regretted that they never seemed to have a solo part; with all that amount of instrument, he thought, and never a tune. The lift gates opened and the man lugged his bass inside. Marcus stood next to him, with the bass between. The lift-man pressed a button, a signal, it seemed, that in ascent, all must be silent. The four of them and the bass watched the lift wall descend behind the grille. When they arrived on the hall floor they trooped out silently. 'See you,' the bass said, as it trundled forward into the corridor, singing with a deep, resonant hum the opening bars of the concerto. The player turned round and winked at Marcus, who followed Manders and Sousatzka into the artists' room.

The room was stuffy and the nervousness of the previous night's soloist still hovered round the dirty glass on the table, the half-filled jug of water, and the ruffled cushion on the chair. A black upright piano stood in the corner, the lid sealed and dusty as if it had never been opened; as if no artist had taken the risk of a last-minute run through. Manders took off his coat, as if to assert that he was in charge; Madame Sousatzka noticed the manoeuvre and did likewise, although like most spreading women, she depended on her coat for cover-up.

'They'll call you when they're ready,' Manders said to Marcus. He was an old hand at the routine. 'The conductor will probably want a word with them first,' he added to Madame Sousatzka. 'That's what usually happens,' he said with the air of an expert.

Madame Sousatzka went over to Marcus where he sat on the edge of the table. 'You remember, my darrlink,' she said, turning her back on Manders, 'in the second movement.' She sang a phrase, outlining the melody in the air with her finger. 'Don't forget, my darrlink, it is only the echo. Very, very soft. You will hear the orchestra. You will play the echo without touching it. Listen to it. An echo is wonderful. An echo, it happens. From God it comes. It is His approval. I will leave you now,' she said. 'I will sit in the hall and listen. But we both listen, yes darrlink? We are together.'

Madame Sousatzka put on her coat. She felt she could well afford to leave Marcus alone for a while with Manders. She kissed the top of Marcus's head and started for the door. Then, as an afterthought, she said, 'If something you don't like, Marcus, with the conductor, you say. If too fast, you say; if too slow, you say also; if too loud, and so on.' She opened the door. 'And the cadenza of course. You don't play it. No necessity. You play only the last few bars with the trill.' She suddenly remembered her dream that morning. 'Count the trill quietly,' she whispered. 'The conductor will look at you to come in.' She walked down the corridor.

Marcus ran up her. 'Stay with me till they come,' he pleaded. 'I just can't wait here.'

A little green-coated man rounded the bend of the corridor.

'Look, he's coming,' Marcus whispered.

The man beckoned to Marcus. 'Come on, laddie,' he said, 'they're all waiting for you.'

Madame Sousatzka gently pushed Marcus into the green man's keeping, and she went into the auditorium. She made for a seat in the second row on the piano side, so that Marcus would not look at her.

Marcus was threading his way between the 'cellos. One of the players leaned over his instrument and patted Marcus on the back as he passed. Marcus turned round to smile at him, and his eye caught the thick wall of double-bass players, and their solid immobility frightened him. He wished for the first time in his life that he'd never played the piano. He felt his hands clammy and a liquid fear in his stomach. He put out his hand to clasp the conductor's rail. He didn't think he could make the piano without some support.

The conductor stretched out his hand and guided Marcus over. 'Better than being at school, eh?' he said.

The orchestra laughed dutifully. Marcus didn't think it was very funny. In fact, at that moment he would have willingly opted for a life-sentence at school in preference to his present occupation. Somehow Marcus found himself seated and adjusting the stool. He wiped his hands down the sides of his suit and placed them for confidence on the keys. He saw them reflected in the shining black wood. They looked so small and stunted that he was convinced they were not his own, and he had to take them away quickly and see the reflection disappear in order to convince himself that they were his. He looked up and his eye caught the conductor's, but only because the conductor was directly in his line of vision. But the look was as decisive as a faint nod at an auction sale, and the conductor raised his baton. 'I'm not ready,' Marcus wanted to shout, but he knew that, feeling as he did, he would never be ready. He lifted his fingers to the keys, looking at them only for a moment to get his bearings, and then, staring at the infinitesimal tip of the conductor's baton, he played the opening chord.

The first solo drew an audible gurgle of joy from Madame Sousatzka. Marcus heard her and the trembling left him. During the first movement, Madame Sousatzka saw Manders tip-toe into the hall. He was seething with anger at not having been notified. He made a note to see the green man after the rehearsal. He climbed the steps to the terrace stalls, seating himself in the middle where he could be seen.

The orchestra had reached the beginning of the cadenza and the conductor leaned over to have a word with Marcus. Madame Sousatzka half rose from her seat. Then sadly she sat down again, realizing for the first time that Marcus was no longer with her. Marcus started playing a few bars before the final trill. She covered her face with her hands and counted. At the end of the trill Marcus looked up at the conductor, and the orchestra arrived punctually to see him through the end of the movement.

The concerto rehearsal lasted an hour; that is, a little longer than its actual running time. It was obviously a work with which the orchestral players were very familiar, and which they played in run-through mood, having left their vibratos in their dinner-jackets. They were like long-practised midwives to whom birth and delivery had ceased to be a miracle. When the concerto was finished, they clapped on their instruments with one hand, feeling in their pockets for their cigarettes with the other. 'Seen the paper this morning, Harry?' Marcus heard a violinist say. 'Looks like your shares have dropped again.'

Manders was tripping down the steps towards the platform. Madame Sousatzka got up and managed to reach the platform at the same time. They both went towards Marcus, eager yet hesitant as if by some error they had both drawn the winning ticket in a lottery. Madame Sousatzka was the first to reach him. He took her outstretched hand. 'I must play more, and more,' he said. 'It's wonderful.'

'You will, my darrlink,' she said sadly, 'but you have so much to learn yet. For many concerts, you are not ready. Sousatzka knows, my darrlink.' She grasped his hand in hers, and felt it suddenly grow cold. She knew at that moment she had lost him.

Number 132 Vauxhall Mansions started to prepare for the concert at four o'clock in the afternoon. Madame Sousatzka had arranged a little party for Marcus and his mother, together with Jenny, Cordle and Uncle, for after the concert. She was still undecided as to whether to ask the Manders. With Jenny's help she had prepared a table of food and covered it with a damp white cloth. Of the left-overs, she made an informal tea-party in the kitchen for the residents.

Mrs Crominski was going to join them at the house an hour before the concert. Out of nervousness, she wanted to put off her participation until the last moment. She wanted desperately to be with Marcus, to go to the rehearsal with him, to help him into his evening dress. But she was afraid she might break down in front of him. So she had decided to keep out of the way.

Madame Sousatzka and her tenants had assembled in the kitchen for the tea. All of them, except Marcus, were in dressing-gowns as a preparation for getting dressed. Uncle was collecting pennies from Cordle and Jenny for a bath. It was a great occasion for her. Her dressing-gown had once been chiffon, and bright blue, but little remained now either of its texture or colour. And it clung un-chiffon-like to her and she to it like a touchstone of a fading memory. Her hair was rolled tightly into curlers, clinging to her scalp like a cap of serrated cardboard. Cordle's dressing-gown was what is known in the trade as 'serviceable', and indeed it looked as if it had done yeoman service for years. It was red with a corded edge. A large brown burn had replaced the pocket. But he kept his hand in the hole notwithstanding, just to keep up appearances. Jenny's dressing-gown was new, and it looked more like a loose dress. It was short and buttoned down the front. She had a large stock of dressing-gowns. Marcus always saw her in a different one. The garment that enveloped Madame Sousatzka would, in any other setting, have been called a mackintosh, which indeed it was. But here it looked no more out of place than Uncle's, which had originally been born in a boudoir.

Madame Sousatzka sat at the head of the table with Marcus by her side. Uncle slipped into the wall bench next to Cordle and Jenny began to pour the tea. 'What you wearing, Uncle?' she said.

'The black.'

'Which black?'

'*My* black of course.' Uncle was behaving like an *haute couturière*, fighting off the Press before an opening.

'I'm wearing black too,' said Jenny, 'the one with the frilled sleeve.' Jenny was more forthcoming.

'We'll all be in black,' said Madame Sousatzka as cheerfully as she could. 'I also wear mine.'

After this announcement, nobody spoke, and the silence continued throughout the meal. Occasionally, someone asked for the sugar or a sandwich.

'In six hours' time,' Marcus said suddenly, 'it'll all be over.'

'How did the rehearsal go?' asked Cordle. He hadn't seen Marcus or Sousatzka since their return and he was aching to know how Marcus had gone down.

'It went well, of course,' said Madame Sousatzka. 'But

why ask? It only goes well. A good orchestra, too.'

'Yes, you should have heard them,' Marcus chimed in enthusiastically. For a moment he'd forgotten all about the concert. He felt that it was already over.

'We will,' said Uncle, reminding him.

'Yes,' he said thoughtfully, 'but I mean, all on top of you. So close. And to be playing with them. Once it starts, it's a wonderful feeling. It's just that walk from the end of the platform to the piano. You walk, and walk, and you don't seem to cover any space. That's terrible.'

'It'll be different tonight with an audience,' said Cordle. 'Have a sandwich.' He wanted to put Marcus at his ease. 'Don't look at the piano while you're walking. Look at the orchestra, or your feet, or look at the conductor and smile if you can, and the piano will seem to come to you.'

Even the thought of the walk made Marcus tremble. He decided to practise it. If he opened the door of the studio, and walked from the first floor down the stairs through the hall to the piano, it was about the same distance. He told Madame Sousatzka he was going to practise a little, and he ran upstairs to the first landing. He tried to imagine himself behind the green curtain that cut off the platform from back-stage. He counted three and imagined the curtains drawn back. He looked at the banks of flowers on the banisters and nodded to the back-desk of the violins at the bottom of the stairs. He tip-toed on the black and white tiles of the hall floor through the violin desks, and reached the leader of the orchestra at the studio door. He stretched out his hand to take the conductor's who reached out to him from the piano. Then he sat down. 'Well, that was no trouble,' he thought, but he realized that all he had done was to walk from the first landing to the studio. He banged his elbows in a fury on the keyboard and rested his head on his hands in a solid agony of nervousness.

Madame Sousatzka came rushing to the studio on hearing the noise. 'What is it, my darrlink?' she said, going up to him.

Marcus didn't lift his head. 'I wish it were all over,' he said. 'I wish I'd never learnt the piano. Why can't you leave me alone?' he shouted at her suddenly, the tears streaming down his face.

'You have the talent,' Madame Sousatzka said quietly. 'A gift you have. From God you have a gift. And a gift is a responsibility. You have not to worry. I know you have not to worry. D'you hear me?' she said, her voice a little louder. 'I know you play well, and when Sousatzka knows, she is right. Sousatzka has never been so sure. Never in her life. She knows it plays well,' she thundered at him. His nervousness had infected her. 'For nearly a year you come here,' she pleaded with him, 'every week Sousatzka give you the heart, the soul, the life even, to bring the music out. I should leave him alone,' she whimpered, suddenly quiet, 'I should leave him to his school, his arithmetic, his geography, he should grow up a fine man, in the advertising perhaps, an executive even like Manders he could have been,' she spat out. 'A man in the middle, a dealer,' she hissed. 'I should leave him alone. I should myself play. I should be in the Festival Hall. Nobody gave me the life, the soul, the music. Sousatzka gave you everything, my darrlink,' she broke down, the tears running down her cheeks. Marcus daren't look at her. He felt her hand on his head. 'No, I shouldn't be in Festival Hall,' she said gently. 'You are playing there for me, and it will play for you, like it would play for me. Tonight we will listen together. Don't practise any more, my darrlink. Sousatzka knows you are ready.' She knew she would have to admit it sooner or later. She also knew that as far as Marcus was concerned, the admission was now too late.

'I'll never be ready,' he said.

When Marcus was dressed, he sat at the piano in the studio, staring at the keys, not daring to touch them. He heard a rapping on the glass panel of the front door. He knew it must be his mother, and he felt suddenly excited that she was there. Then he wondered what she was rapping the glass with, and the fear that it might be her shopping-bag took the edge off his excitement. Grateful for something to do, he ran to the door.

Mrs Crominski stood there shyly, trying to stifle a smile

that threatened to dissolve into hysteria. She was fidgeting with the metal clasp of her new handbag, which she had obviously used as a knocker. Marcus looked all around her and found no sign of the shopping-bag. Having ascertained that it wasn't with her, he was able to look at her properly.

She waited for him to say something about her hat, but he was silent. She no longer wanted him to comment on it. 'So wonderful you look,' she said. 'Your poor father should only see you.' She slid her little finger underneath her veil to wipe away a tear.

Marcus was staring at her hat. It was brown. Undeniably. So was her coat. A new coat, but brown all the same. He knew that if he looked at her feet, they would be brown too.

'You like it?' she said timidly, pointing nervously at her hat.

He put his arm round her and brought her inside. 'Let me look at you,' he said.

Mrs Crominski couldn't bear it. 'What's to look?' she said. 'You like or you don't like.'

'I like,' he laughed. It was the veil on her hat, and the silk stockings, that had conquered his objections to the colour. Veils and silks belonged to Jenny's world, and Uncle's and Madame Sousatzka's. His mother had qualified for membership. He felt suddenly free. 'Madame Sousatzka,' he called, 'Momma's here.'

He took her into the studio, confident that her membership would be a permanent one. But as he watched her sitting in the chair, awkward, not knowing where to put her new shoes, hotly blowing at her veil, unaccustomed to her trappings, he knew that she was dressed up for the part, and that when the play was over she would be just brown again.

She opened her bag and brought a small packet wrapped in tissue-paper. 'Marcus,' she said, 'your father gave me this. I should give it to you, he said, when you're grown-up. Tonight I give it to you. I want tonight Poppa should be with you.' She opened the packet and brought out a plain gold watch. As she put it on Marcus's wrist, he winced with the pain of loving her. He longed for some sign of the old brown woman, the woman who embarrassed him, who shamed him, who wrung out in him all the twisted feelings he had learned to accommodate. 'Something also I brought for you to eat at the concert,' she said. 'Perhaps you should be hungry.'

Gratefully, he tore open the second parcel. Three scraped raw carrots. Vegetables, vegetables, vegetables. With a great sense of relief, he was back in battle.

They all went to the concert together. Mrs Crominski and Madame Sousatzka took Marcus back-stage, and left him in the artist's room to the half-full jug of water, the dusty upright piano and a new suit-full of tremblings. He looked down at his knees jutting out from under the hem of his short black trousers. He caught sight of the black silk bow on his patent shoes, and he felt sick. He could only imagine what he looked like, because he'd avoided looking at himself in the mirror. Manders had bought him this suit. It had no doubt gone down on his expense sheet for publicity. Marcus felt hired in it, and he resolved never to wear it again. He wandered over to the table and poured himself a glass of water, because he felt it was expected of him. The water made him sweat even more. There was a telephone on the window-sill and Marcus wondered why it was necessary in the artist's room. He picked up the receiver, but it was dead. He sat down limply in the chair and waited. He could hear members of the orchestra tuning up in the corridor outside. He heard one of them laugh, and he was convinced that they were laughing at him. Someone blew a long shrill note on a clarinet, and Marcus thought of the football match he'd been allowed to watch when his school was playing a visiting team. He loved football, but of course, with his handicap, he couldn't play. He might injure a finger, his mother told the headmaster. He'd be taking a risk with tennis too, and cricket. He could swim, of course. After all, the headmaster had said, the little chap's got to have exercise. He remembered the school swimming gala. Being the fastest of the swimmers, he was chosen to swim last in the relay race. The last swimmer of the opposing team had already taken off, meeting their own third swimmer half-way down the pool. Marcus clung to the marble edge with his toes, his arms curved outwards, ready for the dive. When the third swimmer touched the bar, Marcus plunged into the water. His opponent had already completed three-quarters of the length. They began to shout his name from the stands, dividing the two syllables like two tom-toms beating him along the pool. The black and rubber head of his opponent seemed to be bobbing towards him, and suddenly, driven by the beat of his name, he knew he was going to win. It seemed he wasn't swimming any more. He was moving his arms and legs, but something had taken over, and he only came back into his body as he touched the rail a few seconds before his opponent. 'It swam well,' Marcus thought to himself. 'Perhaps I am ready.'

Manders walked into the room without knocking. 'You look wonderful,' he beamed. 'It's a perfect fit. Hair looks good, too,' he said, stepping back to get it into focus. 'Unkempt enough for a schoolboy, but not scruffy enough for a second-rate artist.' It was obviously a rehearsed line, and was probably at that moment circulating in the numerous handouts Manders had sent to the Press. 'Just came to wish you good luck,' he said. 'I'll be around in the interval.' He bounced out of the room, well pleased with himself, and Marcus knew again that he wasn't ready.

He suddenly missed the noises in the corridor, and he opened the door of his room. He could hear the audience clapping, and it sounded like a thunderbolt. He closed his eyes, which were smarting with fear, and he gripped the door-knob to control his trembling.

The main body of the orchestra was assembled on the platform. The rank and file took a surreptitious look around the hall and, as if they had seen all the hundreds of faces before, returned disenchanted to their instruments. In the almost-silent last-minute tunings, Manders entered the hall. He tripped up the stairs, eyeing his takings with a look that told them he was responsible for everything. Then he sneaked into his gangway seat, folding himself like an impermanent pleat next to Mrs Manders, who looked as if she was not expecting him. He leaned over and greeted the

Sousatzka party alongside him, giving them a general wink which might have meant anything. His late entry and ostentatious movements already singled his row out as a source of attraction, and there were whispers of 'Manders' and 'Sousatzka' from the people behind.

Madame Sousatzka clutched her programme, holding it to her as if it were trying to get away. When the leader of the orchestra came on to the platform she clapped with one hand against the programme. Jenny, who sat next to her, clapped vigorously as if the concert were at an end. Uncle had her arms clasped about her as if she were pulling herself together. Cordle, on Madame Sousatzka's right, placed his large hand on hers in a gesture of confidence.

Mrs Crominski sat at the end of the row, immobile. Her coat was still buttoned, and the silk of her gloves stretched taut over her clenched fists. Her feet were tightly crossed in a rope-climbing position, so that the new leather of her shoes whistled occasionally as they rubbed against each other. When she made an effort to relax, her body set up an overall trembling and she would stiffen again to avoid embarrassment. She clutched at her programme, not daring to open it, for fear it would slip from her fingers.

The leader bowed to receive the applause, and the sub-leader, for whom it was obviously a question of dead man's boots, glowered at his feet behind. But as the leader took his seat he turned to his partner, and for a few moments they indulged in what seemed to be a very friendly conversation. Suddenly, and at no given signal, everybody was quiet. The curtain at the end of the platform was invisibly drawn across and a little man, a veteran of the rostrum judging by the tired look of his tails, hopped up the steps like an old blackbird. The orchestra looked at him with some surprise, as if he were not the man who had conducted the rehearsal in the morning. Nevertheless, when he had taken his bow, they shrugged themselves into a standing position for the National Anthem.

The initial drum-roll literally frightened Madame Sousatzka out of her seat. She dropped her programme and stood trembling from head to foot as if she were wearing a corset of built-in semi-quavers.

Jenny, who had never been to the Festival Hall before, wanted to show her enthusiasm, and she opened her mouth to invoke the Lord to save the Sovereign. She had called upon the Almighty in her deep contralto, and was just about to tell Him what to do, when she realised that she was quite alone, and unwilling to take the whole of the responsibility on her shoulders – after all, she wasn't even a relation – she decided to hold her peace.

Uncle cheated a little, humming the tune quietly to herself. During her marriage and the diplomatic rounds with Paul, she had heard it often enough. She raised her eyes slowly to the roof and whispered, 'Paul, they're playing our tune.'

Madame Sousatzka looked upon the Anthem as a respite, and hoped patriotically that it would go on for ever.

Cordle used the music to ask God to save himself. He felt guilty, as if he were using someone else's telephone, and he looked around, wondering if he'd been found out. He caught Manders's eye and knowing look. 'They always do this,' it seemed to say. 'I have to go through it every concert. I'm an old-timer, you know. It's only a formality.'

When the Anthem was over the tympano player patted his drum as if he was patting a horse after a good gallop. The audience sat down and rearranged their clothes and programmes. There was a rustle of paper as they confirmed for the hundredth time that they were to be treated to the Leonora Number Three. The unison opening put them at their ease and prophesied that there would be no difficulty in listening to the overture. It might even be a pleasure.

Jenny was clinging to her seat with fascination, not so much at the music as at the paraphernalia of the occasion. In particular that part of the audience that sat behind the stage, facing the conductor. A woman in a red pullover in the front row kept nodding her head at the conductor as if in approval, and an old bearded man next to her, sitting immediately behind the drums, stared blankly in front of him like a mute, as if the percussion of the National Anthem had paralysed him. She looked up at the organ, and the countless pipes that sprawled like a plumber's paradise across the upper wall. She started to count them, but after the first dozen they blurred and became two-dimensional. She took another general look at the audience behind the stage. So many people, she thought. I must know some of them. She thought of all the people she had met during her working life. Hundreds of them. Freds and Bills and Toms, even a Eustace, she remembered. But to none of them, not even to Eustace, could she put a face. She remembered only beards or stubbles, horny hands and the occasional acne. Her acquired blindness was acutely compensated for in her sense of touch. She imagined herself groping around the audience with her fingers, greeting each familiar touch. But would they know her? She knew she could recall the faces of the teachers of her childhood, but would they recognize all their pupils? She suddenly grew afraid that in the vast hall a Tom, Bill or Fred was staring at her, and she covered her face with her programme. She was too innocent to know that her clients came to her equipped with the same blindness, born of the same necessity.

The sound of a distant trumpet-call from the orchestra cut off her wandering thoughts, and for the first time she began to listen. She found it hard to concentrate, and she tried reading her programme. 'The music is suddenly interrupted by the sound of a distant trumpet-call.' That must have been it, she thought, and found that the programme notes ended only a short paragraph later. One paragraph to Marcus. Suddenly the trumpet called again. It sounded nearer this time, but it was a harsh note, and off-key, and in no way corresponded to the 'sound of heroic calm' of the optimistic programme note. Two more lines to go. She read them hastily. 'The end of the allegro symbolizes triumph and victory.' She recognized the victory as the full orchestra took up the melody. She looked at the programme hopefully, but there was no doubt that the notes had come to an end. There was a two-inch white gap, and Marcus was over the page.

The audience began to applaud, a formal, polite acclaim, neatly timed for an overture, and when it began to wane Mrs Crominski, Jenny, Cordle, Uncle and Madame Sousatzka simultaneously began to clap again, encouraging the applause, no doubt in the hope that the orchestra would give an encore. But no one took up their clapping and the conductor was already leaving the platform. Jenny took out her pencil, and solemnly ticked off the overture on her programme. Then quietly, and with determination, she turned the page. She looked at Madame Sousatzka, who had folded her arms lightly on her lap. Her programme had dropped to the floor, and as the conductor disappeared from the platform she turned round and looked at the audience, preferring to read on their faces what was happening on the platform, rather than face it herself. Her eye caught a posse of fat starched ambulance women, seated near the exit, their faces a composite blank. They certainly weren't there for the love of music. Stolid, immovable, there for their job and keeping the law, rather like long-suffering policemen in a controversial demonstration in Trafalgar Square. Their faces betrayed the void stare of duty, and Madame Sousatzka turned back helplessly to look at the platform. She stared at the green curtain solidly drawn, and she felt the fear that lay behind it.

Marcus stood there alone, with the green canvas wall in front of him. He felt the conductor's hand on his shoulder. 'Are we ready?' he said. Marcus didn't remember answering. He remembered being convinced that never in his life would he feel more alone. The usher drew the curtain, holding it aside for them to enter, and in that second when Marcus saw the vast audience as if through a wide-angle lens, and the foreground of flowers that half hid them, he knew that this moment was lonelier still. The conductor ushered him forward to the first step.

Mrs Crominski involuntarily relaxed, and trembled like a train. A woman sitting in front of her, who had been set in motion by Mrs Crominski's trembling, turned round to look at her. 'It's my son,' she said, by way of apology for the vibrations. She pointed to the small figure on the platform. 'Is my son.' The woman gave an understanding smile, as if she was prepared to be shaken like a cocktail throughout the concerto.

Madame Sousatzka leaned backwards in her seat,

pressing herself into the upholstery, trying to embed her whole body into its resisting frame. 'Don't worry, my darrlink, this part is the worst. When you reach the piano it is over, and there is only the playing.'

Marcus climbed the first step. He heard the beginnings of the applause, unleashed by a single loud clap, which somehow or other he recognized as Cordle's. Cordle had told him to look at the piano, and the ground between him and it would disappear. But he was afraid to look anywhere but at his feet, because he could not rely on them to take him where they all expected him to go. Then, suddenly, his fear made him impatient and he took the next steps two at a time, and found that he had reached the back desk of the first violins. The two players had turned round to watch him, their fiddles standing upside down on their knees like stunted 'cellos. This was their moment. It was a moment that made up for years of back-desk frustration, for years of following the bowing of the men in front, and hoping to God they were doing likewise. For years of being automatically accused, for whenever a conductor detected a false note it was always towards their desk that he would turn a raised eyebrow.

They stared a Marcus, smiling, and he couldn't help but see them. Then, like a disciplined miniature army, they raised their hands in which they held their bows, and cocked out their thumbs. Their movements were perfectly timed and symmetrical, for it was a regular routine with them. Every single soloist who played with their orchestra was greeted with their smiles and signs. Even the greatest, who needed no luck at all, even the idolized celebrities, who could have happily performed like pigs and got away with it, all were treated to the same send-off. Marcus smiled back at them, and his smile embedded itself into his face like a moist stucco. He moved forward and reached the fourth desk. The two players sat immobile, their black backs stiff, their coat-tails drooped over their chairs, so that they looked like two transfixed swallows. Marcus looked at the jacket on the player on the inside, and saw a long fair hair clinging to it. He raised his hand automatically to take it off, and as he touched it, he felt that its removal would bring him bad luck. He wanted it to stay there as a talisman. It was only then that he noticed how his fingers were trembling. He swallowed, and it hurt him under his arms. His whole interior body felt like a nettle sting, as if his nerves were crying out to be scratched. He noticed as he moved forward that the foot of the inside player on the third desk was turned slightly outward, just enough to block his path. Marcus was convinced the man was trying to trip him up. He boiled himself up into the conviction that they were all against him, and when he reached the second desk and saw a mute on the violin stand, he was convinced that the orchestra were a bunch of saboteurs. He could remember no passage in the orchestral score of the concerto that called for a mute. They had had a secret meeting, he decided, they were going to give him as faint an accompaniment as possible. They didn't think he was worthy. He shivered. 'I'm not ready,' he said to himself. 'Where is the piano? Is the conductor still behind me? How long have I been walking? When can I start to get it all over with?'

By now, he'd reached the first desk. The sub-leader was sitting motionless, and by the shape of his back, Marcus knew that he knew the soloist was just behind him. He was sitting there, just like Jenny every Friday night, before Marcus surprised her with his hands over her eyes. And as he thought of Jenny, his body grew warmer and his fingers grew still. He put one hand on the piano stool and bowed to the applauding audience.

'You feel better now,' said Madame Sousatzka. 'Just one bow, my darrlink, and sit down. You are ready. Sousatzka says you are ready.'

Marcus sat on the piano stool. He fiddled with the knobs on each side, from force of habit. The audience was silent. Marcus looked up at the conductor. He nodded, and Marcus felt for the G Major chord. He took a deep breath, as he knew Madame Sousatzka in the audience was doing, and as he breathed out the opening chord dropped from his fingers with surprised finality. In the short introduction that followed and the final run to its conclusion, he gradually detached himself from his playing. When the orchestra entered for the first time, there was a gradual stirring in the audience, as a relief from the tension Marcus had created.

Madame Sousatzka gently eased her pressure off the chair. Uncle put her hand on Sousatzka's elbow. 'All's well,' she whispered. She quickly looked at her programme as if at a time-table, checking that she had three movements on leave. She could safely board the train to Paris having seen that all was well at home. The faint background of the concerto was quickly attuned to the wheels of the train, the station calls, the hotel bells, and the Embassy waltzes.

Cordle put his hand across her, as if her seat were vacant. 'He's wonderful,' he whispered to Sousatzka, and he leaned back, settling himself into a scrutiny of the various sections of the orchestra. It was the 'cellos particularly that appealed to him. They, more than any other instrument, seemed to be an integral part of the player. The long black finger-board appeared to him as an extension of the player's tongue. Hitherto, the tongue had played no part in Cordle's osteopathic methods, and he resolved there and then to include it on his charts. He set about thinking what colour would be appropriate. Surreptitiously he felt for his notebook and a bunch of small coloured crayons he always carried with him. He spent the concerto experimenting with his colours.

Manders at the end of the row was planning Marcus's future. He looked across at Cordle's notebook and the coloured indefinable blots on the page. He'd never officially met Cordle, but as part of the Sousatzka retinue he accepted him readily as an eccentric. He looked over at Madame Sousatzka and saw her staring at the ceiling. He looked up to see what had drawn her attention, and a few heads behind him did likewise. But Manders found nothing, and he attributed the tilt of Sousatzka's head to some profound meditation. And he was right.

Of all the people in the party, only Sousatzka was listening to the concerto. But not to Marcus. Once she had seen him off at the start, she was confident he would play brilliantly. As Marcus was playing, she was listening to her old Pachmann recording in her studio. She knew every nuance of that recording, and when Marcus's interpretation did not coincide with it, it interrupted her enjoyment. In the middle of the first movement there was a slight crack in the record which had stretched itself across several revolutions. The rhythmic jump of the needle in the section had become part of the music for her, and she missed it in Marcus's plastic hi-fi playing. Now the record was clean again, whizzing round in its 78 speed until the chord that introduced the cadenza. The agonizing silence that she had felt all the morning before the rehearsal was much shorter on the Pachmann recording, and he had started on his cadenza while there was still silence in the hall. The audience were shifting in speculation. The resigning chord was like the end of a *pase doble* when all the toreadors retire from the ring and leave the arena to the matador alone. When Marcus began, Pachmann was way ahead, and Madame Sousatzka had difficulty in concentrating on the recording. Marcus's cadenza was a fading echo of Pachmann's and gradually the echo was too distant to be heard. She could hear only the recording now, drumming her fingers on her black velvet knee, marvelling at his strange accentuation, joyfully anticipating the final triumphant trill. At the turn of the trill, the orchestra thundered in to clear away the spoils. The recording ended, and the needle slithered over the grooveless slate. Madame Sousatzka could not immediately reorientate herself to the Festival Hall, and she heard with horror that Marcus was still trilling. She started to count, quickly at first, to make up for the time she'd lost through her fear. But the orchestra had made their entry, and people around her were sighing with satisfaction, either with the playing or in anticipation of an interval. When it came, Sousatzka heard the scratching needle. She picked it up and turned the record over. The orchestra didn't give her enough time. Marcus had started on the second movement before Pachmann could get going. She decided to take off the record and listen only to Marcus. She glanced at Jenny's open programme. In the margin, Jenny had drawn three little boxes to represent the movements of the concerto, and Sousatzka noticed with a smile that the first little box had been shaded in.

The dark sad tones of the Andante took Uncle back to the moonlit rivers of Europe, where she and Paul had spent their happiness. The melody suggested to Cordle a deep purple, and softly he rubbed his crayon into a newly outlined tongue. Madame Sousatzka found the melody depressing. It seemed to prophesy her final loneliness. She knew that the vitality of the final movement would be strong enough to offset it, so she could afford for a while to indulge in the sadness that the music evoked. The piano and the orchestra were having a discussion, the piano anticipating arguments with youth and impulse, the orchestra gently remonstrating. At times the piano would offer a challenge, and the orchestra would take up the gauntlet with fear of their victory. And then they would turn to discussion again, gently pesuading each other, the orchestra resorting to pizzicato in its persuasion. But the piano always managed to get the upper hand, and in this unequal struggle, Madame Sousatzka saw herself opposed to Marcus. She knew that in the end she would lose him, if not to Manders then to someone else. She wondered how she could ever replace him. He had exhausted her like the leasehold of her house, which she couldn't afford to renew. She felt she was dying, with Marcus strong and surviving at her bedside. In the short cadenza that interrupted her vision, his music was stormy and feverish, then suddenly calm. The orchestra, on its entry, had become tamed, and shifted, martyr-like, into a minor key. With that modulation, Madame Sousatzka felt she had yielded up her spirit and the piano phrase that cloaked the end of the movement fell over her like extreme unction.

There was no pause before the final movement, and Jenny had to read quickly through the programme notes. 'Notice,' they advised her, 'the subtle canon between the clarinets and the piano.' She wanted very much to oblige, but the word 'canon' bewildered her. She had known plenty of canons in her time, and none of them had been subtle, and she didn't quite see what they would be doing here along with a clarinet, an instrument which, in any case, she couldn't recognize. And quickly, before the Rondo began, she shaded in her second box.

The gaiety of the last movement infected the whole audience. Some were thinking of where they would dine after the concert, others of a visit to the artist's room, of autographs, handshakes, and telling the tale in drawing-rooms afterwards. Others wondered whether it was raining outside, and how difficult it would be to get a taxi.

The Sousatzka row seemed suddenly electrified. Manders was beaming. He knew from the feel of the audience that Marcus was a success. Even Uncle had returned from the embassies, and Cordle put away his tongues. Jenny was eagerly but sceptically awaiting the arrival of the canon.

Madame Sousatzka quickly resurrected herself, and felt the general enjoyment of the audience. Marcus was practically dancing in his seat, the elevated pedal springing from the soles of his shoes like a fixed punchball. Sousatzka looked at his body and the slight curve in his back that was accentuated while playing in the bass section of the piano. She realized that he had never played so well, except perhaps at the 'salon'; that he would reasch a stage when he would depend entirely on having an audience. The thought didn't disturb her too deeply because of the irresistibly happy nature of the music. 'It plays well, my darrlink,' she whispered.

'It's nearly over.' The thought flashed through Marcus's mind with a certain regret, and in the loud tone of the ending he suddenly remembered his mother's words before the rehearsal. He'd forgotten to make a point of remembering his soft parts. Had they been soft enough? He'd eat the carrots in case they hadn't. Why couldn't he be like Peter Goldstein, who ate carrots like a rabbit? Why did he have to lie to her? Tomorrow they'd go together into her brown world and he'd make it up to her. I wish I could play it through all over again, he thought.

'You must be sorry,' said Madame Sousatzka to

herself, 'that it is nearly finished.'

'I want to give concerts tomorrow, and the next day. So many concerts. So many orchestras.'

'You will give many concerts, Marcus. It is only the beginning.'

'Madame Sousatzka, listen to the 'cellos. I wished I played the 'cello.'

'Listen, Marcus, how the 'cello understands you. The piano and the 'cello, they are close friends.'

'I like this conductor, Sousatzka. He understands Beethoven. D'you think they will ask me to play with them again, Sousatzka?'

'The conductor loves you, my darrlink. He will ask you again.'

The conductor, too, was indulging in those thoughts that occupied his mind each time he reached the final coda. 'Will they ask me again, I wonder? I hope the boy likes me. Must give him a good hand-shake afterwards. Perhaps a kiss, too. Depends on the reception he gets. Mustn't overdo it. He'll go a long way, this boy. Worth sticking to.'

'I want to play all the Beethovens, Sousatzka, the Tschaikovskys, the Brahms and all the Mozarts.'

'You will play more concertos, Marcus. Tschaikovsky, Brahms. Everything but Mozart. For Mozart you are not ready. Only Sousatzka can make you ready for Mozart.'

The audience were beginning to close their programmes, anticipating the end of the concerto from the stirring fortissiomo of the full orchestra, rather like a film audience who recognize a long-shot of a cinemascopic sunset as a cue to reach for their coats.

The clapping began almost before the orchestra finished. And when the playing was over, Marcus sat quite still, his head bent, listening to the unfamiliar sound of applause and trying to understand that it was for him. Before Jenny could join in the clapping, she had to settle things. She shaded in the third little box in the margin and ticked off the work for good. Then she closed her programme, put her bag on the floor, slightly rolled up the sleeves of her dress, and offered her contribution.

Cordle had stood up, shouting 'Bravo's'. The man behind him was obliged to stand up too, because Cordle blocked his view of Marcus, likewise the man behind him, and so on in a single slanting line right to the back of the stalls. Uncle threw her arms round Madame Sousatzka, congratulating her on her achievement. Marcus was standing, bewildered, and bowing in quick jerks to the audience. The conductor took his hand and they bowed together. The applause swelled, and the conductor kissed him. He'd decided it was worth it. Marcus began to walk off the platform, but the volume of applause did not decrease.. When he was once again behind the green curtain, the little green man clapped him on the back. 'You'd better go out again,' he said. 'They're calling for you.' He drew the curtain aside, and Marcus ran up the steps. As he passed the player on the fourth desk, he noticed again the long fair hair on the back of his jacket. The hair had bred during the performance and two or three smaller hairs lay nearby in a fresh bed of dandruff. Marcus paused to remove the parent hair. He didn't need it any longer.

The applause was thunderous. Madame Sousatzka looked round at the posse of ambulance women. They sat demurely, their hands clasped on their laps. Strictly impartial. It was then for the first time that Madame Sousatzka began to applaud. 'Darrlink,' she shrieked, and Marcus heard it through the clapping. He smiled in acknowledgement, and bowed again. Then he turned and bowed to the audience behind and to the orchestra. The conductor summoned the orchestra to stand and Marcus shook the leader's hand. Everybody seemed mightily pleased with everybody else. The critics in the audience got down to their jottings. 'The boy will go far,' wrote one. He was obviously on trial with his paper and he didn't want to commit himself. Another took out his cliché book and ticked off, 'well-deserved acclaim'. One critic, probably the mouth of a committed paper, wrote 'a miniature Richter' on his programme. Another critic with literary aspirations wrote 'a velvet suit filled with genius'. He was rather pleased with that one, and decided to get a photograph to go with it. He looked at the last item on the programme, and seeing that it was the Beethoven Fifth, he decided that nothing could go radically wrong with that one. So he could go home and write up his piece with the help of his programme notes.

The applause waned slightly, and a body of isolated people in the hall suddenly reinforced it. Marcus came back again. It was the fourth time. There was a shout of 'Oleh' from a very Enlgish-looking gentleman in the audience who, had he had a hoof in his pocket, would surely have thrown it.

Throughout the applause Mrs Crominski had sat immobile, her hands clasped together. And as the applause subsided and people began to leave the hall for the interval, she uncleaved her hands and gently and almost inaudibly clapped them together. She wanted to be alone in her applause. She noticed that Manders's seat was empty, and Madame Sousatzka was hurrying down the aisle towards the exit. She smiled to herself at their haste. Although she was excited at the thought of seeing Marcus, she felt no pressing necessity to get to him first. She was confident that of them all, she would receive the best welcome. But at this thought, she wondered whether in fact he would be pleased to see her. He'd liked her hat, hadn't he? But the others. Madame Sousatzka and Mr Manders. They'd been in on it from the beginning. They'd been to the salon, they'd been to the rehearsal, and they were with him now. 'But I'm his mother, aren't I?' she said aloud. She got up quickly, furious at herself for having waited so long.

When Madame Sousatzka had reached the artist's room Marcus was sitting on the table with his back towards her, and Manders was bending over him, whispering. When they saw Madame Sousatzka, Marcus reddened slightly. He went over to her and kissed her. 'It was wonderful, my darrlink,' she said. 'You enjoy it?'

He was panting with excitement. 'Oh, Sousatzka, it was marvellous, and Mr Manders says I can play a lot more. I can have thirty concerts a year, he says.'

Mrs Crominski knocked at the door and it was

Manders's authoritative voice that asked her to come in. She was angry with herself that she had knocked and given someone the right to grant her entry. She walked boldly into the room.

Even Mrs Crominski was surprised at the way Marcus received her. He practically leapt forward, and kissed her affectionately. 'Momma,' he said. 'Momma, did you like it? What was it like out there? Were you nervous? D'you feel better?' He was hugging her all the time. He glanced over his shoulder and saw Madame Sousatzka looking at them. He immediately withdrew from his mother, holding her at arm's length. He noticed that his embrace had dislodged her hat. The veil was largely concentrated around her ear and it looked browner than ever.

'I don't think I have the pleasure,' Mrs Crominski said, nodding at Manders. For Mrs Crominski, everything and everybody was a pleasure to be proved otherwise.

'This is my mother,' Marcus said tonelessly. He remembered the pride with which he intended to make this introduction, and he was saddened by his inability to show it.

'Mrs Crominski,' Manders said expansively, turning his back on Madame Sousatzka. 'It is indeed a great pleasure. How surprising it is that we have not met before. I fully expected you at our little salon, when Marcus played so delightfully. We had a grand party,' he rubbed it in, 'you would have been so proud of him. My wife was most disappointed you couldn't come.' He turned to nod at Madame Sousatzka, assuming she was keeping the score.

Mrs Crominski glanced at Madame Sousatzka, too. 'I was thinking I wasn't invited,' she said triumphantly.

'Oh nonsense,' Manders said. 'We're not formal about this sort of thing. We don't send out invitations. And after all, you are the boy's mother. What you reap,' he said parsimoniously, 'you are entitled to sow. And much more will you sow from our seed here.' He rather liked the metaphor and was prepared to flog it to death. He put his arm round Marcus's shoulder. 'A great harvest,' he went on mercilessly, 'but he must play, play, and play again.'

'You mean more concerts he should give?' Mrs Crominski said.

'Many more. Thirty a year at least.'

Madame Sousatzka stood up. She took Marcus's hand and pulled him towards her. 'You cannot play so much,' she said. 'At least, if you play so much, you cannot play well. With thirty concerts a year, there is time only for worry, for rehearsal. No time for the lesson. And you must always have the lessons. You play well, my darrlink, but I know you will play better. Sousatzka knows. At the moment, perhaps I let you play two concerts in the year.'

Mrs Crominski gasped. '*I* let, *I* let, d'you hear?' she marvelled.

'Every week I am giving the boy music,' Madame Sousatzka insisted. 'You learn something with Sousatzka, Marcus, yes?' She held him close to her. 'Sousatzka gives you the life, no?' she pleaded with him to confirm it. But he was silent. He couldn't imagine ever living without Madame Sousatzka, but he wanted concerts, too. Why couldn't he have them both, and his mother and Jenny and Cordle and Uncle and Manders?

'If I don't go to school,' he said, 'and I do nothing else but practise and have lessons, I'll still have time for concerts.'

'He's left school already,' Mrs Crominski marvelled again.

'Madame Sousatzka,' Manders interrupted. 'I don't want to use this time to discuss these matters. But one thing is certain. If you don't allow Marcus to give concerts, many concerts, I can't handle him.'

'Who's to allow? Who's to allow?' Mrs Crominski stepped in, begging her rights. 'For Madame Sousatzka, Marcus is not ready even for this concert.'

'I know, I know,' Manders warmed to her, 'but when the crop is ripe, it must be reaped.' Old Manders was back on the farm again. 'Not ready,' he laughed, 'you heard the applause out there. They'll want to hear him again. They know what they like. The public always knows.'

'They know what you know,' Sousatzka shouted at him. 'Nothing.'

Marcus sat between them, trembling.

'You agree he played well?' Manders refused to be brow-beaten.

'Of course he played well. My Marcus cannot play bad. But those people out there, they clap anyway. Even if he play like . . . er . . . like the other boy on your books last week, I don't say the name. You know who it is. Believe me, Manders, that boy has money. That's all. No talent he has. He pays you to give the concert, he pays the orchestra to play with him. He is a prostitute. You know that word, Manders?' she threatened him.

Manders lost his temper. 'You're jealous, that's what you are. You're jealous. You're afraid to let him go.'

'I want to play,' said Marcus simply.

Through the door, they heard the familiar victory opening of the Beethoven Fifth.

After the concert, a queue formed outside the artist's room. The door opened and Manders came out, letting in the queue like a cinema commissionaire. Mrs Crominski and Sousatzka stood behind Marcus as the first people congratulated him. Jenny, Cordle and Uncle were in the first batch. They approached Marcus together, kissing him and Sousatzka and whispering excitedly in a huddle, excluding all those waiting in the queue. When they had finished, they stepped aside and sat on the long couch alongside the wall, thus establishing themselves as close friends of the artist's. They looked on benevolently, as the men and women came to offer their congratulations. A little man went up to Marcus shyly, and whispered something in his hair. Then he stepped back and brought forward a mountain of a woman, holding her away from him with an outstretched arm, as if exhibiting her, eyeing her with pride and with satisfaction as if he'd made her himself. She looked at Marcus and smiled. And then she plunged forward and kissed him on both cheeks, panting loudly and breaking out into an endless stream of pure Russian. Marcus nodded occasionally and smiled. The voice flowed on over a series of sudden equidistant waterfalls, and there was no indication that she was ever going to stop talking. Suddenly, her little owner stretched out his hand, and marched her away in the middle of a sentence, as if she were a musical box which he had overwound and which had begun to repeat itself. She was followed by a man in parenthesis who stepped forward, took Marcus's hand, let it go, and disappeared without saying a word. Suddenly Manders reappeared with his wife, and they took up their positions next to Marcus. Young boys and girls were coming forward with their programmes to be autographed, and Marcus moved over to the table to sign his name. His mother followed him. The Manders and Madame Sousatzka now remained together in a little group.

'It's a wonderful turn-out,' said Mrs Manders as if she were opening a church bazaar.

'He's been a great success, and he deserves it,' Manders said. 'If I have my way, he'll go far.'

'Why shouldn't you have your way?' his wife asked with feigned innocence. She was itching for an argument, expecially one in which she was personally not involved. She had enough contempt for her husband to enjoy seeing him bested in a quarrel, and not enough respect for Madame Sousatzka to think that she could do it. 'You're his manager, aren't you?' she baited. 'His future's in your hands.'

'It's not as simple as that, my dear. It seems I have some opposition.'

'But surely not Madame Sousatzka,' Mrs Manders said, turning to her. 'Surely you're not going to stand in the boy's way?'

'In his way, I shall not stand. In his way as a pianist, I shall not stand. That is why he must learn and practise and have the lesson. The concert is not everything,' she said.

'But a few concerts,' Mrs Manders said. 'Surely one or

two a year will not harm the boy's playing?'

Madame Sousatzka smiled. 'Oh no, one or two concerts. Very good. But thirty? No. He is not the machine, my Marcus.'

'Who said anything about thirty?' said Mrs Manders, turning automatically to her husband.

'I said,' he said defiantly. 'If the public are to keep him in mind, he must appear. Continuously. He mustn't be forgotten.' Manders was getting angry now. He felt that he was outnumbered. 'Don't forget,' he said, 'he need never have been discovered in the first place. It is only because of me he's here tonight.' This thought had been in his mind all day, accompanied by the determination never to voice it. He regretted it immediately he had spoken. Nothing he could have said could have infuriated Madame Sousatzka more.

'Because of you?' Madame Sousatzka whispered. She had decided to play her trump, and she was going to play it slowly and quietly. 'Because of you?' she repeated, 'or because of Jenny?'

Manders's mouth dropped open. Madame Sousatzka prolonged the pause. Give it time to sink in, she thought. Mrs Manders stepped backwards out of line, in order to watch them both. 'Jenny?' she breathed. 'What's it got to do with Jenny?'

'Ask him,' said Sousatzka. 'He knows so much about everybody on his books. Also Jenny is on the books, Mrs Manders. The private books. The diary,' she added, in case she didn't make herself clear. 'Marcus owes it to you, does he?' she said to Manders. 'You have taught him the music. You have given him the soul. Yes, Manders?' She was almost crying now, sensing that she had lost everything. 'You gave everything to him, yes? The career, the life, the gifts. He owes it all to you, of course.'

'You know I didn't mean it like that,' he said. Mrs Manders was staring at him. 'Jenny?' she asked again.

'Yes, Jenny,' Sousatzka answered for him. 'She plays the piano like your husband plays the piano. She knows about the music like your husband knows. She lives in my house. But she is not my pupil. She has herself the pupils. Your husband is one of them. In fact, he is her favourite. And she does not teach them the arithmetic, Mrs Manders.' She was at pains to make herself clear. As she looked at Mrs Manders she could not bear to see the quiet pain creasing her face. She herself could no longer hold back her tears, some of which flowed for Mrs Manders too. She started for the door. She stood for a moment behind Marcus, listening to the woman in the queue whose turn had at last come, and who was making the most of it.

'I was moved to tears, to tears, to tears,' she was saying. 'You are a pianist to the finger-tips, to the finger-tips, to the finger-tips.' She obviously carried round her own built-in echo chamber.

Madame Sousatzka managed somehow to reach the door. The corridor outside was empty, except for one violinist who was dusting the belly of his violin with a yellow duster. She walked down the corridor and found herself again in the empty auditorium. She climbed the steps to the stage, walked slowly across, and sat down at the piano. She stared at the empty hall, then at the seat she had occupied. She shuddered to find it empty. The emptiness of all the seats appalled her. The vast hall was like a desert, politely littered with a few programmes, tickets and sweet wrappers. The boxes along the sides looked like empty drawers that thieves had ransacked and left open. She had often imagined herself sitting at this piano, especially lately in her day-dreams. She had never seen herself in the process of playing. Her dreams always began with the last chord of a concerto. Then she would sit for a moment listening to the applause. Then the bowing, and the shaking of hands, and the clapping that never stopped. The dream was always the same, and the only variation was in the dress she wore. She never saw the audience, or even the orchestra. She saw only herself at the piano and heard the chord and the clapping.

She closed her eyes. She was not completely sure

whether she was in the hall at the piano or day-dreaming at home. The sense of isolation she felt was common to her dream and her present reality. She listened for the clapping, and waited in the silence for it to start. When she opened her eyes and heard the silence she realized that her day-dream, her most frequent and most satisfying, had been destroyed. She had tested it against reality and it had failed. She wondered desperately how she could fill in her time at home. Suddenly she remembered Manders and the pain on Mrs Manders's face when she told her about Jenny. He'll punish me, she thought. He'll take Marcus away from me for ever. She heard a movement behind her, and she was frightened in case it was Manders. She turned around and found the little green man, who was collecting the stands. He recognized her from the rehearsal.

'You must be very proud of your son, lady,' he said smiling.

'I am,' she said. 'No mother could be prouder.'

'Must be a worry, though,' the green man said. 'All that talent. Still, I wouldn't say no to a boy like that. I expect we'll be seeing you here quite often after tonight's performance,' he said.

Madame Sousatzka suddenly felt cold towards him. 'I must go,' she said. 'Otherwise they lock me in.'

When she reached the artist's room, she heard a whisper of voices inside. She opened the door quickly, and noticed immediately that Jenny wasn't in the room. The visitors had gone and Marcus was putting on his overcoat. Manders was standing by the dumb piano, red in the face and sweating. Mrs Manders lounged calmly at the table. She was obviously waiting until they got home. Uncle and Cordle stood almost soldered together for safety. When Madame Sousatzka came in, they both stepped towards her.

'I've come to a decision,' Manders said, looking at Sousatzka. 'The boy has to choose. I can't handle him as long as he is having lessons with you. Either you give him up completely and let me handle him as I think he

151

should be handled, or I wipe my hands of him. And I doubt very much,' he added, 'if any other agent in town will take him on.'

Mrs Crominski had not overheard the revelation about Jenny, and she wondered why Manders had come to such a decided judgment. 'I can persuade, I think,' she said. 'Is not necessary, Madame Sousatzka shouldn't teach my boy. And also he will have the concerts. After all, if not for Madame Sousatzka, Marcus isn't here tonight.'

'I've said what I have to say.' Manders was adamant. 'Business is business. There's enough worry handling managements and other agents in this cut-throat trade. I can't take on teachers as well. No. I've made up my mind. You take him away from Madame Sousatzka, or he finds another agent.'

Madame Sousatzka looked at Marcus and he tried to look away. Suddenly she understood what was going to happen. She knew that at that moment Marcus was drunk with his success, and he needed more to feed on. She began to pardon him for the choice she knew he would make. 'You're a little boy,' she said, forgiving him.

'I'm not a little boy,' Marcus suddenly shouted. He was glad that Madame Sousatzka had given him reason to complain. 'You've always treated me like a little boy. You won't let me go.'

The tears were rolling down Madame Sousatzka's face. 'I have already at this moment said goodbye,' she said.

Marcus stared at her, and as she turned to walk out of the room, supported by Uncle and Cordle, he made a move to follow her. 'Madame Sousatzka,' he called. 'Uncle. Cordle.'

Mrs Crominski put her hand on his shoulders. 'It's for the best, Marcus, you'll see.' He threw her hand away from him, and he looked at her and Manders with hatred. Manders managed a weak smile. 'I'll take you home in my car,' he said.

Madame Sousatzka was sitting in her studio. She had only just come home, and Cordle and Uncle had gone to their own rooms. She thought with disgust of the table of curled sandwiches in the kitchen, and wondered painfully whether Marcus would come back for the little party they had arranged together. She heard a car draw up outside the house. Yes, yes, who else would come to the square at this hour? She heard the car door open, and whispers of many voices. Yes, they had all come. Manders and his wife, Marcus and his mother. They were laughing now, and she tried to identify the laughter with any one of them. 'This is Vauxhall Mansions,' she heard a woman's voice. She tried hard to convince herself that it was Mrs Manders. Yes, she'd never been to the house before and she was glad they'd found the right square. 'Ours is the next on the right,' the woman went on. 'Sorry, Sammy.' She heard the door slam again, and the car purring away. She waited for its drone to leave the square alone.

Then for the first time, she sobbed aloud. She hunched herself up in her chair, her hands over her face, giving herself up to the red, wet, strangling agony that seemed to pump itself into her body, melting bone and muscle in its hot, unquenchable thirst.

In the morning she awoke, swollen, with the sad and certain knowledge that she was still warm.

13

Weeks passed and Sousatzka heard nothing from Marcus. She bought all the papers advertising musical events, in the hope that he would be playing somewhere. Even Jenny was of no help. Manders hadn't contacted her since the concert. Very often Sousatzka had wanted to suggest another session with the glass, to find out what and how Marcus was doing. But she knew that the glass was only for advice, and to use it as a detective would have insulted its purpose.

Every night she would sit at the piano, going over Marcus's old music, recalling his fluency or difficulties in each phrase. She was like a discarded mistress reading old love letters. And every day she told herself to pull herself together. There were her other pupils, but none of them was bound to her like Marcus. She taught without heart.

Her lethargy had infected Cordle too, and he spent his time re-examining his old rejected theories, wondering how much their rejection was justified. He took out old copies of a newspaper which had long ago reported his osteopathic methods. And he read the little paragraph over and over again.

Upstairs, he heard Jenny go about her business, and on Friday nights her light went out very early. In the basement, Uncle's unsolved crosswords accumulated and the door that led to Marcus's room was open, revealing the bed, unmade as he had left it. And from top to bottom of the house, they day-dreamed more than ever before.

About three months after the concert Madame Sousatzka was giving a lesson to Paula, a new pupil, a talented eight-year-old, with an over-ambitious mother. It was all Madame Sousatzka could do to keep the woman out of the lessons, and she always waited outside the studio door, breathing heavily through the wooden panel, with her hand, no doubt, on a stop-watch.

Madame Sousatzka spent the lesson, as she did all her lessons, trying to pretend that the pupil was Marcus, trying to transfer to them all the love she had given him. The pain of his departure still nagged at her, and there were many moments when she wanted to stand up and scream 'it's not fair'. She was worried, too, about the letter she'd received that morning from the ground landlords of the house. It informed her that their surveyors would be coming the following week to examine the house and to assess the repairs that would have to be carried out. The diminishing lease had worried her for a long time, but as long as she knew that the whole square was worrying for the same reason, she could shelve the problem till it became acute. She knew it was insoluble. She had not enough money to carry out even the most minor repairs to the house, and the time was running out. They had offered her the freehold, but at an unthinkable price. The thought of selling it assailed her like a wound and she tried desperately to put it out of her mind. She thought she would speak to Cordle about it, though why, she couldn't imagine.

Paula was playing a scale and Madame Sousatzka suddenly heard the front door crash open, followed by running steps across the hall and up the stairs. Cordle was in, Jenny was in, and so was Uncle, and there was no one else who knew how to open the front door without a key. She got up quickly and went into the hall, almost knocking Paula's mother over as she opened the door of her studio.

'Who was that?' she asked breathlessly.

'A man.'

Madame Sousatzka made for the stairs, but the woman barred her way.

'Madame Sousatzka,' she said, 'you are in the middle of a lesson. You can go up afterwards. It was probably a friend of one of your tenants.'

Madame Sousatzka turned back to the studio. She was suddenly sure that the visitor was someone from the ground landlord. Who else could barge into a house as if it were his own? In which case, she preferred not to confront whoever had come in. She returned to the safety of the studio and tried to concentrate on the lesson. But the letter had said next week, she thought. No official authority could make such an unofficial entrance. It couldn't be a surveyor. Paula was labouring with her scales and although Madame Sousatzka heard the jerkiness of her rhythms, she couldn't concentrate sufficiently to correct her. Suddenly she heard Jenny's voice screaming from the top of the house. Then the heavy thud of someone falling downstairs. Madame Sousatzka got up quickly and told the astonished Paula that her lesson was over. She hurriedly pushed the child's music into her case and more or less shoved her out of the room in front of her.

Mother was waiting. She looked at her watch. 'She's not had an hour yet, Madame Sousatzka,' she said.

In a panic to see what had happened, Madame Sousatzka decided to lose no time on this woman. 'How often do you count the hour over the hour? I don't hear you complain then. You stand there all the time counting minutes on the watch. I am not breaking the record, Missus,' she shouted at her on her way up the stairs. 'For the five minutes, I give you back the money.' She rushed upstairs to the first landing.

Cordle was on the floor in his white coat, massaging a massive hulk on the floor. 'Is he dead?' Sousatzka asked. The identity of the man could come later.

'No, just a bad fall.'

The man on the floor made an attempt to get up. He managed to stand by supporting himself on the banister. He turned round to find Sousatzka staring at him.

'Manders,' she gasped. 'Felix Manders,' she laughed, 'the great impresario. Manders, the thief,' she waved her arm over the banisters. 'Come, Uncle,' she invited her, seeing her at the foot of the stairs. Uncle had somehow made the journey from her basement room to see what had happened. 'Look what we have here, lady and gentleman.' She nodded at Cordle. 'The great Felix Manders. Ah, it will be in the paper. Felix Manders, the music middle-man,' she spat out, 'the dealer, kicked down the stairs in the house of Madame Sousatzka, the celebrating teacher of the piano. Sit down a little, Manders,' she coaxed him. 'You are not well. The shock is too much. I will ring up your wife. She should come to take you away.'

Manders was nursing his shoulder. 'I beg you, Madame Sousatzka,' he managed to blurt out, sitting down on the bottom stair.

'Ah,' Sousatzka laughed, 'Felix Manders is begging. Come here, Uncle,' she called, 'have the front seat. This is my concert, my management, and here,' she pointed at him, 'is the latest one on my books.'

Uncle came slowly up the stairs and stood beside Sousatzka. Cordle was squatting on his heels massaging Manders's shoulder with a fixed 'pain knows no frontier' look on his face. They heard Jenny's door open and her light footsteps running down the stairs. Manders tried to turn his head, and he shielded his face with his good arm in anticipation of another blow.

Jenny leaned over the banister. 'Here,' she shouted, 'you left your business behind,' and she flung a half-open briefcase on to his head. The contents spilled out and fluttered around him, pamphlets, brochures and contracts. A folded brochure landed on his knee, and Madame Sousatzka was able to read '*Management. Felix Manders Ltd.*' She picked it up to look at the other side. A large sad photograph of Marcus stared back at her. Uncle gripped her arm to support her. But she shook her off. The agony of Marcus's departure returned and gave her strength. She bent down, and lifted Manders bodily from the floor. She steadied him on the top of the flight of stairs leading to the hall. Then she screwed up Marcus's picture in one hand and with the other she pushed Manders down the stairs. He rolled over on the threadbare carpet, and landed with a groan on the coconut mat in the hall.

'All my good work,' Cordle reproached her. But even as he spoke he was smiling.

At the sight of Manders painfully putting himself together in the hall, Uncle giggled, and Jenny leaned over the banister and started to laugh aloud. Sousatzka joined in too, and Manders slunk out of the hall, not caring to retrieve his briefcase, and out of the front door. They saw his shadow hobble painfully down the front steps.

'We won't see him again,' Sousatzka said.

Jenny's laughter trailed into a sob, and they heard her going back into her room. Uncle took a deep breath and started her return journey. Madame Sousatzka watched her disappear. She uncrumpled the paper in her hand and spread out Marcus's photograph in front of her. The creases had inserted a smile into his face. She smoothed them out against the wall as gently as she could, until Marcus was sad again. Her head drooped and she gave a deep sigh.

Cordle put his arm round her shoulder. 'Come and sit with me for a while,' he said. She let Cordle take her into his room. He sat her down on the low couch, and switched off the light above her head. He stood in front of her, his hands resting on her shoulders, and lightly massaging the back of her neck. 'Lie down and relax,' he said. 'I'll help you.' He lifted her feet on to the couch and she lay down on her stomach, her head resting on the small pillow at the top of the bed. Cordle worked his way around the shoulder-blades, and as he pressed he saw the tears fall on to the pillow as if he was, with his manipulations, squeezing them out of her. 'You must forget about Marcus,' he said gently. 'There are other things. Other pupils. There's so much more for us to do. New methods to be examined, practice, work, people and love.' He drove each example into her back with his thumbs. He let his hands come to rest alongside her spine. 'You should marry, Sousatzka,' he said flatly. 'You're lonely. You need companionship. You need help. You need love. You have so much love to give.'

Madame Sousatzka turned round and sat upright on the couch. Cordle took his hands away and stepped backwards away from her. She looked at him steadily for a moment and then she smiled. It was the first genuine smile Cordle had seen on her face since the concert. 'Who would I marry, Cordle?' she said.

Cordle was silent. Although the situation had arisen quite naturally, he was astonished at the turn it had taken. He thought of himself as Monsieur Sousatzka, and a sudden thrill of pleasure forced him to sit down and steady the trembling in his body. 'I have nothing to offer you, my dear, except respect and admiration. I am lonely too and groping. Groping in a jungle of bones and muscles and colours for some understanding. There have been moments when I knew you understood, and I've gone back to my work with renewed confidence.' Cordle suddenly realized that this was the real speech of his day-dreams. His fluency, such as it was, surprised him, and the moment he became conscious of it he began to stutter and stammer, the words strangling in his throat. 'Madame Sousatzka,' he blurted out, 'this is the point of it all. When Marcus went away, we both lost him. Perhaps we will find him again, if we come together. Sousatzka,' he whispered, 'D'you think you could marry me?'

Sousatzka got up and came towards him. 'You are a good man, Cordle,' she said, touching him on the shoulder. 'I must be by myself for a while. I have so much to decide. I tell you.' She left him trembling in his chair and went down to the studio.

She had wondered, when Cordle had proposed to her, whether she was happy. She would only know in recollection. She sat down at the piano and began to play. Cordle opened his door and listened. She was playing a Mozart sonata, and in the abandon of her playing, he decided he was entitled to some hope.

He didn't see Sousatzka for a few days after the incident, but he noticed that she was playing more than ever before. Sometimes the music was melancholy, and she would often break off in the middle to practise a scale or a study. Meanwhile, he worked on his charts and the occasional pupils. Jenny's customers went upstairs, and Uncle restarted on her crosswords. The house was alive again, despite the fact that it had but a short while to live, but it was living at a feverish pace, like a knitter who, seeing her wool running out, knits fast and furiously.

On the fourth day after the proposal, Cordle was colouring one of his charts when he heard Sousatzka stop playing in the middle of a study. He waited for her to start again, but he could hear the silence quite clearly. Since the proposal he had left his door open, and he heard her coming up the steps to his room. He tried to get on with his colouring, feigning concentration on his work, like a young lover trying to appear casual. He heard her come into his room and shut the door. He turned round to welcome her.

'I was thinking,' Sousatzka began. Cordle knew the verdict instinctively and he wanted to delay it.

'Sit down,' he said. 'You're playing a lot lately. I have my door open. I love to listen to you. Sometimes you play like an angel. You inspire me,' he panted on. He was going to make it hard for her to reject him. 'I myself have done so much work in the last few days.' He stopped, breathless. He'd run out of his defence, and he stared at her dumbly.

'You have made me very happy, Cordle,' she said, 'when you ask for me to marry. That is very good for a woman who has been reject. That is stimulus. That is tonic. And I work. You hear me. Every day I work. But you know, Cordle, I am not the one for the marriage. We are good friends. Always we will be good friends. You help me. I am grateful. Cordle, you must not be disappoint. I will never marry. Not to nobody. You are my great friend, Cordle. Give me the hand. For ever we will be friends.'

Cordle stretched out his hand and smiled at her. He was surprised at himself that he felt no heart-break at her refusal. But the idea of marriage, once formed in his mind, had whetted his appetite. And as he was holding Madame Sousatzka's hand, he made up his mind as soon as she was gone and the coast was clear, he'd go downstairs and see Uncle. He stood there smiling at her, his thoughts treacherously in the basement.

As Madame Sousatzka smiled, her thoughts were elsewhere too. Not that she didn't feel genuine friendship for Cordle. She did. His sudden proposal had freed her from despair. She was concerned with the reasons why she had turned down his offer. It was not because she didn't want to get married. She had lied to him. It was because she saw him, as she too often had seen herself, a failure who, to disguise his lack of success, had evolved in his work a 'method'. The Cordle 'method'; the Sousatzka 'method'. They were both strangled admissions of failure. And although she realized that her 'method' was questionable, it had produced Marcus, and this thought saved her from depression. She was still smiling at Cordle when they parted. Each of them felt a certain relief at having gleaned from an experience only the best, without having to exploit all its precarious advantages.

14

The day the surveyors were expected, Madame Sousatzka received her bulletin of forthcoming musical events. She opened it slowly, anxious, yet dreading to find Marcus's name. The pamphlet fell open on the middle-page spread, with a large central picture of Manders, stapled down the nose. '*Impresarios*,' the title read, '*First in a series. Felix Manders*.' Half-way down the first column, Madame Sousatzka saw Marcus's name in heavy print. She shut the book quickly, not daring to read what she hoped and feared to find. She looked out of the window, hoping that the surveyors would come, to give her an excuse to postpone reading. But apart from several FOR SALE notices that sprouted from scattered houses like white flags, the square was empty. She turned up the corner of the middle page and peeped inside. She caught the tail end of Marcus's name again, and quickly looked away. But she knew that she would have to read it. The fact that his name was in the book at all was confirmation of what she half dreaded, the news that he was giving concerts. She opened it squarely on the piano and read it sadly and without haste. It announced that Marcus would give a series of six piano recitals of the works of Mozart, the last three of which were to be broadcast. She read on, not allowing herself to register the composer. Later on in the year, it said, he was to tour the European capitals and make a series of recordings. Manders, it concluded, had 'high hopes' of him.

She read the article over and over again. The news that he was playing Mozart pained her less than the fact that he was going away. For a swift moment she was happy at the thought that he must come to say goodbye. She would at least see him again. But at the same time, there was the equal possibility that he wouldn't come at all. She picked up the book, and shutting her eyes, wandered about the room to hide it, so that she could never find it again. She stuffed it on a shelf, recognizing full well the large music lexicon which obscured it. She kept her eyes shut, making her way towards the window. She felt the sun on her cheeks, and hoped that it would disappear before the surveyors arrived.

But they came at mid-day, when the sun was at its height. It was particularly hot that day, although Madame Sousatzka had prayed for rain as fervently as a drought-sick farmer. In the rain, many imperfections on the outside of the house were camouflaged. The water that dripped from the pipes could be ascribed to natural causes, whereas in the blazing sun not only could you see the lone drip dripping, you could hear it too. And as Madame Sousatzka watched the surveyors approach the house, she heard the pipe calling them, and they stopped and nodded to each other knowingly.

They reached the bottom of the front steps and automatically looked up at the sky. Then they turned about and marched across the road to find a better vantage point. They positioned themselves against the railings in the middle of the square opposite Madame Sousatzka's house. They looked up again. Madame Sousatzka saw them pointing to her roof and again nodding to each other. She remembered the damaged guttering that for four years she'd intended to repair. It was only visible from the other side of the road, dangling half-amputated over Jenny's window. She naïvely thought she might have got away with it. She looked at the unbroken straight line of the guttering on the house opposite, and was offended. They hadn't conformed. Straight guttering and healthy pipes were the uniform of freeholds, and if you wore it in Vauxhall Mansions, you were living a lie.

She watched the men as they craned their necks upwards, pointing from time to time and exchanging looks of horror. They might have been looking at a gallows. They started to cross over, still looking upwards, and Madame Sousatzka had the fleeting hope that a car would swerve into the square and run them over. But they arrived hale, and still nodding, at the bottom of the steps. As they climbed to the front door, they prodded each step in front of them with their umbrellas, as if they suspected a land-mine.

They reached the top surprised, and Madame Sousatzka saw one of them press the dead bells.

She gave herself time to hear it, and then went to the door. She felt suddenly very alone, with an enormous responsibility. Jenny and Cordle were in their little rented rooms and Uncle was in the basement, and she was alone and without Marcus. And Marcus was going away. As she walked through the hall she noticed the large cracks along the skirting, and the sunken area along the tiled floor. They suddenly disgusted her. She wanted to go on the side of the surveyors, to have Cordle answer the door, or Jenny or Uncle, so that she could upbraid them for their neglect. She hoped that they had an least tidied up their rooms for the visitors. She daren't hope too much of Uncle. God knows where she had stuffed her hoard of newspapers. She opened the door timidly.

'Good afternoon, Madam,' they said together. 'Doesn't the bell work?'

'Of course it works.' Madame Sousatzka defended her dead bell. She hoped they wouldn't test it.

'We're from Cameron & Hodge,' they said, as if a dual partnership required dual representation. 'You do expect us?' came a solo.

'Of course. Natural,' said Madame Sousatzka, as if she had nothing to hide. 'Of course I expect you. I have from you a letter.' They had begun to come in, their umbrellas well in front of them, prodding for dry rot in the thin air.

'Shall we start in the basement?' Madame Sousatzka asked them cordially. She wanted to get Uncle over with.

'I think we'll start at the top, shall we?' said one heartily. 'Get the climb over.'

The other one nodded at his merry fellow, and led by Madame Sousatzka they dawdled up the stairs.

'Lovely day,' the hearty one said conversationally. 'They don't build houses like this nowadays,' he said, as if sound building were a corollary of fine weather. He prodded the wall with his stick. 'Solid stuff, this,' he barked. Madame Sousatzka turned and smiled at him.

As they passed Cordle's door, Sousatzka could hear no sound. She was sure Cordle was hiding. They reached the top and she heard scuffling in Jenny's room. She hurried to Jenny's door, and knocked on it to give her warning. She opened it before Jenny replied. Jenny was with a client.

'But it's early,' Jenny stammered. 'You said you were starting with Uncle.'

'Get dressed,' Sousatzka hissed, and she shut the door quickly.

The men were behind her, each with one eyebrow raised. They certainly had a team spirit. 'She won't be a minute,' Madame Sousatzka said calmly. 'She is clearing her table.'

'We haven't come to inspect the crockery, have we, Frank?' the cheery one joked to his companion.

The heartiness of the man was slowly wearing Madame Sousatzka down. She forced herself to smile. 'Are you very busy?' she asked, without much relevance.

'Up to our necks,' George replied on behalf of both of them. 'Always busy with property. I'm not telling you a word of a lie, Madam, but we've got three hundred and fifty houses falling in a couple of years. And that's just in this area.'

Madame Sousatzka could almost hear the earthquake. 'You like your work?' she said, stalling for time.

'Well, it's like this,' said George, 'the work's all right, surveying and that sort of thing, but when it comes to doing a job like this, it's sort of sad. People who've lived in houses for generations having to get out because the lease is up, and they can't afford the freehold. Now Cameron & Hodge, they've got to do it, I suppose. Good firm to work with. But I'm not married to that company and I think it's immoral.' His companion nodded his head, sombrely.

'Take the other day, for instance,' he went on. 'There was this old lady, she must have been close on ninety, wouldn't you say, Frank?'

'And the rest,' said Frank, who felt he ought to contribute something.

'She'd been born in that house, Madam, and she'd got to go. It's the law. That's the worst part of our job. Now, I'm not married to Cameron & Hodge,' he said, divorcing himself once more from same, 'I can say it. It's immoral.'

Jenny must be dressed by now, Sousatzka thought, and

she knocked again at the door.

'Come in,' said Jenny's cheery voice.

Madame Sousatzka let the two men in before her, and she followed them. Jenny's room, as always, was neat and tidy. She was sitting in front of her gas-fire, filing her nails. The client was fixing bookshelves which Jenny had hastily dismantled.

'Make yourselves at home,' said Jenny, as she would to any client. 'Don't mind Mr Holmes. He's just fixing my bookshelf for me.' Mr Holmes did not turn round, in case his face would betray his utter lack of skill in carpentry. He hammered on, with what was left of his soul, deep in his work.

The two men poked about the skirtings with their umbrellas. They fumbled along the walls, tapping with their sticks, like two blind men anticipating a crossing. For the second round George, who was in front, got down on his hands and knees. Frank followed him like a shadow. George poked his finger into a large hole in the base of the skirting, and murmured 'Ah.' Then he followed the crack with his finger right up the wall as far as he could reach, slowly bringing himself up from the floor. He traced the rest of the crack with his umbrella. 'That'll be the roof,' he said to Frank. 'Make a note of it.' George was obviously in charge of diagnosis.

Frank opened his brief-case and pulled out a long roll of paper. It was rolled into the centre from both sides like a Jewish scroll. He laid it on the floor, holding it down in the centre with his knee. He unrolled the section on his left and scanned the various columns for the correct heading. Not finding it there, he did the same with the section on his right. Madame Sousatzka had to move out of the way in order to give him room. He found what he wanted at the foot of the end column. He took out his pen and solemnly put a red tick in the appropriate square. He looked up at Madame Sousatzka and smiled. First point to them. He let the scroll roll towards the centre and carefully replaced it in the case.

George had by now reached the window frame, and he had come into his own. Window areas were as happy a hunting-ground as basements. 'Dry rot,' he cooed, '*and*,' he added, licking his lips, 'woodworm.' Had the whole house crumbled at his touch, he couldn't have been more delighted. 'Make a note of that one, Frank,' he said. 'Most interesting.' With another smile at Madame Sousatzka, Frank took out the scoreboard again.

After a half-hour's examination every possible disease known to wood, brick and lead had been diagnosed in Jenny's room. Frank's score-sheet, which he had taken out and put away a hundred times, was covered like a rash with tiny ticks.

'We won't be troubling you any more, Miss,' George turned to Jenny. 'I think we've got all we need. Get a lot of mice up here, I suppose?'

'I've never seen one,' said Jenny.

'Funny,' said George, 'Lots of holes.'

Jenny was indignant. 'I've been here ten years and I've never seen a mouse.'

'All right, lady. Take it easy. Maybe you heard one.'

'I'm sure you're wanting to see the rest of the house,' Jenny said, opening the door for them.

George looked at her gleefully, as if she answered a requirement in his 'damp clause'. 'Make another note of those holes, Frank,' he said.

Suddenly they heard a crash from the other side of the room. Mr Holmes, whom at his own request everybody had ignored, felt the need to stand by Jenny. He dropped the bookshelves he was still fixing on to the mantelpiece, and waving his hammer in his hand he said with authority, 'If Miss Boxhall states that there are no mice, I see absolutely no reason on earth to disbelieve her.' Frank and George gaped at him. It was his accent that disturbed them; it seemed in no way connected with the hammer in his hand.

'What are the holes there for, then?' said George, who was the first to recover.

'For air,' said Mr Holmes, waving his hammer theatrically.

'Make a note of that, Frank,' said George. 'Twenty-five holes, for ventilation.'

'I think we go downstairs,' said Madame Sousatzka. She

was smiling to herself. The whole examination suddenly appeared to her to be ridiculous. If they had found so much fault with Jenny's room, which she considered to be the best in the house, what would they find when they eventually made the basement? She followed them down to the half-landing.

'Let's see the plan,' George said. Frank drew another chart out of his case and spread it open against the wall.

'Let's see, now,' said George, pointing to a square, 'we're here, at this point, aren't we?' Madame Sousatzka leaned over to confirm it.

'That's right,' she said triumphantly. 'We're here.' It was the first time she'd seen the plan of a house, and it meant nothing to her, but she saw no point in disagreeing with the examiners.

'Well then,' said George. He was already dribbling in anticipation of another victory. 'If we're here, and it's here on the map,' he said, screwing his finger into a little black square, 'if we're here,' he repeated, 'what, Madam, has happened to the lavatory? Now you can't deny it, can you?' he said, before Madame Sousatzka could offer an explanation. 'It's here, in black and white, a lavatory. Now where's it gone?' He made Madame Sousatzka feel as if she'd stolen the lavatory and hidden it under her pillow. She remembered that years ago Cordle had wanted to extend his room to store his charts, and he'd had the lavatory taken away and the wall pulled down. 'It's gone,' Madame Sousatzka said simply.

'You admit it was here?' said George. Frank had taken out his scoreboard without waiting for George's instructions.

'Oh yes,' said Madame Sousatzka, 'I remember it very well. But you see, very simple, we didn't want it, and Mr Cordle, he lives in that room,' she pointed down the stairs, 'he want bigger space. So we pull down the wall and we take away the lavatory. A very good man did it. Very expensive. But Mr Cordle,' she smiled, 'he is professional man. He need the space.'

'It's got to go back,' said George with finality. 'In 1860,

168

when this house was built, there was a lavatory on this very space where we're standing.' Madame Sousatzka moved away from them. 'It's got to go back. People've got no right to take things away. What people think they can get away with with these leaseholds, is astonishing. It'll have to go back.' George had obviously remarried Cameron & Hodge. Meanwhile, Frank was scribbling frantically in his notebook, ticking off on his chart, like a zealous schoolmaster marking the work of a genius.

George walked defiantly down the stairs. He was getting belligerent. Mr Holmes's accent had set him off. Always in the course of a survey George would switch sides, so that by the time a job was completed he was ready to worship at the shrine of Cameron & Hodge, gloating over evictions, hob-nobbing with the bailiffs, and ordering the replacement of a hundred useless lavatories, sheds and entrances, according to the rule of the book, 'everything shall be left as found'. He banged on Cordle's door with his fist. 'Shifting lavatories,' he muttered. 'What next?'

There was no answer. George turned to look at Madame Sousatzka, but she didn't see him. She was far away; she was thinking of the dressing-room adjoining her studio, which years ago she'd converted into a bathroom. Marcus used to love that bathroom because of the shower. At the thought of Marcus the expiration of the lease became meaningless. She suddenly hated these men. She didn't care what they said about her house. She didn't care about the house any more. She cared for Jenny, and Cordle, and Uncle, and the music Marcus had made from her and the ulcerous hole in her heart.

'There is no need to bang like a hooligan,' Madame Sousatzka said quietly. 'Perhaps he is out, Mr Cordle. You will see the room. I will take you. You have not come here to examine the people, remember. You have to make the report, the report of the house. I am not a criminal. If the house is bad, it is because I have not money. That is not a crime.' She moved towards them to open Cordle's door, and George stood aside quietly. He looked at Frank, who noncommittally shrugged his shoulders.

There was no one in Cordle's room, and Madame Sousatzka was convinced he was hiding somewhere. She opened his cupboard and his one suit, its hanger wedged in the door, swung round in her face. She clutched the dangling sleeve, as if Cordle were inside it. There was no sign of his white jacket. He must have it on. He must be in the house somewhere. He never went out in the street with his white jacket. She began to worry about him. She needed him, with these men and this examination. 'Cordle,' she whispered into the closet, as if he were a pet kitten that would emerge only at a familiar bidding.

'It's all right, Madam,' George said, friendly again. 'We won't need Mr Cordle. Have to take down some of these charts, though,' he said, 'with your permission.'

'I will take them,' said Madame Sousatzka. She didn't want strangers to handle Cordle's work.

'As you wish,' George said, and they stood aside and watched Madame Sousatzka as she carefully lifted the charts from the wall.

'Is he a doctor, or something?' Frank wanted to be friendly, too.

'Yes,' said Madame Sousatzka. She was not prepared to go into the matter and she went on rolling up the charts. When the walls were stripped she stood in the corner, holding the charts to her. She watched the men as they examined the room. George measured, prodded and peeled, while Frank scribbled and ticked. The men were silent. George no longer expressed any enthusiasm over his discoveries. In fact, he seemed suddenly bored by the whole business.

'That's it,' he said after a short while, 'let me help you put the charts back.'

Madame Sousatzka sensed his change of heart and she allowed him to help her. When it was finished, she opened the door for them to leave first; she looked round the naked room, still aware of Cordle's presence. 'Thank you, Cordle,' she whispered, 'We're going now.'

As they reached the first landing, the 'phone rang. When a 'phone rings in a lonely house, you don't answer it automatically. Like Madame Sousatzka, you listen a while to its ringing. She would wonder who it was. She would think of half a dozen unexciting people and hope it wasn't one of them. She would give her ear wholly to the sound of the bell, and enjoy the concrete knowledge that somebody wanted her. She would approach the 'phone and stretch out her hand, testing the caller's patience, savouring the rhythmic insistence of the caller. Once she had over-tested, and the ringing had stopped as her hand touched the receiver. She was furious at herself for missing the call and she spent weeks of vain enquiry to find out who it had been. Since that time, she would pick up the 'phone promptly, to acknowledge her presence, but she would wait a few minutes before saying 'Hullo', in order to prolong her excitement. Now, with George and Frank immediately behind her, she couldn't play her private game. As she lifted the receiver, she half hoped it would be the wrong number. It was a pity to waste a telephone call under such conditions. 'Hullo,' she drawled, bored as a habit-worn telephonist.

'Madame Sousatzka?' a small voice both questioned and answered at the other end.

Madame Sousatzka caught hold of the coin-box that held the money. 'Marcus!' she gasped. Frank and George looked at her and saw her stagger slightly, her face a pale yellow. George stopped forward to hold her.

'Is there anything wrong, Madam?'

'Go away,' Madame Sousatzka screamed, 'I must be by myself.' The men turned to walk down the stairs, staring behind them. 'No, my darrlink,' Madame Sousatzka was saying, 'Not you, my darrlink, I was talking to someone else. Is all right with you, Marcus?' The colour had returned to her face, the yellow rinsed out with her tears. 'Yes, of course,' she said. 'Tonight. Eight o'clock. I wait for you. Is all right everything now,' she said, almost to herself. 'I wait for you, Marcus. Is all right.' She heard Marcus put the 'phone down, and she stared at the receiver in her hand. 'Is all right,' she said, laughing to herself. 'Is all right, Jenny,' she shouted in the direction of the top storey. 'Is all right, Cordle,' she ran towards his room, relaying the good news through the door. As she came downstairs and passed the telephone she picked up the hanging receiver and replaced it violently, as if she wanted to break all communication. She didn't need it any more. Everything was all right again. She ran past the men in the hall and leaned over the basement staircase. 'Is all right, Uncle,' she yelled, 'is all right.'

It did not strike her as odd, that none of the tenants had answered her. It didn't matter. She came towards Frank and George, who couldn't fathom the change in her manner. She looked at them both with a feeling of great love. 'Is all right now,' she said gently. 'Is everything all right with Madame Sousatzka. Come, I show you my room. My piano, my life,' she said, opening the door. 'You go about your business,' she said, 'I go about mine. I have so much to do. I have a lesson. An important lesson. A great pianist. I must get everything ready.'

She started to sing as she opened the large kidney lid of the piano, as if to air it after lack of use. She removed the velvet band that covered the keys. She busied herself with the music, selecting pieces from the various piles. She opened a book of studies and placed it on the stand, gently turning up the corners to facilitate the turn-over. She began to giggle with excitement. With her two hands she played a scale the length of the keyboard, chromatically, so that every note would be run in. She followed this with a number of arpeggios and chords, testing the keyboard for varying tones, warming it up, as one cranks a car engine on a frosty morning.

Frank and George, their business forgotten, stared at her, bewildered. They watched her as she sat at the piano, twirling the stool higher and higher.

'Oh, I forget so soon,' she said. 'Please, Mister,' she said, going over to Frank who was the shorter of the two, 'would you please sit on the stool and make so is the right height? You are like my Marcus. I mean only in the height you are like him.' Frank let himself be led to the stool, and as he sat down he started to adjust the seat. 'Is comfortable?' Madame Sousatzka asked him when he'd stopped twiddling.

'It's all right,' he said. 'I like a seat with a back, myself.'

'Not for the playing,' Madame Sousatzka laughed. 'Is right for the playing? You can reach the piano?' Frank stretched out his arms and rested his unkempt long-nailed hands on the keys. Madame Sousatzka looked at them, horrified. 'Is all right,' she said quickly, taking his hands away. She stared at the range of notes his hands had covered and she desperately wanted to wipe them clean. She felt Frank was like a tramp who, just for kicks, had taken a nap on a virgin bridal bed.

'Thank you,' she managed to say, 'now all is ready.'

'Give us a tune, Madam,' said George, 'while we get on with the job.'

Madame Sousatzka closed the lid of the piano. 'Not now,' she said. 'Everything is ready. Must not disturb.'

'Pity,' said George, disappointed. 'I like a drop of music myself.'

'Will it be very long? The house business, I mean,' Madame Sousatzka was getting impatient. It was already three o'clock and she wanted to savour the waiting time alone.

'About an hour, I should say,' said George. 'Come on, Frank, get cracking. I'm going to need that plan again.'

Frank pulled it out of his brief-case and spread it over a chair.

'Now let's see,' said George, 'where are we?'

Frank pointed with his pencil. 'We're here,' he said gaily. His services as a stand-in had given him confidence. 'Entrance floor. Front room.'

'So this door should lead to the dressing-room,' said George, his hand on the door knob.

'Correct,' said Frank, who had suddenly assumed seniority. 'Absolutely correct.' He went over and opened the door with confidence, only to be faced with a rusty old-fashioned geyser and the beginnings of an off-white bath. He shut the door hastily behind him, thinking that he had mispointed the place on the map. But George was a thorough man. He wanted to check on everything.

'Hullo, hullo, hullo,' he said, opening the door and greeting the geyser in triplicate. 'What have we here? A bathroom. How nice.' He was dating Cameron & Hodge again. 'No sign of a bathroom on *my* map, Madam. This *is* 132 Vauxhall Mansions, isn't it?' he asked disdainfully.

'Yes, it's a bathroom all right,' said Madame Sousatzka. She could think of nothing else except Marcus's promised visit. 'Yes, I wanted a bathroom, so I built the bathroom. Very good man. Very expensive. But I understand. I take it away, yes?' George was annoyed to have the wind taken out of his sails so quickly. 'I take it away,' Madame Sousatzka went on. 'I take away the bathroom on the ground, I put back the lavatory on Cordle's floor. I mend all the pipes. I take away all the damp. I mend the roof. I kill worms in the wood. I do everything. You send me the catalogue. I do it.' She wanted them very much to go away.

'All this is going to cost you a lot of money, Madam,' George persisted. With this surprise bathroom he had good grounds for an argument. He wanted to scold her. He wanted to tell her that she had no right to play about with the law. Even if she was pleading guilty, he was not going to let her off without a reprimand.

'Every penny I will pay,' said Madame Sousatzka with enthusiasm, and no doubt, had she had the cash, she would have thrust it into George's hands then and there.

'Yes, but it's not that easy,' said George, hanging on to her guilt. 'This sort of thing isn't done, you know. Cameron & Hodge' – he almost crossed himself at this point – 'take a dim view of this sort of thing. Isn't that right, Frank?'

'That's right,' said Frank sadly, and he managed a sidelong smile at Madame Sousatzka to show her what side he was on.

'It'll all have to go,' George argued, as if someone were trying to shout him down. Madame Sousatzka said nothing. George tried again. 'The geyser, this bath, the lavatory, it'll all have to go,' he decided. 'There's no provision for a water system here on my map.'

'As you say,' said Madame Sousatzka.

'It'll cost you a pretty penny,' George gurgled. 'Can't go against the law for nothing.'

'I have said already,' said Madame Sousatzka, tired now, 'that I will pay for everything. What d'you want with me, Mister?' she said quietly. 'You want also my blood?'

George looked at her as if he thought it wasn't a bad idea. 'As long as we understand each other,' he said. 'Get out the book, Frank, and take all this down. Everything I tell you.' George had begun to sense Frank's wavering loyalty. Frank had his book and pen ready and George bent down, dictating in his ear in whispers. He'd done all he could to humble Madame Sousatzka. Now he was going to try and make her afraid.

But Madame Sousatzka did not even look at them. She was re-sorting the music on the piano, testing the distance from the stool to the keyboard, and heartily wishing they would go away. She heard George's whispers growing louder and more angry, so she set the metronome going to drown them. George dictated louder, competing with the rhythmic tick and bell of the machine, but Madame Sousatzka set it faster, and the bell, now ringing at each alternate tick, put George off his stride completely.

'We will finish at the office,' he yelled to Frank. 'Now let us go to the basement.'

Madame Sousatzka turned off the metronome and announced herself gaily at their service. 'I lead the way,' she said. 'The stairs is a little shaky. Frank, if you want to write it down in the book, there is dry rot here too. Very dry. Also bad drains. Put it all down for Mr Cameron and Mr Hodge. Is very important.' Frank pulled out his notebook automatically. He was a man who would have taken orders from anybody.

'I will tell you what to put down, Frank,' said George. 'That is my job. I assure you, Madam,' he said to her back as he followed her down the stairs, 'I shall not miss anything. This basement,' he added, 'I shall go through with a tooth-comb.'

'Who's there?' Uncle shouted as they came down the stairs.

'We are here,' Madame Sousatzka shouted back. 'We come to look at the dry rot.' By now, she didn't even care whether Uncle had bothered to clean up her room or not. In fact, she rather hoped she'd left it in its usual state. She heard scuffling inside Uncle's room. She must be tidying up after all. She went into the room without knocking. 'Don't

175

bother, Uncle,' she began to say. And then she saw Cordle.

He had been on his knees by Uncle's rocking-chair, and he was beginning to stand up. When he saw Madame Sousatzka the blood rushed to his face in a violent blush, sensing that he could have given time for the grass to grow. Uncle giggled nervously. Madame Sousatzka tried desperately to convey to them an understanding smile. For a moment, she forgot about Marcus's telephone call, and a swift pang of jealousy pricked her. She hadn't wanted Cordle herself, but she didn't particularly want anyone else to have him. But more than anything, she didn't want their pity. She remembered Marcus, and she wanted to deal out her happiness to them like a card in Snap. 'Marcus is coming back,' she said quietly.

Uncle and Cordle, relieved to change the subject, came towards her, taking her hands in theirs. Frank and George tried to circumnavigate their reunion, dodging around the circle they had formed in the doorway, trying to get into the room and on with the job.

'Did he telephone?' Uncle asked, breathless.

'Yes, ten minutes ago. He wants to see me. He wants a lesson. He comes at eight o'clock. I wait for him in my room. He's come back, Uncle,' she whispered. 'Cordle,' she said touching his shoulder, 'Marcus has come back to Madame Sousatzka.'

'I will get my couch ready,' said Cordle happily, 'and put on a clean overall. We will all go back to work, Sousatzka. Uncle, find the draught board and make his bed. Oh, Uncle,' he laughed, 'we shall all be happy again.'

'We shall start to live,' said Madame Sousatzka, solemnly, 'all of us.'

'If you can spare me a moment, Madam,' said George disdainfully. He stood, quizzing the map in his hand, like a tourist lost in a grotto. 'Perhaps you will tell me, to save us time, where on this floor you have installed the lavatory, the bathroom, and the shower.'

'Here is nothing installed,' said Madame Sousatzka proudly. 'Here is exact as Mr Cameron and Mr Hodge left it.' She spoke in reverent, hushed tones, as if the basement were an important historic ruin. 'There is no water here.

Mr Cameron's and Mr Hodge's convenience is in the garden. From here is a long walk.' She intended to give George his money's worth. 'Here in the basement is untouched. Genuine period. Oh, I made a mistake,' she confessed. 'I modernize the ruin just a little. I put in the gas. I'm sorry. I take it out again. Then real genuine.'

She paused to give George a chance. He did the only thing that was left to him. He ignored her. He turned to Frank and started talking to him in highly technical terms. Frank looked uncomfortable, but he felt sorry for George and he pretended to understand everything he was saying. After all, they worked as a team and they must stick together. He even jotted down a few meaningless phrases in his notebook. Then George got busy with his tape, and his plumbline, while Frank pulled out his large sheet of paper, and with his red pencil he ticked away all house diseases like a madman. He thought of the application form he'd had to fill in when he'd applied for the job. 'Do you suffer from any of the following?' it had asked. 'Please put a tick where applicable.' Had he ticked them as he was ticking now, he would have succumbed to epilepsy, tuberculosis, venereal disease, diphtheria, malaria, and several unheard-of maladies. He wondered fleetingly how many applicants owned up to their maladies, or whether they suppressed them like poverty. He stopped ticking for a moment, suddenly overcome by a feeling of guilt. It was not his business to diagnose the diseases of a house. It was the house that was applying for life, and for Frank this house had suddenly become personalized. The house was Madame Sousatzka, and all those odd people who surrounded her; the blonde up in the attic, and these two crones in the basement, and Madame Sousatzka herself, who not so long ago in her studio had given him his first break. He closed his pen and put it back in his pocket. Even without one more tick the house was condemned twice over, and how often could one demolish a house? He folded up his paper and watched George as he knelt on the floor, prodding the boards and the skirting like a punch-happy boxer, whose victim has long since surrendered.

Madame Sousatzka was still huddled in the doorway

with Uncle and Cordle. She was repeating for the tenth time her conversation with Marcus on the telephone. And Cordle was asking her the same questions over and over again. 'Did he sound happy? Did he mention Manders? Did he ask about me? Or Uncle, or Jenny?'

'No, he hadn't,' Madame Sousatzka told them. 'But tonight everybody will see him. Marcus is coming home.'

'I'll go to my room to wait for him,' said Cordle. 'Are you coming, Uncle?'

Uncle looked at Madame Sousatzka for a moment, as if asking her permission.

Madame Sousatzka smiled. 'You wait with Cordle, Uncle,' she said. 'I will wait for the men to leave my house. Then I wait for Marcus in the studio.'

Uncle was drawing on her long stored-up energy. There was no hint of dismay at the thought of the journey in front of her. Madame Sousatzka watched them go upstairs together, and she knew that their need for Marcus had lessened and the surplus had been added to hers.

The two men were in the process of packing up. 'We'll be back,' George said to her, in case she thought she was seeing the last of them. 'Can't possibly do the whole job in one visit. We'll be back tomorrow,' he added, 'and we'll probably have to come again after that. Probably with Mr Cameron,' he said, lowering his voice with respect.

'Yes, of course,' Madame Sousatzka said, 'very often, I like you to come. Special Mr Cameron.' She was willing to entertain them to her dry rot every day for the rest of her life, if only they'd go away now and stop robbing her of her waiting time. She wanted to sit down and organize how she would spend it. She didn't want to think about it. She wanted to sit down with paper and pencil and write it down. It was part of the pleasure of waiting.

Frank closed the clasp on his brief-case. George was taking his time, gathering up his papers and tools one by one. Madame Sousatzka started to walk up the steps, hoping that they would follow her. She looked at her watch. Four hours of waiting were still left to her. She tried not to think too much about it. She wanted to wait until she was completely alone. She heard them coming up the steps behind her, and suddenly she wanted to delay them. The anticipation of waiting for Marcus had already exhausted her, and she wanted to postpone it, as if the waiting itself were the sole object of her excitement.

'Please,' she said to Frank, who was first at her side, 'would you like both of you a cup of tea?'

'A cup of tea?' said George, on his guard. 'It's not usual, you know. Not in this business.' He made Madame Sousatzka feel as if she'd bribed a policeman.

'I was in any case going to make one,' she said flatly. Frank smiled. He wanted a cup of tea very much. 'But of course,' said Madame Sousatzka, 'if you think it is for other reason, then I like it better you shouldn't have it.'

'In any case,' said George, 'we've got another job. We're late there already. Well, I won't say goodbye, Madam,' he said formally, 'we'll be seeing each other again very soon.' He opened the front door and let Frank out in front of him.

Madame Sousatzka watched them disappear down the steps. She closed the heavy door, and turned to face the empty hall. There was now no question that she was alone. She couldn't postpone it any longer. She would have, there and then, to begin the waiting.

15

She sat at her desk in the studio with a blank sheet of paper in front of her. It was just after four o'clock. She drew a line down the centre of the page, dividing it into two columns. She knew from experience that the hours of waiting were long and they needed to be divided. So she wrote in the first column, 4.15 to 4.30, and opposite, she wrote. Make tea. The next quarter of an hour was assigned to the drinking of the tea, and a further quarter of an hour was generously allowed for clearing it away. That would occupy her till five o'clock. She chewed the end of her pencil, considering what activities she could indulge in to while away the remaining three hours. But she knew that whatever she did, she would be waiting all the time, and that nothing was more important than the act of waiting, that nothing should interfere with it, or take priority. She felt that she was insulting Marcus in trying to occupy herself till he came. With sudden decision, she firmly crossed out her tea arrangements with her pencil, and wrote very simply, in huge letters, FROM NOW UNTIL THEN – WAIT.

And so the waiting began, with Madame Sousatzka, her hands in her lap, her watch flopping like a sick pendulum over her bodice, and staring, as Uncle so often stared, at the wall, and a patch on the wall, and the infinite isolated patches within each patch. After a while, she lifted up her hand to catch her watch to look at the time. But she quickly put it down again, as if she were about to cheat and had thought better of it.

She transferred her gaze to another wall, and found it, not surprisingly, similar. Her hand rose again, fingering the face of her watch as if it were braille. And as she touched it, the temptation was too much for her, and she slyly looked down. Half past four. She put it to her ear, hoping that it had stopped, and in spite of hearing its reassuring tick, she shook it violently.

She got up restlessly and went over to the shelves of bound music. She turned her head sideways and squinted at the book spines. She noticed that the books were in no particular order, but that she knew their disorganized state intimately. Mozart was next to Bach, because she felt they would be happy together. Suddenly she thought she would reorganize the shelves into some conventional alphabetical order. She ran her finger along the shelves, looking for a composer who satisfactorily began with A. She found some music by Arne, tucked away unplayed on the bottom shelf. She pulled it out and gave it pride of place at the beginning of the top row. The rest of the shelf, and the one below, was taken up completely by the Bs, and she found enough music to satisfy her new form until she came to the letter E. She went through all the remaining music and could find nothing suitable. She was beginning to like this new system, and she didn't want it disturbed. Although she disliked his music intensely, she longed for even a sheet of Elgar to contribute a link to the chain. A pile of Cesar Franck lay alongside, waiting to be called. She thought of leaving a gap and filling it in later, even if she had to buy some Elgar, but the idea of postponing the completion of the pattern made her angry.

She was aware for a moment that time was passing, that perhaps in her activity, it was even passing quickly. She didn't want to cheat Marcus out of any of the waiting time due to him, so she abandoned the task gratefully. It was all Elgar's fault, anyway. She shoved the music back into its old recognizable chaos, and she returned to her chair to wait.

She leaned forward, so that her watch swung from her chest into her line of vision. This way, her seeing the time was accidental. Five o'clock. The last half hour had gone quickly and she was tempted again into more activity. She got up, smoothing down her dress, as if she had visitors. She went over to her desk and drew a large irregular circle on a piece of paper. Out of this circle she made a clock, marking the division of minutes with lines from the centre.

Then she started to count. She counted in German; she felt it more reliable. She shaded in the first minute when she reached sixty and then started on the second. But she didn't trust the rhythm of her counting, so she set the metronome as a guide. In this way she shaded off four minutes with her pencil, but the whole business had begun to bore her. She might as well wait and do nothing as wait for the metronome to tick off its quota. She screwed the paper up in her hand and threw it away. Then she stopped the metronome, and the relief of the sudden silence in the room tided her over for the next five minutes.

She opened the door of the music cupboard that was lined with a full-length mirror. She looked as casually as she could at her watch as it swung gently from her neck. She held herself rigid to keep it still. Then she stared at it through the mirror. It took her some time to decipher it in reverse, and when she happily realized that it was a quarter to six she looked round the room innocently, like a schoolgirl after a successful piece of cheating. She approached the mirror and studied her face. She screwed up her nose and poked out her tongue. She came in closer and licked the cold surface of the mirror. Her breath had left a film of irregular shape, and she modified it with her finger to give it form. She had begun to like the face-making game, and she puffed her cheeks out, and lowered her eyes with her thumbs, trying to achieve the depths of ugliness. She rushed to her handbag and fetched a comb. She combed all her hair over her face, and parted it over her nose, giving herself a moustache and a beard with what was left. 'Oh, I'm so sorry,' she said to herself, pursing her lips and closing her eyes. Then she dilated her nostrils with contempt, and pulled down her lips. For this face, she said, 'Mr Manders, you are a nobody.' She threw back her hair, and parted her lips. 'Marcus, my darrlink,' she said, stretching out her hands towards the mirror. Then she flung her arms open wide and made a deep bow. 'How do you do, Mr Cameron and Mr Hodge.'

She began to laugh and feel the beginnings of her happiness. But in the moment of being aware of it, she knew that she had hours still to wait. Without any shame, she looked at her watch. Ten minutes to six. She must go back to her chair and her waiting. She wondered for the first time how she would receive Marcus. She resented having the thought, because now she would have to deal with all its possibilities.

She got up restlessly, and rushed to the door of her room. 'Marcus, my darrlink,' she cried, throwing her arms around herself and rubbing her nose in his imagined hair. 'No,' she said to herself, shaking her head, 'I will be angry.' She watched him come into the room and she sealed her lips lightly. She followed him with her eyes as he went to the piano, and sat down. 'It's not so easy, Marcus,' she said, 'to come back. You broke my heart.' The memory of her broken heart made her laugh, and she couldn't finish the act. 'Marcus, my darrlink,' she said, running over to the piano.

It was still light outside and the paper-boy who delivered regularly in the square at six-thirty had not yet arrived. The waiting had come upon her again. She opened the door of her room and stood in the hall. She listened to the others and in the silence she heard their waiting. She came back into her room, calm with the sense of company, and she sat in her chair for a long while, her mind unbusy.

It grew dark as she sat there. She knew that time was passing, but she felt safe because of the others waiting. It was like waiting late at night at a bus-stop, with people in front of you as proof that the last bus hadn't gone. She looked at her watch and saw that it was a quarter to eight. The imminence of Marcus's visit shattered all her calm, and she wanted to be active again. She held out her hands in front of her, spreading her fingers. She would baptise her fingers in the names of some of her pupils. The little finger was Rosemary, because her technique was weak. She took off her ring from her fourth finger and christened it Basil, because Basil, she felt, had the greatest potential. The middle finger she called Victor. She could think of no reason why, but she was getting tired of the game, and she wanted to finish it quickly. Paula was the index finger, because it pointed, and reminded Madame Sousatzka of Susan's mother, who counted the minutes outside the door.

She closed her fist with her four fingers and lovingly caressed her thumb. 'Marcus,' she whispered. She clasped her thumb with her other hand, holding it before her in a gesture of interrupted prayer. She closed her eyes, and for the first time since the telephone call, she let her happiness embrace her.

It grew dark outside and behind her closed eyes Madame Sousatzka saw the sudden light of the street lamp outside her house. She opened her eyes immediately, and without need to recollect when and where she was, she grasped at her watch in fear. Ten past nine. The panic didn't creep on her; it pounced on the soft pad between her shoulder-blades, and straight through her heart like a panther. 'He didn't come,' she screamed. 'No, he's not coming,' she corrected herself, as if it were less final. She wouldn't allow herself to lose hope. She ran outside her door, thinking perhaps he had knocked and was waiting her reply. But the emptiness was there, as if fixed for ever in the walls, along with the noise of the others' waiting. Her legs trembled as if, like a grasshopper, her ears were in her knees, but all they recorded was the screaming pitch of silence.

He's had an accident, she decided. He said he was coming. He wouldn't have 'phoned if he didn't want to come. She wondered whether she should ring the police but she was afraid to leave her room in case she missed a second of his absence, which had now become a tangible void in the studio. She moved over to the other chair and looked at her watch. Half past nine. How quickly time passes, she thought, when there is no need to wait for it. The waiting had been his coming, and now he was gone. She closed her eyes, and only when she felt the hot tears on her cheeks, did she realize she was crying. The pain of his first parting was fresh again, and all the wounds that time had healed had reopened. Marcus hadn't given time, time. She wanted to sleep and to forget, but she was nagged by the hope that he would still come. She thought of closing the piano and putting all the music away, so that he would come without any purpose. But she was too tired and too hurt to move. She wondered whether she should go to bed. Perhaps he would come if she weren't looking, if he knew she wasn't waiting for him. She leaned back in her chair and closed her eyes; her watch slipped sideways over her shoulder, her mouth opened slightly, and her half-clasped hands fell apart on her lap.

Upstairs, Jenny was painting her nails, while the crumpets curled in front of the gas-fire, and the half-empty kettle whispered with steam. Below on the next floor, Cordle sat, huddled next to Uncle on the couch. His new white coat was now unbuttoned, and they sat staring at the chart over the door, like two old-age sparrows keeping their vigil.

Madame Sousatzka stirred in the dark, and in her half-sleep she clutched at her watch around her neck. Not finding it, she woke up suddenly and grasped it from over her shoulder. The hands sat neatly on the twelve, and she knew that it was the end and time to start all over again. She looked out into the empty street around the square of dying houses. She noticed without much pain that yet another house sprouted a FOR SALE sign. One on a short stick, like the hand of a timid pupil who, not being too sure of the answer, thinks it safe to put up his hand in a surrounding sea of upstretched arms. As she turned to draw the curtain, she saw the house on the far corner of the square. A new notice had sprung up in the garden, as if from a magic bean. 'SOLD,' it said, in large triumphant letters. With one word, each house had been condemned, and Madame Sousatzka knew that all hope had been drained out of the square. She stared at the word for a long time, chilled by its treachery that injected her with its cold virus of despair.

She went over to the piano and closed the lid, and she put the music tidily away. Then she crossed to the window, and the notice stared back at her for a long time.

Occasionally during the night, Madame Sousatzka wondered why she still stood at the window. She was numb beyond fatigue. She shifted her feet from time to time, but she moved them as if they were not part of her. She felt a decided separation between the three portions of her body. She could feel her heart beating, and she listened to it with detached curiosity. She felt her head stretched high by headache and tears, and when a stray night-bird settled on a lamp-post opposite, she felt she was looking down on it. She spread out her arms, letting the passing hours dry her out, out of her sadness and out of her soreness. And like an immutable scarecrow, she saw the roofs of the houses opposite gradually assume a skyline in the growing light. She still saw the notice in the garden of the house on the corner. She saw its separate letters, but could find no communication with its ensemble, as if the night had immunized her from the square's surrender. She became suddenly and sadly conscious that she still had hope.

The postman brought one letter, and it lay on the hall floor in its solitude and importance as if sent by special delivery. Madame Sousatzka opened it without any preliminaries. When she saw that it was from Manders, she took it into her room. She saw and understood the notice again, and she drew the curtains so that the room was almost dark.

My dear Madame Sousatzka, it read,

Marcus wanted to come and see you yesterday to tell you of our decision. But he was afraid you would be angry with him and he has asked me to write to you. I have many concerts lined up for him in the following months, and I have great hopes of his career. But meanwhile, as you said, he must continue with his lessons. After great consideration I have decided to send him to Miss Mabel Larks, L.R.A.M.(Hons.), A.R.C.M.(Dip.), to further his studies. She has been highly recommended. Marcus wishes to add a note.

Yours very sincerely,
Felix Manders.

Madame Sousatzka turned the letter over without giving Manders's news time to register.

Dear Madame Sousatzka, it said.

Please don't be angry. I know you will understand. I hope it plays as well for Miss Larks as it played for you.
Love from Marcus.
P.S. Tell Cordle my back back is getting better.

186

Madame Sousatzka sat for a long time with the letter in her hand. 'Cordle,' she whispered to herself, 'his back is getting better. He's gone to a letter-lady who makes his back better. And you know, Cordle,' she laughed sadly, 'what he plays with the better back and the letter-lady? Mozart, he plays.' She stared at the postscript, which was magnified by her tears. And all her separate sadnesses, the torture of her parents, Boris, Marcus, and now Miss Larks who had taken her place and straightened his back, collided in a clot in her mind. The realization that there was no limit to human endurance deeply offended her. By all the laws of nature, she should have died of a broken heart long ago.

She was not surprised at the smile she felt gathering on her face, any more than she would have been surprised by a day-break. She drew the curtains to let in the light, and she opened the piano lid to its upmost. She began playing a scale. 'Not with the fingers, Sousatzka,' she said. 'With the belly, the chest, the shoulder, the arm. Nothing you will get from the fingers, Sousatzka. Nothing. They don't know how to do, and who will tell them, these ten poor little worms? Once again, Sousatzka, to a scale there is no end and no beginning.

'Listen, Sousatzka, how well it plays.'

Also available in ABACUS paperback:

FICTION